DUBAI SANDS

by Edward Flaherty

The sixth and final novel in "The Landscape Architect" series

Don't want to think about it?

...when landscape is more powerful than shelter...

...than humans.

EUROPE
MANNLICHEN
PORT KOPER
CJ'S GO-ROUTE
How did CJ get to Fujairah in the United Arab Emirates?
Long route and even longer story. Here's the summary:
His wife had been killed in the strange Mannlichen debacle.
A person of interest, he had to escape from Switzerland. ...over land and sea... on the run for a month... then he landed in Fujairah.
ASIA
MIDDLE EAST
SUEZ CANAL
NORTH AFRICA
FUJAIRAH
TROPIC OF CANCER
BAB AL MANDEB

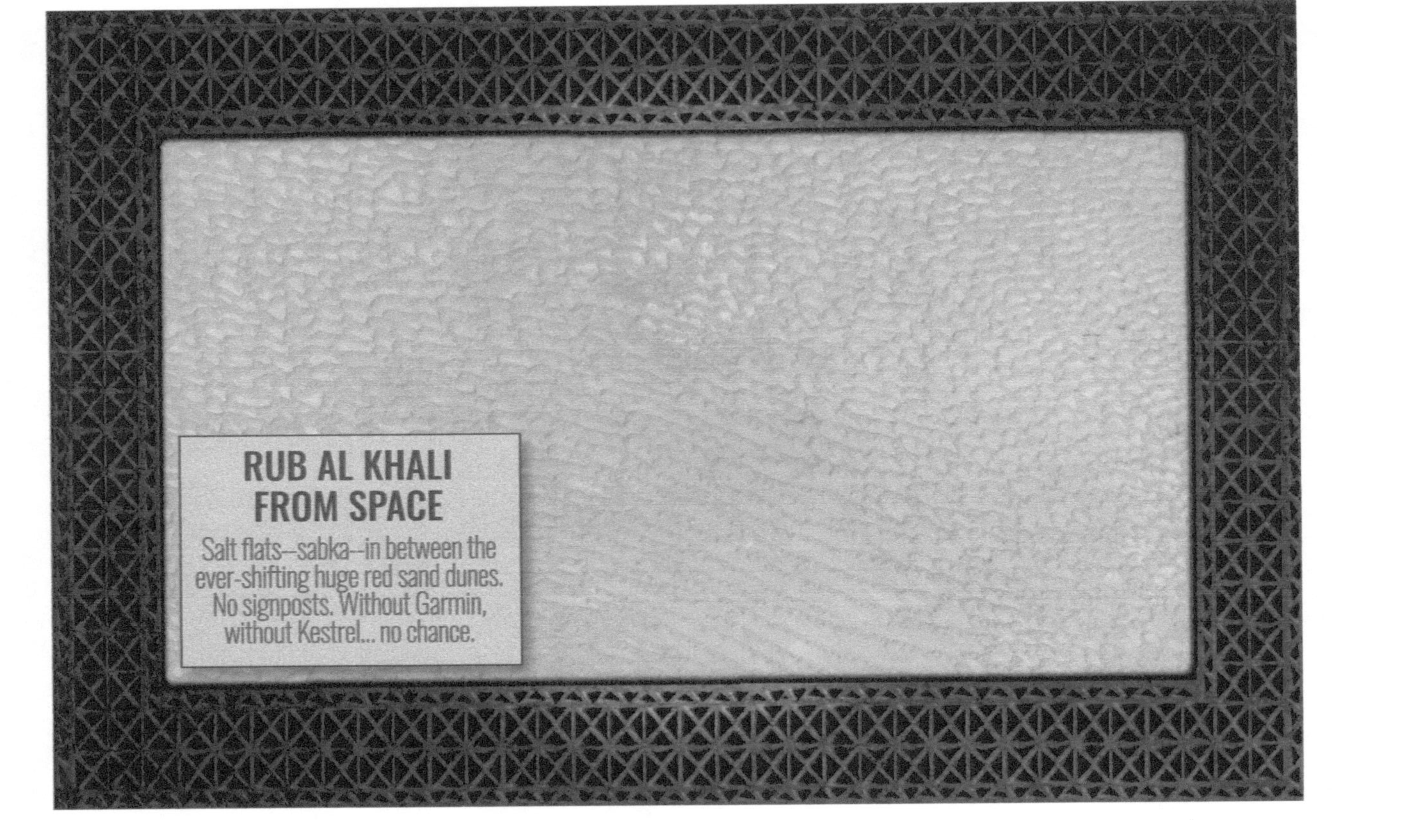

RUB AL KHALI FROM SPACE

Salt flats—sabka—in between the ever-shifting huge red sand dunes. No signposts. Without Garmin, without Kestrel… no chance.

LIWA QSAR COMPLETE
A protective micro-environment to observe and study the Empty Quarter.

Preface

Disasters have vexed CJ's personal life and professional landscape architecture career. And indeed another disaster has brought him to Fujairah in the United Arab Emirates. He must rebuild his professional career and recover his personal life.

Only one thing stands in his way—the Rub al Khali, the Empty Quarter.

Is that a landscape challenge... or... ?

CJ will tell his own story; and you can decide.

Edward Flaherty

Contents

1-Coming Up For Air

Under Water

Tramp steamer south out of Port Koper, Slovenia. Day after day. I didn't know how many days. Didn't know where I was. In over my head.

Sick, not from anything I ate—sick, not seasick—sick, vomiting all over my cabin. Again and again. Retching till nothing... but hurt. Living in a hideous nightmare where emotional storm waves drained my life force. Emotional waves and sea waves—waves pounded me.

Each wave was unpredictable and more intense than the last. And the emotional swells? Nauseating—more retching. I couldn't keep track of time.

It was... I don't know... it had been a couple horribly stressful weeks since Bree, my second wife, died in that "discover-the-ancient-gold" Mannlichen debacle in Switzerland. Bree was shot, died in a hail of gunfire around a Swiss military centre. While only watching, she and I had done nothing. Two friends of ours were shot attempting to illegally enter the centre in an historical yet foolhardy hunt for ancient gold from the crusade era; and I was on the run—the Swiss were after me.

But the Swiss were the least of my worries. From deep inside came those waves, swells, throbbing emotional hurt... Bree was gone. She had enabled me to finally overcome, after decades, the hurt, the loss of my first wife Sachy and our three young kids from their horrendous death years ago in an automobile accident in Albuquerque.

I owed Bree so much... and now, Bree... she's gone. So many emotions dragging me under... destroyed, ruined, hopeless, nothingness.

I clambered out of my cabin, up on deck. Didn't help. Sun, sand, wind, narrow channel. The Suez Canal and the Sahara. Blowing sands rasped my head. Powerful emotions suffocated me like swirling desert sands. No shelter inside or outside.

My personal life had been torn out of me. I had no oxygen, only hurt. I had to heal, protect, wrap myself so that my body, mind and intelligence could not linger on the bleeding, the throbbing wound that Bree's loss had inflicted. And my professional career? It had always been my source of sheltering cocoons. But the Swiss police were after me. My professional career would be in danger for sure.

Talk about cocoons—I needed a big one. My cocoons had always been in my professional world. And after that Mannlichen debacle, I wasn't sure that I even had a professional life. Professional? It doesn't count, I'd lost Bree, nothing else mattered.

I'd been at sea, physically and emotionally, continuously for too long. No solid footing. My emotions had taken control. They had their way with me; and they were relentless. I've never known such internal pain. It had been 24/7 hell.

My escape route from Switzerland had me on that rusty bucket of bolts local cargo freighter—that tramp steamer port to port from Slovenia, the Adriatic, the Med, the oppressive Suez Canal. Would it ever end?

I knew I had to traverse the edges of the Arabian Peninsula around that most enigmatic landscape—the Empty Quarter. And before landfall I would be closer to India than I would to Europe—never with sea legs—never in peace.

***

Fujairah

Fujairah UAE (United Arab Emirates) wasn't my goal.

It was my final destination on my international escape route, as dictated by my longtime personal friend and information-gathering colleague, JeanClaude. He had programmed it onto the burner phone he gave me should I run into trouble in the Mannlichen adventure. And trouble found me indeed; but I was safe—emotionally shattered but safe. After a month at sea, my goal was get my head straight, move forward.

And I had been really at sea in more ways than one. Fujairah was a destination that meant nothing to me. Nothing except landfall after 30 days at sea.

Nobody talks about Fujairah. But I had familiarized myself with it, not long ago when I was in the UAE, on a hospitality project in Ras al Khaimah, RAK. On the Gulf of Oman, Fujairah is the only Emirati city on the UAE outside of the Persian (Arabian) Gulf, free from the physical and political restrictions of the Strait of Hormuz.

The city of Fujairah is in the Emirate of Fujairah, like New York City in the State of New York. The cities of Dubai and Abu Dhabi also are in their own individual Emirates with the same name—Dubai and Abu Dhabi. Fujairah, Dubai and Abu Dhabi are three of the seven Emirates in the United Arab Emirates.

Travelling between the Emirates is like travelling between states in the US or cantons in Switzerland. There are no physical or administrative boundaries.

Fujairah? Why Fujairah? I don't know. It was just supposed

to be a safe touching down point for me. I certainly never thought about what to do if I landed here. But here I was.

My professional and personal lives had been uprooted. What to do? I needed to sort out all of that. I couldn't stop thinking about Bree. But I needed to think about the basics of life—food and shelter. I needed work.

My past project, at Queen of Sheeba in Dubai on the Palm Jumeirah, was near the huge landmark, that famous landscape of Atlantis the Palm. I needed a large, complex project like those to get my head straight. I needed to ensconce myself in my trustworthy professional cocoon, to get stuck in. Dubai was the place.

At Fujairah Port, after disembarking, I walked to passport control. I, Christopher Janus, with my original identification documents that my old friend and handler JeanClaude had returned to me with my international go-route escape package, entered the UAE without a problem.

My original ID? That's a strange story—years ago, Egypt, the Sahara, walkabout searching for the Pharaonic landscape—I'd long put all that behind me. But JeanClaude had explained I should get rid of all my Charles Jacobs ID if the Swiss were looking for me. So I did. Dumped everything, including the burner phone, in the Gulf of Oman just before docking at Fujairah.

Exiting at the Port Entrance, I asked a policeman how I could get to Dubai. He spoke English, pidgin English—maybe he was Pakistani. Why do I say from Pakistan? First, the geography—check the proximity. Second, Pakistan is a Muslim country. And third, when I was working in RAK, I learned that many Pakistanis came to work on this side of the UAE in nurseries at the mouths of valleys, where the subcontinent weather patterns bring occasional seasonal moisture.

He said, "Take taxi Ajman University, take bus Dubai International." Decades in this region have taught me to understand so many dialects of pidgin English. I knew Dubai International as DXB. I had come in and out through it when I did the RAK and Sheeba projects.

I had to cross a street to get to the taxis. And I felt for the first time the thrill of a strange landscape. I was on the ground on the eastern edge of the Arabian Peninsula. It had its own character. Modern but not flash, wide multi-lane, traffic-engineered, well paved, well-signed roads and intersections. Sand everywhere. Cloudless, blue sky. Unbelievably bright sun. And virtually no plants at all—no trees, no shrubs, no grass. Found the taxis and one took me to Ajman University bus station. The bus traversed some barren mountains and then sand desert. Three hours later I was in Dubai, at DXB, Dubai International Airport.

I had learned from my decades in this region—all the oil-rich Arabian Peninsula countries, with their oil wealth, sought dependable energy, dependable water and gardens. Dubai was the same and I needed to get a job.

As part of my international escape package, I had only limited cash. I had no credit cards, no links to my past "Charles Jacobs" resources. My cash would not last more than a month. And I had no income. With luck I hoped to find a large project which could become a cocoon that would help me get some kind of professional normality and hopefully emotional stability back in my life.

***

Mall of the Emirates

On the elevated Dubai Metro monorail system, I bought a one-way ticket at DXB and rode the Metro to the Mall of the Emirates (MOE)—a central location in New Dubai. I'd always wanted to spend time there but neither my Queen of Sheeba project nor my RAK project allowed me the free time. Indoor Ski Dubai snow slope and so many diverse uses and activities—a huge air-conditioned urban centre in its own right—I looked forward to seeing if it had the facilities to set me up for job hunting.

The mall was teeming with activity. I saw the ski slope and 3 plus levels of shops. I looked at an information board. They advertised 80 luxury stores and 250 flagship stores. I couldn't count all the retail outlets—easily over 500 in addition to over 100 restaurants, coffee shops, and fast-food outlets. There were all the international fashion shops, male and female Emirati clothing shops, grocery stores, home supply stores, carpet shops, perfume shops, jewellery and watch shops, pharmacies, telecom outlets, a social program centre, and a cinema. Additionally, there were two hotels connected to the mall.

When I worked in Los Angeles (LA), southern California (SoCal), I thought I'd seen the best of the developed-world malls—lots of shops and food places, great architecture, first-class interior design, fantastic craftsmanship and welcoming landscaping... but here, the MOE outdid by orders of magnitude, in size, store variety and customer volume, any I'd ever seen in SoCal.

And it was crowded even on a mid-week workday in the mid-afternoon. Crowded at this time? I learned that so many of the larger construction projects were active 18-24 hours a day—shop when you have time.

In an Apple store, I bought an iPhone. At a telecom kiosk, I bought a data plan. Then I found a busy, good size Indian restaurant with an all-you-can-eat buffet. Sat down to eat and do some research.

I found that one of the hotels attached to the Mall had reasonably priced rooms. I booked a room in that hotel, then at nearly 6PM, I went to check in. I paid in advance. JeanClaude had me take $10,000 in cash for my international escape—I thought it was way too much; but lo and behold it all was necessary. Check-in went smoothly. Smoothly? Until I got into my room.

I sat on the edge of my bed. Job was one thing but... the hurt descended on me. It overcame me. Flattened. My emotions, hidden by my travelling in Dubai, now returned with a vengeance. I just sat there, head in hands.

I had not come out of the emotional cloud shock of having lost my second wife. Bree had died in my arms just like Sachy, my first wife. Did I still carry that curse? The curse from Morocco. The curse that the shaman from New Mexico supposedly removed 25 years ago? Bad juju—was I still carrying bad juju? But... but... what about Bree? The hurt was filled with unknowns and uncertainties.

What happened in that Swiss Alp Mannlichen debacle? In the very heart of the Jungfrau Region landscape, the landscape of Byron, the landscape of Tolkien? What happened when she... disappeared?

Disappeared? I hadn't processed that. I didn't know what to make of it. Did it actually happen or was it just my imagination? Did her spirit, soul and body really get absorbed into the majestic Swiss stone pine—into that landscape? So many thoughts, so many loose ends...

I wondered about the guys, our friends, Garrett and Faf, the private sector mercenaries who went with us to the Mannlichen. On the day, it all happened so fast. ROCKSTAR over the comms, gun shots, then quiet. I figured they were dead or captured. With all the shots, it was most likely they had been killed. How many times can I rethink those days, those hours, those minutes? Are they still alive? Captured? Are the Swiss really after me? And what if they found Bree's dead body on the edge of that forest? What if her disappearance really was my imagination? Too much!

I stood up for a moment, staggered over to the minibar, unlocked it and found a bottle of beer and a small bottle of Seagrams. Boilermaker! I chugged the Seagrams and followed it with the beer. Still an unquenched thirst. I needed more. I called the *chef de l'étage* who within a half hour was able to supply a 375ml bottle of Seagrams and four bottles of Heineken. I had him add the charge to my room.

***

Drunken Sailor

Boilermakers—downed them like water. I struggled over my situation. I remembered what Bree had warned me about working on the pirate coast in a country where the majority of people were contract labourers away from their homes and families. The boilermakers started getting to my head—pirate coast of a country? The UAE? I had done some research before my previous projects here.

I recalled my research and dug deeper online... around the edges of the Empty Quarter, its history and the most prominent Western explorers of the last 200 years: Burckhardt, Wallin, Burton, Bell, Lawrence, Thomas, Philby, and Thesiger.

They were all about the mysterious sands... but the tribes of the UAE and their history? What is the mystery? Of all the explorers, only Thesiger connected both the Emiratis and the sands. I remembered Al Ain Oasis, Liwa Oasis, Salalah, the Empty Quarter and the people he encountered at the edges of the Empty Quarter.

Pirate coast? This is, was and always has been a landscape of spice and incense. But the harsh life of pearling and annual retreating from the cruel climate into the oases made for an impossibly difficult life. Pirates raided dhows. Tension abounded until 1971 when Sheikh Zayed united the Trucial States into the United Arab Emirates as it is today.

My thoughts on local history were dry and lifeless. I downed another boilermaker. I was wracked by my realities. I had hacked off my career, my wife, my life...

I was both numb and hurt. Melancholic music in my head

wrung out onto the floor whatever job-related plans I had. Getting closer and closer to the edge. I wasn't clear in my mind. I felt my soul had gone mad. I broke from my family, broke from my wife, broke from my job, now I'd broken from myself. I knew the risks at Mannlichen, or imagined I knew the risks. And did it anyway. It hurt everywhere.

I forced myself across the room, opened the curtains, looked west toward the Arabian Gulf coast. The sun sets fast in the tropics—not like the northern temperate zones where the sunset lingers. I was watching it set beyond the 5-star destinations on the Gulf. At the twilight's last gleaming, I downed another boilermaker. And I didn't know how many more.

It was 2am, fear was gone; and so were the Seagrams and Heinekens. Was I slipping into the twilight zone... my own madhouse... where might I go if I go too far?

My head was heavy. I had been running for over a month. I was tired, physically and emotionally. I was alone in a hotel, in a single room, in a new place. Alone. Deeply alone. I couldn't take it. I fell back on the bed, rolled over, and collapsed into unconsciousness.

Then other-world dreams began. Bree was out in the haybarn garden. I was inside exploring her labelled glass jugs of mead that she kept under the staircase.

"CJ, can you give me a hand out here."

I went outside to see what she was doing. "Sure, what's up?"

She had her beekeeping suit on. "I'm harvesting honey and beeswax."

"Honey I understand, but beeswax?" I'd never paid much attention to her beehive, out back next to some protective shrubs.

"Me and bees... got started on the wrong foot in my grandfather's garden. How I remember it—I wasn't much more than five when, looking at the flowers in his garden on a warm early summer day, I bent over to smell a flower's fragrance. Never saw the honeybee. The bee took issue with my nose. Bee sting on the nose. Massive pain for the little boy. Baking soda plaster, the whole bit. So I keep my distance. Anyhow..."

"I use the beeswax as a base for some of my cremes and unguents," she said.

"What do you need?"

She handed me a large stainless-steel tray and said, "I've got to select a frame. When I find the one I want, I'll set it on that tray you're holding. You wait holding it while I put the top back on the hive."

I stepped back while asking, "Do I need bee protection?" I was worrying.

"No, these bees are settled here and they don't get stirred up easily. Just stand there without threatening movements—you'll be okay."

She opened the hive box and began inspecting one frame after another. I had never seen so many bees. Like a densely packed high-rise, and they all were busy and buzzing. I stepped back further.

Bree knew how to lovingly joke with me. It was a heartfelt pleasure for me when she did.

"What's the matter, CJ? International traveller, expatriate mercenary, met your match, a one cm insect?

"Here's a good frame—see that waxiness..." She had a bee brush and started brushing huge quantities of bees off the frame into the hive. It was getting too much for me. Anyhow in one smooth motion, she finished with the bee brush and reached over to me, placing the frame of beeswax and honey with maybe 15-20 confused looking bees on the tray I was holding.

"Just wait there while I close up the hive and we will take that frame to another side of the haybarn for processing. You okay?"

That was the last word I heard. The bee buzzing overwhelmed me, I didn't feel a sting but I certainly imagined them. I wanted to run, but I couldn't. I was frozen in place and buzzing kept getting louder and more furious.

Then I woke up. It was morning and my room phone was buzzing. Buzzing way too loud. The phone's buzzing kept my dream alive. Had to stop that buzzing. I leaned over and picked the receiver from the bed table. It was already 9AM but I had all the curtains drawn tightly. No light except from the clock and phone.

"Hello?"

"Hello, CJ is that you?"

***

Eileen

"Who wants to know?"

I was totally bothered—Bree, Garrett, Faf, the bees—and I had been sleeping soundly.

"Who wants to know?"

"Have you forgotten, Morocco, Casablanca, the California nursery, the Trump Golf Club in Palos Verdes, our time in Kuwait?"

Only one person knew all that, Eileen. I was mixed up. The loss of Bree had torn my heart so deeply that logic, memory no longer functioned normally. But Eileen? Yeah, a friend.

"Eileen?"

"You've got it. Thought I'd check in."

"Check in? I'm confused. I just woke up."

"Just woke up? Perfect. You're in the MOE, why don't we meet for breakfast on the ground floor at the Paul Café, say at 10AM? Can we do that? Just the two of us?"

I didn't know what to think; but a friend is a friend and I needed to talk.

"10AM at the Paul Café? I can do that."

"See you there."

"Got it and thanks for the wakeup call."

I didn't know what to think. I hadn't expected any calls. And Eileen? What could that mean? Analysis Corp.? Will? Info gathering? Could they be tracking me? How did they know? Could this be about jobs?

These questions already took my mind off Bree and the Mannlichen debacle. But all I had to do was let the name Bree float through my mind and the hurt resurfaced worse than ever.

I needed breakfast and getting out of my room was a good thing. I cleaned up and headed to the Paul Café.

When I met Eileen at Paul's I reached out my hand to shake hers but she came right in, hugged me and gave me a squeeze.

"I'm so glad to see you are safe, CJ."

I stepped back and looked at her. She had aged well. She was fit, pushing 6 feet tall. She was dressed as always with toreador pants and a large Texas cowboy style shirt, not tucked in—just like when I first met her years ago in Casablanca where she had a gun concealed under her shirt. She looked good. But I was slow, uncertain, not normal.

Paul's wasn't crowded. We chose an out-of-the-way-table in a quiet corner. When we sat for breakfast, my appetite was under the emotional influence of Bree's death. Little appetite. I ordered a continental breakfast—coffee, juice and bread. Eileen took coffee only.

"All social chit-chat aside, Eileen, how did you know I was here? And why did you contact me?"

Eileen took a sip of her coffee before she started. "A wire from the Swiss Police to Interpol came across our desk. Two weeks ago, your name, Charles Jacobs, and Bree's name were identified as persons of interest in the deaths of two international mercenaries who were killed in their attempt to enter a secure military site, Mannlichen, in the Berner Oberland.

"I knew all about your identity change after Cairo, so I flagged Charles Jacobs and Christopher Janus in our communications watch list. I knew you entered in Fujairah and that you had registered in the hotel here in the MOE."

I listened carefully. I understood. "But why?"

"Why? You and I have serious history. That counts. And Will? He likes you."

Will Clendenon had set up my projects in Saudi Arabia, Egypt, Turkey and Bahrain. Three years ago, when I left Analysis Corp., Will and I parted on good terms.

"Will? Is he here in Dubai?"

"Until recently, he's in Qatar now. But tell me about yourself and Bree, is all well? Why is she not here with you?"

Was I going to tell it all?

"She's gone. She died the same day as those two mercenaries. She had saved my life and I couldn't save hers. I have been on the run since that day. Been at sea most of the time until, as you know, I landed in Fujairah. The details... I don't like to talk about. But I am hurt. Two wives each died in my arms. I'm looking down a dark tunnel... if you hadn't called I would have just stayed in my dark room... all I have left is my work, and after that incident in Switzerland, I don't know if I even have any professional life left."

"There might be a couple ways I can help you..."

Oh no, I thought, the Analysis Corp. again.

"In return for... what? I don't ever want to be in the same room as that pushy son of a bitch, Alan, the handler that tried to take advantage of me in Yenbo, Cairo and again in Bahrain—that guy is off the charts."

"Not at all, I know what he put you through. If your professional world doesn't work out—listen. Your current Charles Jacobs ID will get you nothing but trouble because the Swiss are chasing it. So... I know for sure your Christopher Janus ID and passport are clear. And if you want to startup your banking world again, I can assure you that the local branch of CitiBank will set up a secure (including the US) international account for you, no questions asked... but after your Sahara walkabout all the rest of your professional record as Christopher Janus is gone. If you want to work here, I can arrange a driver's license and a work visa that will let you work for anyone here in the UAE. And if that doesn't pan out..."

She paused for a minute. I had no idea what was coming; but she and I had form and were close from Casablanca and Los Angeles. I was listening.

Then she continued, "Nothing to do with Alan but in my work I need people on short notice for anywhere in MENA (Middle East and North Africa) to clean up problems, messes, like janitors. It's not landscape work but it's work and if work can get your mind off the recent horror..."

"Work, yeah, I need work; but my strength and best cocoon is landscape architecture work. I'd like to look around here to see what I can get. I'd like that driver's license and visa you offered... and I'd like to keep in touch. What you've shared has helped me understand better what happened on the Mannlichen in Switzerland."

She paid our bill and we walked the MOE up to the indoor ski slope. We paused there and watched a ski instructor teach a class of 8 how to ski.

"Looking for work here in Dubai—you should know that Alan is deeply involved in the expanded Atlantis the Palm project—so don't even try there. What do you plan?"

"Good question. My insides are all shook up. I'm still in emotional shock. I'm going to go back to my room and quietly think through what you've shared with me. And then I don't know. Maybe start looking for work, maybe go look at Souk Madinat Jumeirah, on the Gulf coast, not far from here. I've always wanted to go there. I can't stay in my room. I've got to keep busy. Maybe we can go for dinner there tonight, I've heard there are nice restaurants on an *abra*-only canal."

"Yeah, there are some nice restaurants there, if you are still into vegetarian meals, you should try the Magnolia, or is it the Plumeria, it's a flower name. It's five-star quality. But as for your invitation—thanks but I have work to do. Here, take my card. Get in touch with me anytime if you have questions... or want to talk about working for me if you need an income... or when you've settled maybe we can get together socially..."

"Thank you for everything. I really needed some deep root stability... being with you today has given me that." I smiled and looked into her eyes. She returned my smile and then I asked, "You're not moving to Qatar as part of Will's team, are you?"

"No, I've got my own team here in the UAE. So it will be easy to get together."

She gave a hug and a tight squeeze as we said goodbye. She went her way and I returned to my hotel room. I thought. I felt. A lifeline.

***

Magnolia

My head was still unsettled about everything that had happened on the Mannlichen. Lost my loving Bree. Lost friends. All dead. Uncertainty. Haybarn, my home, finished. I figured I had to make my new life here in Dubai. Being stuck in my hotel room was not a solution. If I could fill my life here... maybe...

That evening I decided to go out to Souk Madinat Jumeirah—always wanted to go there for that restaurant Eileen had recommended, Plumeria or Magnolia. The Souk Madinat—I could see it from my hotel room and read about its old Arab character with modern Dubai convenience.

I had to take a taxi to get there because it was not on the Dubai Metro line. The souk is a modern take on an old Arabian medina and is interconnected by 3km of lazy waterways and surrounded by lush gardens. I walked through the souk area until I found the placid, palm-fringed waterways where I rode a traditional wooden *abra* boat (like a water taxi, driver and quiet electric power), the only way to get to the "healthy food" restaurant I was seeking. The weather was clear, warm and peaceful as I rode to the Magnolia restaurant where I could eat outdoors creekside or indoors.

9PM—outdoors uncomfortably warm and humid. I was looking for an air-conditioned indoor table with a good view. The indoors was quiet and peaceful, but there were too many people. So I went back outdoors. Creekside was beautiful—nobody else outdoors. I wanted to be alone and quiet so... I figured might as well get accustomed to 9PM too warm and humid. Welcome to Dubai on the Gulf.

I sat outside and quietly and slowly worked through four delightful courses of artistic vegetarian fare. It was a pleasure to see each plate arriving but by the end, I was hankering for an espresso and a Lebanese sweet. While I was thinking about it, who did I see walking toward my table? JeanClaude Thibault. I hadn't seen him since Interlaken almost two years ago, the day he set up my international bug-out should I get in serious trouble on the Mannlichen adventure—as I did. I wondered how he knew I was here.

Before I could answer, JeanClaude stood next to me reaching out his hand saying, "Kismet, *mon ami*, Kismet!"

We shook hands heartily—two old friends. I thought he was in Papua New Guinea. This wasn't a coincidence... or was it?

***

JeanClaude

I first met JeanClaude in Yenbo, Saudi Arabia, some fifteen-odd years ago when he was introduced as Alan's Analysis Corp. boss. He was a hands-off boss who replaced Alan, a guy always in my hair.

I didn't really get to know JeanClaude well until a bit later when we bumped into each other as speakers at an ASLA (American Society of Landscape Architects) conference. In our own ways, we were both into plants and the landscape. Easily we became friends and he, via Analysis Corp., was my trustworthy handler in the passing years as I did projects in MENA.

JeanClaude was an explorer. I was a builder. We were friends, even though our clatteringly different approaches to the landscape often belied that friendship. Nevertheless, JeanClaude was happy to see me and greeted me saying, "Well, my old friend, long time no see. You're looking a bit stressed. Have the Swiss Alps let you down? Wait a minute, are you here as the 'Surveyor of Fabric' on some new mind-boggling landscape extravaganza? Or... did that adventure with you and your wife fall apart?"

I didn't know what to say... hurt from the loss of Bree came bubbling up all over. Then I realized the only reason I was safe in Dubai was the bug-out setup that JeanClaude had given me with that burner phone back in Switzerland. My head was spinning.

"JeanClaude, there is too much. I need an espresso and we need time to talk."

"No hurry, take time. Compose yourself."

He was understanding as always. He said he knew another place here in the Souk Madinat and we caught an *abra.*

Along the way, JeanClaude shared what he had been doing.

"It's about, as always, ethnobotany. I've been on and off years working on the edge of the Empty Quarter mentoring a Sheikh's young son who was going to the USA for education. I check in with him from time to time."

In my mind I recalled JeanClaude's background. He might be able to help me move my professional career forward.

JeanClaude Thibaut, a forty-nine-year-old Belgian, was a confirmed bachelor who found his pleasures in the "hair-shirt" explorations of cultures, of marginal groups beyond the edge of mainstream society—people still in contact with the land, with the old ways—Bedu, Berbers, true Gypsies, Calusa fisherfolk descendants and similar humans in the distant backwaters of lesser developed countries.

He examined human relationships with plants, through landscape, language, music, life. He was a very broad-scale ethnobotanist. He did not write for publication, did not have a PhD; but he did keep extensive multimedia digital archives, all collected first-hand: stories, songs, movies, images, along with plant-related artefacts—amulets, charms, talismans.

In a wealthy entrepreneurial Belgian family, he took birth in the Belgian Congo where he spent the early years of his childhood. He was a polyglot graduate of international schools in Brussels and Gstaad. Following formal education at the University of London, he had travelled and visited all major botanical institutions in Africa and Pre-Columbian America, gathering ethnobotanical information before his first post with the International Union for the Conservation of Nature. He became a director there. But he had since retired to focus full-time on his personal ethnobotanical research activities. His info-gathering with the Analysis Corp., when I first met him in Yenbo, Saudi Arabia, was only a part-time, sub-contract activity.

At five foot eleven and 165 pounds, he looked popularly slender and athletically lean. He had a self-effacing presence, and a manner of dress and hygiene making him as at home meeting and greeting in a five-star Monte Carlo resort, as in a *majlis* tent on the edge of the Empty Quarter. He was not shy about sharing the realities of the groups he studied. And there was no polite way to describe his most unusual first-hand experiences of old, almost forgotten ways of human interactions with plants in the landscape.

Threads of ambiguous tension often interlaced the substantial grounds of agreement between JeanClaude and me. Stubs of awkward conversation... mostly friendly... mostly the hidden subtleties of cross-cultural joking. Always good for a chuckle.

Those subtleties were built from JeanClaude's frequenting of the boundary edges between humans and plants—inspired by his attraction to the writings of William Blake, Aldous Huxley, Carlos Castenada. No question, JeanClaude's roots and his life were "over the edge" of the day-to-day, the traditional, the mainstream Western culture. I could not really imagine how he got into the intelligence business, where we started our relationship in Yenbo, Saudi Arabia.

We got off the *abra* at Al Makan. We sat next to a noisy water fountain and ordered two espressos plus a plate of baklava. Before speaking, I slowly chewed the honey-soaked baklava then sipped my espresso. I took a deep breath and started.

"It happened. The Mannlichen adventure. Bree got shot, died on the spot. I grabbed my go-bag and burner phone then hit the road. That was about a month ago. All your notes got me through the tough spots and here I am. But I still have to get through the loss of Bree. I must have bad juju—two wives have died in my arms. Wives who gave me a personal balance that my professional life needed. JeanClaude, it took me two decades to get over the loss of my first wife and our three kids. And Bree got me over that. Now, a month ago, she was taken away from me. I can't talk about it anymore. I've got to get into my professional work—it has always been a cocoon to protect me from instability in my personal life. That's where I am now."

I took another sip of espresso. I looked into JeanClaude's eyes. He was listening closely. He drained his espresso before he began.

"Okay, let's take steps forward. What kinds of projects have you had since we last talked?"

"I've been fixing problems on short term contracts... a bunch of projects in the Gulf Region..."

"Stop! Bingo! That's the direction, CJ! I see a future professional direction for you right there! Fixing a bunch—that's your handle—you're a fixer, an Arabian Peninsula specialist who can beat time and cost expectations—a fixer. Lots of Westerners can't handle the work out here. You're the exception."

JeanClaude understood my predicament. He suggested how to package my professional future.

***

The Fixer

Well, JeanClaude got me into an improved mindset. He encouraged me to look into my experience and prepare to move forward as specialist landscape fixer.

What could I do as a fixer? I'd confront difficulties and challenges, then solve them in impossibly short time frames within strict budget limitations. What kinds of difficulties and challenges?

My specialization? I build fine gardens—five-star resort destination gardens. Not the high-minded megalomanic design that I have dreamt about; but practical, attractive, get-it-done design and installation. I work in a rarely defined, but critical gap—the gap between the air-conditioned carpet world of the planners, of the designers—and the oppressive, 50°C sweaty world of the people who, piece by piece, build those very large and complex iconic projects in the oil-rich Middle East.

The gold ring? Get them built and beautiful, so that they can begin the return on investment on opening day as scheduled. My most recent noteworthy example of success was the Queen of Sheeba Resort Complex on the Palm Jumeirah, a 1,000-unit mixed-use resort destination with its A-level international celebrity "Hollywood to Bollywood" opening media event.

My specialty has been external finishes. These are the things of the first impression, that must look good. The external finishes are the magnets that "wow" people from their first view, and then pull them on through the front door. They must be beautiful, fresh, healthy, seductive, and breathtaking! If not, I won't work again. Reputation is everything.

Some developers plan for this. Others do not. For the developers who do not plan, a real-time anarchic mash-up ensues, rupturing cash and resources; and me, I get called in at the last minute, with panic all around.

***

White-Collar Mercenaries

As a fixer I have had to weigh into the following kinds of complexities—structures, personalities, processes and... the unpredictables.

White-collar mercenaries... experienced international professional consultants, planners, engineers, managers in design, construction, maintenance... what is their life blood? Large international projects! It's all about reputation for success... and money.

Theoretically, each project has a repetitive structure, a dependable structure that each white-collar mercenary has learned to manipulate to advantage. In other words, there is a very general outline, a linear sequence for international project activities—planning, design, engineering, construction and operations.

But it is never so clear cut. There are many subsets and always unexpected complications. What? Why? Able to manipulate the structure? Which structure? That differs in every country and on every job—figuring that out is the first complication. And then each personality carries his own complications. These complications are exacerbated by the lack of locally established and fixed process guidelines, locally established and dependable consultants, contractors and material suppliers. So what is it then? These are free-for-alls where every manager must be a bully to succeed.

Yogi Berra had it right. He said, "In theory there is no difference between theory and practice, but in practice there is."

It's straightforward, and it's not; but it has to work. Ironic once. Ironic twice. Confusing in the end.

That is why only experienced white-collar mercenaries can tough out these iconic large international projects. Mercenaries who, even in the most hostile environments can meet the often-unachievable cost and schedule requirements... to succeed on opening day.

***

Players and Processes

Once you understand the structural context–cultural and regulatory, the following "simple summary" explains what happens on a project. There are three players. Number one, the Owner/Developer–the Owner/Developer has the money and property to develop the project. Number two, the Consultant–the Consultant does the design and engineering for the project. And, number three, the Contractor–the Contractor builds the project. Then, construction complete, the Owner/Developer moves in and operates the project. Straightforward, right?

Almost...

How can a simple one, two, three–design, build, operate–project process become a twenty or more consultant spaghetti? Here is how it works, in theory and practice, in real life. The Owner/Developer intends to build a certain project, and is the money behind that project. At the outset, at the behest of an Owner/Developer, Consultants drive projects. That is the theory.

The Owner/Developer hires a Consultant, the Prime Consultant for the design and engineering. This Prime Consultant is in charge of herding a team of cats, twenty or more design sub-Consultants, each responsible for unique and specialized aspects of the design. The Prime Consultant translates the Owner/Developer's intent into design documents.

These design documents are a coded set of reproducible plans, drawings, and specifications that translate the Owner/

Developer's intent into a buildable project. The Owner/Developer then hires a General Contractor to build the project, according to those design documents. The General Contractor then hires and coordinates a wide range of sub-Contractors to build their individual specialist parts of the construction.

During construction, the Consultant team provides oversight to assure that the Owner/Developer's original intent is met and built according to the design documents. In the end, though, the practical, real-life reality is, the General Contractor truly drives the built project because he, alone, has the final responsibility for opening on time, all liability, all warranties, for everything built and supplied.

Now, that is the simple traditional outline–the simple project process, the three essential players, and the basic template for all projects.

***

The Complexities

However, with large, complex, international projects, in addition to the usual personality tensions between twenty or more consultants, and another twenty or more contractors, and their materials suppliers, lots of extra layers of management are often added. And me, I see these as problems—each extra layer of management tends to fray the clarity, fray the directness, fray the quality of the project.

For example, the Owner/Developer often hires a Project Management team. Why? To reduce the Owner/Developer's workload. To oversee the day-to-day schedules and activities of the Prime Consultant team and the General Contractor team. Complications arise. Too frequently during the design process, these often-inexperienced design managers, either from the Owner/Developer or Project Management teams, second, third and fourth guess the Consultant. These continuous battles often undermine not only Consultant morale, but also, project quality.

After this, if the Consultant has any morale or willpower left, it is completely burned away by an additional series of reviews—cost control reviews commissioned by the Owner/Developer—another layer of management. I call them "acid washes". These cost control reviews are known as the value engineering process, or VE, for short.

Essentially, VE is when people who know little about either the construction process, the local procurement market, or the local environmental conditions, get a chance to look good by simply lowering the cost estimates. It's easy to do—

less natural stone, thinning the hard materials, less, less, less—smaller trees, simpler way-finding, less interpretative signage systems, less lighting, etc. But this exercise has design quality implications.

These VE people, especially on Arabian Peninsula projects, regularly have no idea about how contemporary social culture, that is, the local people, will use the project and its site. Their VE cost savings belie ignorance of the daily, nightly, seasonal and annual use complexities. Most of the time, the VE result begins a snowballing disaster that ends up in my in-box.

So, by the time a project gets to the site for construction, the Consultant has been severely "beaten up". The original design "mojo" has been torn to shreds. The cost savings schemes have wrung out the design quality and desiccated the design finesse. Is that important? And what does that mean in reality?

It means the Consultant rarely has Western-trained senior people on the job site. And, truth be told, on the job site, the Consultant usually gets abused. They get walked over. They are the last to know and by then it's too late.

So, in reality, on site, the Consultant staff sit in the office, the air-conditioned office and wait on the Contractor—wait for materials submittals—wait for shop drawings—wait for requests for information—wait for requests for inspections—wait for as-built drawing submittals. There is no aggressive problem solving. There is nobody "on the ball". They are all drinking Nescafe, chai or just sitting and waiting.

All of this happens, in this part of the world, as 45-50°C temperatures and sand blasting windstorms "conspire" to make sure no Consultant ever leaves the air-conditioned site offices to visit the actual work in progress! Thus they open more doors to undermine the final result design quality. These are additional quality gaps that I often fill, along with my re-instilling and re-kindling of the high-quality landscape design concept that the Owner Developer still expects.

Mind you, this happens as the Owner / Developer's financial, public marketing and brand image are all under pressure to have opening day festivities occur exactly when originally promised at the outset of the project construction—two years earlier. Even though everyone knows unexpected problems arise during construction. So it's always a major time squeeze causing huge pressure on all, especially the Consultant. The Consultant has been battered. The Consultant has become fatigued. This has been what I have come to expect.

The Consultant, however, is in business to make money through repeat work with clients. So, to maintain a professional reputation and steady workload, the Consultant needs to apply reasonable attention during the construction.

This is my work environment. This is the complexity that structures my work cocoon. I love getting into it.

***

Desertification

After giving some structure to the services I planned to offer, I short-formed my CV for use on my mobile. Then began my contacts. First I talked to the landscape contractor from Sheeba to find out who was who and what was happening in Dubai. I learned there were a slew of small to medium sized landscape architecture offices plus at least two large American AEC (Architecture Engineering Construction Management) offices centred in Dubai. They both had landscape architecture groups.

I visited a couple of them. Interesting. There were none of them staffed with Americans. Egyptians, Filipinos, Thais. Among the seniors here and there were Brits, Germans and a few Yanks. But they were all seeking work via the two largest UAE developers in Dubai. The ones that developed the islands like Palm Jumeirah and Palm Jebel Ali–huge projects. So I went to see them.

I realized, after talking with a couple of the largest Dubai developers, that I had placed myself into a niche market that they did not recognize on the front end of projects. They were interested in the landscape architect designer/manager market. And further, these large UAE developers had copied the current western-world management systems along with their politically correct/inclusive approach rather than proven field experience. In my interviews I was regularly interviewed by technical people who obviously had less than 5 years' post-graduate experience.

I brought more than 3 decades of experience to the table

and faced questions suitable for recent graduates. That was surprising and a bit disturbing considering the impressive size of the projects, their timelines and budgets. I thought there couldn't be a good fit for me. I was right. Never heard back.

My go-bag finances were drawing thin and I had come up with nothing. I called Eileen and talked about finances and getting by. Wanted to stay in Dubai instead of flying around MENA on short notice.

She brought up a low-level support job in the US Consulate in Dubai—pitching mail—would be enough to afford a Dubai Metro all-zone silver pass and an efficiency studio flat. "I can get you in under my team without the usual State Dept 'BS'. It would be low pay—grade 7, and part-time 4hrs/day, six days/week. There's not a lot of mail these days but we do get lots of packages—you'd be sorting our stuff out of the State Dept. mail bag."

Well, I took her offer and in a month I set myself up in a small efficiency flat in Al Barsha less than 5 minutes' walk to the MOE. And before long I was "settling-in" to Dubai. I still had sand in my shoes. On one side that was true; but on another side, I was still having dreams, dreams that were alive with Bree. Dreams that emotionally carried over into my daily life.

One night I had a dream in which my wife Bree wasn't buying my new work in the Arabian Peninsula. She brought up her own North Africa experiences in the Sahara inland from the Mediterranean Sea—the ones she first told me about that night in Casablanca. Then she brought up that oh-so-strange story of my college friend who had gone off to fight in the first Gulf War and... well, I don't want to repeat it. Suffice it to say that he had a bad episode in the Empty Quarter—the stuff of nightmares.

It didn't make any difference the dream context. The intensity was Bree's presence; and that always dredged up the well of deepest hurt. I needed a job, a landscape job. I had to get stuck into a landscape project cocoon.

I needed to build some beautiful gardens in an impossible place under an impossible deadline. I had to get beyond my dreams of Bree. I couldn't take them. They hurt too bad.

One night after work, when I was relaxing and fretting in my studio flat, my phone started buzzing. Unknown number. I picked up. He asked for CJ and then introduced himself. He was Theuns van der Walt, a Dutch South African Liwa Qsar Project Sponsor in Abu Dhabi. The conversation went like this:

> Theuns: JeanClaude Thibault told me to call you if I got caught in a bind. Do you know him?
>
> CJ: We are good friends.

Theuns hardly let me finish before he pushed:

> Listen, CJ, I have a world-class resort destination in the Empty Quarter with courtyard gardens everywhere, a healthy budget; and I am in trouble! It is screwed up! FUBAR!! You are the best! I need you on this project! You have to fix this for me! You have to come here! You have to make our gardens world class!
>
> CJ: Theuns, understand this, I'm out of the game. I'm retired. I've had enough of these last-minute mashups. And this project, this project... I've heard all about it. And it just has too much noise.

Theuns van der Walt, with mounting aggravation, said:

> What do you need, CJ? Money, autonomy? Just tell me, I will arrange it all; but I need you now. You've got my number. Tell me tomorrow. Let's make this happen.

Well, I played a bit hard to get but the urgency in his voice told me this was what I had been looking for. That evening, I called Eileen to check out the project. She confirmed Alan was not involved and that there were no red flags on it.

Then I asked, "What about my mail pitching? Can I walk away?"

"There are plenty of State Department staff dependents looking for part-time work, I can solve that. Go do your project and get on with your professional life—sounds like a challenging opportunity."

In the morning I returned Theuns' call and we agreed to meet the next day here in Dubai for breakfast in the Spike Lounge at the Emirates Golf Club. I was stoked.

When I laid down to take rest, I thought... Empty Quarter... and all the stories I'd heard about it since way back with my time in Yenbo. I am going to work in the heart of that monster?! I remembered the words of TE Lawrence in the Arabian Peninsula when asked,

"What is it, Major Lawrence, that attracts you to the desert?"

"It is clean," he answered. "I like it, because it is clean."

Hardly had I heard those romantic words when I recalled how the Great Sand Sea of the Egyptian Sahara had tried to rasp away all vestiges of my emotional memories. Empty Quarter? Rub al Khali? May be clean on the surface but down deep... mysteries. Mysteries from before time. Was I ready to be rasped again?

2-Siren Sounds

Emirates Golf Club

Doing business in 21st century Dubai,
for the first-time visitor from the West it is all...
...a mystery, a total mystery...
...who, where, what and how hard to press...
...when to fish or cut bait,
what is a gimme,
and when to putt out.

As I prepared for my breakfast meeting, I thought about what I knew of this new project. From last night's telephone conversation with that pushy bit of gruff, Theuns van der Walt, I figured this Empty Quarter job would be one indefinable mash-up.

This morning I would meet face to face for the very first time with Theuns, my new paymaster. We would establish the terms of agreement, sort out the playing field, and agree the rules of engagement for this project. He scheduled our meeting at a 36-hole, lush, green golf course built some twenty-five years ago on this Empty Quarter coastal edge waterless sand desert... inside a clubhouse that I read was more like 1920s England than 21st century Dubai.

All defied logic. I was on my way to a project already gone "last-minute" mad. A FUBAR project... where good is bad... where black is white... where day is night. I knew that every day on this project would be an unpredictable, to be solved by anything-goes.

And I loved this work.

An oasis node of Western sport culture—the Emirates Golf Club. I had long become accustomed to the Arabian Peninsula proclivity to copy and paste cultural paradigms from Western sport and business. So it was not unusual for me, that same morning, to have over breakfast a business meeting at the Emirates Golf Club.

Theuns van der Walt worked for the project development company, Cultural Tourism Futures (CTF), and his title was Sponsor. CTF held the money and political power behind every part of this US$400 million Empty Quarter project. As Sponsor, Theuns van der Walt was the key operations person wielding that power and money. This much I had learned from my phone call the other night with Eileen.

Sponsor? Here's what I came to learn. Sponsor had become a job title reeking of false financial importance. It was a politically correct jargon job title, intended through words alone to instil high self-esteem, regardless of definitions or how the person performed. In this case, Theuns van der Walt had not one *hallala* of financial skin in the game, but he held the job title, Sponsor. In the old days, the sponsor would have had money in the project. But today the sponsor was actually the project manager.

The bottom line for me on these business jargon issues was simple. If they did not affect my job performance, I kept them on the back burner, without heat. But I did focus on project cash flow and its controlling personalities. Theuns van der Walt controlled the purse strings on this project; and I needed in. I needed control of the landscape budget.

Today in the Spike Lounge at the Emirates Golf Club, the sponsor would brief me about the essential details of the Empty Quarter project's key players, its schedule, and its problems.

***

The Taxi

I had been in Dubai building the Sheeba project only a couple years ago. Since then the pace of the city's growth has been stunning.

The Dubai Metro wouldn't get me directly to the Emirates Golf Club clubhouse, so I planned to take a taxi. I walked 5 minutes to the taxi stand at the MOE. I climbed in and requested, "Emirates Golf Club clubhouse, please."

Dubai taxis were late model Camrys, impeccably clean inside and out, drivers uniformed in pressed trousers and pressed dress shirts with epaulettes and ties. The taxis were metered, and regularly checked—all very neat, all very dependable.

The driver said, "Welcome!" And we were off. Before long, we were driving Sheik Zayed Road, Dubai's main limited-access freeway, close and parallel to the coast, the main connector between Dubai and Abu Dhabi. On the ride, it was all New Dubai—so much recent construction. But inside the taxi, the driver became my focus.

His driving was smooth and controlled, no tailgating, no nervous braking, no maniacal lane changing, no speeding.

He asked, "You American?"

"Yeah, how'd you guess?"

He said, "Accent," and at once continued, "you know Smokey and Bandit?"

I thought... Smokey and the Bandit... Burt Reynolds... early 1980s...

Before I could answer, the driver continued, "My handle, PakiBanditOne. I am Pakistan. I save money this work to buy back home truck."

I smiled and chuckled to myself, remembering Pakistan's long-favoured status with the United States. In my home-made pidgin English, I had to ask, "In Pakistan driving school, is there rule to beep horn every time you start driving, every time you change lanes?"

With pride, PakiBanditOne said, "No, that is India. Pakistan learn driving like Smokey and Bandit."

I softly chuckled about the inherent contradictions between safe driving techniques compared to those of Smokey and the Bandit... then I lost track of the conversation. I had become hypnotized by the futuristic overhead Dubai monorail, with trains riding high along the edges of Sheik Zayed Road. They were sleek, blue, driverless, digital trains with a Japanese bullet train profile. They moved effortlessly from one elevated, gleaming metallic, space-station pod in the sky to the next. Watching them was even more fun than riding in them.

Whether they would ever significantly reduce road congestion, hardly made a difference, because now, the monorail emanated that optimistic Dubai buzz for the future. Even post-2008, it was a sensual buzz. It was in the air, it was live. I felt it. Most cosmopolitan people could feel it. The Dubai buzz was so strong, it energized all of Abu Dhabi, too.

That buzz was the engine that powered local and regional UAE development. People start with unrealistic dreams, then they build them... but I couldn't help second guessing... a 21st century buzz in the inland core of the Empty Quarter? Wasn't quite right. But that was not my call—if this would be my new job, I would just have to make the resort gardens world class for opening day.

As the taxi drove me through New Dubai, I was shocked by the growing forest of colourful, shiny-glass, new 30-40 storey office and apartment buildings! Stunned by the vast number of new cheek-by-jowl skyscrapers!

I noted that almost every building displayed "to let" and "for lease" signs. I looked in amazement at all the sleek, new glass and steel buildings. Those prolific signs, though, could not noise-cancel the buzz; and I liked that. They promised that the free market, in this hustling trading port, will be bargained to reality and continue its 21st century growth... its buzz.

Yeah, I was in the right place to find a new job.

***

Entry Experience

My eyes had glazed over. I was thinking again... I saw my thoughts only... no longer anything out the taxi window. Despite the visual excitement of the gleaming forest of new high-rise buildings connected by the high-in-the-sky, digital monorail, I was still on overload. Bree had resurfaced in my mind. Dead, she was no longer in my life. I was deep purple with hurt inside—not the place to be for my first business meeting on the new project. I had to shake myself—once, twice and a couple more times.

As an expatriate American businessman, I was always early for my meetings. I prided myself on that. I used the time to get an edge, and to learn my way around new places. The Emirates Golf Club was a landmark in New Dubai. I tried to pull myself out of my, to say the least, emotional melancholy. I had looked forward to this trip to the club. Emirates Golf Club had a reputation for first class design. Maybe it would pick me up.

As the taxi pulled in, I recognized the landscaped main entry to the Emirates Golf Club to be much like any "high-end" gated golf course community built in the United States the last fifteen years. Places like southern Florida or southern California. Everything carefully designed. Everything fresh and amply watered green!

Green, I thought, this is just what I need. Refreshment... gardens... landscape... healthy, well maintained. What a relief!

Yesterday, I had done some online research on this golf club. Now as I entered the grounds in real life, I thought about this golf course and how its landscape may have looked before the course, some twenty-five years ago.

I concluded it must have been without any urban development around it. It must have been virgin Rub al Khali coastal edge. The Empty Quarter as it had been before the British... before the Muslims, before the Christians, before the Sumerians. And then we, modern humans, twenty-some-odd years ago, in a place without dependable annual rainfall, built these 6,000 acres of lawn and irrigated them. Every day, 365 per year!

I noted that this golf course had been sustained for twenty-five years on the Rub al Khali coastal edge. That being so, I thought my resort project featuring protected courtyard gardens inland on the Rub al Khali might have a chance to succeed. I started to calculate the numbers. I tried to get my head around how much water per day—and the evapotranspiration rate in winter... almost the same as summer...

But the water... obviously there was no shortage of water. I considered the issue of irrigation water supply. I wondered about the source of the irrigation water at my new project. Was it treated sewage effluent? Was it treated aquifer water? Was it desalinated water from the Gulf?

Big infrastructure was always required to supply dependable irrigation water in these huge desert projects. How else could plants grow where plants had never before grown? If that infrastructure unexpectedly failed, it usually meant death to the plants, like had happened in Kuwait City in the 1990s during the first Gulf War. And if that water provision was delayed on a new project, then the opening day quality of the plants would fail, requiring massive cost upgrades. Enough, I thought. These problems I could resolve on site, when the job is mine.

My historical approach to the social and natural landscape has always been broad and deep. That is how I develop context. I have progressed past my earlier hubris-fired dream of "portals-to-paradise" design. Now my approach to design is practical; I understand what drives, what motivates, what excites humans. I look for local and regional things, as an essential basis for landscape and garden design. Local context drives materials and processes. That has helped me to be successful—to satisfy this region's clients.

The entry to the golf club—smooth, well presented, with its fancy gate house and uniformed security. Followed by a long and winding entry road through the golf course itself. The winding road with its successive vistas intrigued me. It was an engaging rhythm, an engaging sequence of landscape experiences.

I absorbed what I called a "classic belly dance" landscape experience. Veils covering, then gracefully falling away for a brief glimpse, then covering again... so that I hankered for that view.

It was a strong design, well executed. Broad spreading, coarse-textured shade trees making dark tunnels over the entry road... while coarse-textured, large and dense shrubs forbid the view along the sides... then, in the final bend of a curve... dark to light... all opening to bright, dazzling sunlit vistas, over the gently rolling, sensuously manicured lawns—the fairways. I was manipulated by this landscape design... of tension... then relief... then tension again... it was a real tease.

When the taxi dropped me at the clubhouse porte-cochere, the last veils were removed, and the climax absorbed me.

I saw multi-trunk trees. Bundled together in a thick grove, making full bloom umbrellas of soft, yet voluptuous reds, oranges and yellows... *Delonix regia* and *Peltophorum pterocarpum*... nestled on the shoulders of the porte-cochere.

Beneath this well-pruned, high-canopied overstorey was a richly layered understorey. From the edge of the pavement, I saw a gently rolling hummock of variously sized, young *Cycas revoluta.* They took my eyes up to the base of a substantial mass of multi-stemmed *Rhapis excelsa*, lady palms, making up the visually impenetrable, yet gently undulating soft green walls enclosing this entry garden room.

Thrusting strongly, demanding attention, some in front and some behind the lady palms, were well groomed clumps of clear trunk *Acoelorrhaphe wrightii,* stretching up, three, four and five metres.

All in all, this was an exciting planting that recognized shade and deciduous factors in an organic and healthy composition. And more still... this design and its excellent maintenance provided an intrigue—an intrigue ripe with sexual metaphor.

The core of the climax, the decorative focal point of this entry garden room was under the translucent porte-cochere... water and flowers... the archetypal garden experience. Having exited the taxi and climbing three stairs onto a broad terrace just in front of the clubhouse entry doors, I felt a pulsating vibration... the excitement of the burbling water fountain centre piece. My eyes and ears were fully engaged... leaving me breathless... with gentle, heart-pounding pleasure.

I began analysis. Fountain materials... terra cotta colour, light sand blast finish. It was a self-contained modern derivation of the Alhambra's Court of the Lions fountain... similar in size... a comfortable human scale. Between the stylized lions were stacked various sizes of matching terra cotta flowerpots... maybe sixty to seventy pots in total.

Protecting the feet of the lions, the smallest, lowest, most numerous pots, were at the outside edges, filled with the grey-foliaged, yellow-flowered clumping *Gazania rigens.* Then in the medium sized pots, stepping up from the gazania, were every imaginable colour of *Gerbera jamesonii,* florist quality hybrids... hue intensities like explosions of fireworks... strong reds and loud oranges.

Lastly, between the lions, poking up taller than the fountain edge, were the great highlights of dried flowers from *Protea neriifolia* and *Protea cynaroides.* Displayed in tall, vertical terra cotta pots, these accent protea... with stunning floral detail and incredibly large size... reached out, captured and repaid my attention.

Outstanding! A spectacular entry procession, culminating with captivating variety, loud colour, and refreshing water at the entry!

I paused a moment, and looked around to take it all in again... the water, the colour, the healthy aura. The garden had anaesthetized my Bree memories, a relief I badly needed.

I liked this experience. This landscape entry had seduced me while I was in the taxi. And on foot, the garden climax was more fulfilling still.

I knew gardens had to reward with detail. The walking person, the standing person, the sitting person—each had to be rewarded with uniquely crafted detail. Such art! This entry ticked all those boxes. I smiled because I could not take my eyes from the flowers and water... their titillations.

There was activity around me. People entering and leaving the clubhouse. I was out of place with my reveries. I had to pull myself away from the sexual fantasy emanating from that plant-dominated drama. This garden had rejuvenated me. Now, I was ready for work.

I continued to the clubhouse door. Inside, the air conditioning gave me relief to the desert heat I had briefly forgotten. As I paused and looked around, I absorbed an emotional richness that spoke of the 1920s. The heydays of the Western world... the Harry Vardon days, the Cole Porter days. I saw leather, heavily carved wood, curvaceous furniture, classic late Victorian. I saw trophies and displays of golfing paraphernalia in clean Art Deco cases of metal and glass—more pleasures for my eyes.

After the fun of the well-designed entry experience, I recalled another reason why I had wanted to arrive early. I hoped to find the original golf course designer, an unusual character. I had a 10AM with Theuns. It was 9AM.

I had time. I began my search.

***

Vardon Clubhouse

The entry landscape gardens had rejuvenated me. With newfound energy, I eagerly walked the clubhouse. I explored hallways and meeting rooms. I savoured the rich emotions of the place, enjoying the interior decor. I kept an eye open for the course designer and original Club Professional, Bankley Cuthbert, Esquire.

A past member of the Royal and Ancient, Mr. Cuthbert came in the late 80s to help Sheik Mohamed build this course—and stayed. In the underpopulated world of long-time Dubai landscape specialists, Mr. Cuthbert's reputation ran strongly before him.

Successful international projects in foreign countries often benefited from collegial contacts. And I was on the hunt.

I admired the thoroughness and detail appreciation of old-school British landscape specialists. I figured Bankley Cuthbert, Esquire would be a wealth of historical golf and practical horticultural treasures. I hoped Mr. Cuthbert could trot out golf stories from Old Tom Morris, Sir Henry Cotton, JH Taylor. Maybe he would speak of the club's landscape gardens from the aesthetic and horticultural perspectives of Capability Brown, Humphry Repton, Gertrude Jekyll. That conversation promised to be both fun and enlightening–if, that is, he would share it with a Yank.

I was equally interested in architecture and interior design as I was landscape architecture. To me details, inside and outside, were all part of my design analysis and understanding, all part of the user experience. The clubhouse was filled with medium to dark, oak and mahogany wood detailing. The comfortable, well-stuffed, oxblood-red, leather furnishings had to have come from the UK.

But upon my close inspection of the well carved and crafted furniture, I was certain it was not manufactured in the UK. Most likely these fine-quality knockoffs came from either China or Viet Nam, countries whose copies of Western quality furnishings have been improving quickly, almost indistinguishable from the originals, as I had learned some years ago on my Bahrain project. I knew of the Emirati attention to costs and figured these knockoffs probably saved 75% compared to originals from the UK.

I finally found the Spike Lounge on a lower level. I was to meet the sponsor there. It had a shaded terrace. Either inside or outside, the lounge seats provided excellent views overlooking the golf course. Its restaurant offered an "English-fry-up" buffet, every kind of meat, every kind of pork sausage and bacon—this wasn't Saudi Arabia. The breakfast of the Raj—the breakfast against which every doctor warned.

I thought, how can anyone understand the Muslim intolerance for pork and yet find it featured on the menu in this public place? But, as I had long ago learned, the UAE was a moderate country, especially the Dubai Emirate. Pork? No problem. Same for alcohol.

At the end of the buffet was a bar. The bar had ten to fifteen seats in front of a large picture window, providing excellent views of the 18th green. It was a weekday, fewer golfers, more businessmen making deals. I saw, not too far away, standing at the end of the bar, a man silhouetted against the 18th green—an older gentleman—with a 1920s Harry Vardon profile?

That profile looked somehow familiar. I recalled, during my walk from the clubhouse entry, I had passed down two hallways. A hallway of champions, featuring large photos of every winner of the Dubai Desert Classic, over the past twenty years—a veritable who's who of professional golf: Seve Ballesteros, Fred Couples, Colin Montgomerie, Ernie Els, Tiger Woods. And a second hall of photos, commemorating the club captains and the club professionals.

I was now certain I was looking at the silhouette of Bankley Cuthbert, Esquire, the man himself. As in his hallway photo, he wore a flannel shirt and tie, a lightweight v-neck sweater, pleated plus-fours covering his argyle stockings—all in the most sedate of heather colours.

I recalled details from the hallway bio that Mr. Cuthbert, as the Emirates Golf Club's first golf professional, had overseen the original grassing in 1988. In the early 90s, he had overseen the expansion from 18 to 36 holes. According to his hallway bio, he had retired in 1996. He remained to this day in country as the Emeritus Professional, known unofficially as "the oldest member". Judging by his dress, he was certainly a man for landscape stories of unique detail and colour. A PG Wodehouse character. Exactly as I had hoped.

Just then, my cell vibrated with a text. I checked. A text from the Sponsor. He was early, too. Before I finished reading the first text message, Theuns had texted a second time. This time he texted he was at the Spike Lounge buffet and did not like to wait.

***

Breakfast with Theuns

Even though the Sponsor and I had the same objective—opening the project as scheduled and on budget with world-class awe-inspiring gardens—I knew that a personality like Theuns would be a handful. I had already plotted my strategy to get what I needed to succeed on this project. I was ready.

Before I finished reading the Sponsor's second text, my cell vibrated with a call. I didn't pick up. Instead, I looked around and found Theuns van der Walt, the Sponsor, not far away, next to the buffet. We shook hands.

Theuns, giving an aggressive and painfully firm handshake, said, "CJ, pleased to meet you. Glad you made it. Let us begin."

The owner/developer company, Cultural Tourism Futures (CTF), was a well-funded and well-connected Abu Dhabi government quango. I came to know their representative, Theuns van der Walt, well. He was thirty-five, an impressive rugby union player in his youth, and an avid Springbok supporter now. Theuns was five foot ten, and a thick, fit, robust two hundred pounds. He was a focused professional, a real-estate development manager. He exhibited the tenacious qualities of white Dutch South Africans, Dutch East India Company descendants who, over the centuries, had helped build a solid and dependable economic power of a country.

Theuns was always impeccably shaved, head and face, with overall, just the right amount of light suntan. He dressed as if he just came off the catwalk in Milan—conservative and elegant—appropriate sunglasses and no jewellery—Ermenegildo

Zegna—all the way.

But, like many other white South Africans, he was happy to be working outside his home country and had no desire to return. Why? Because of the new black leadership in the country which, in his opinion, had led to a severe cultural and economic degradation. In Theuns' case, it was disastrously exemplified two years ago. While Theuns was in Dubai, there was a racially motivated carjacking in Johannesburg, during which his wife and his young and only child, a son, were ripped from their car and ruthlessly murdered in cold blood in broad daylight on the public street.

Theuns was a man whose impatience and worldly lust could only be the result of the shocking killing of his family, from which he had never fully recovered. I could understand that, having lost my own.

It was not yet 10AM; but outside the temperature was 39°C and rising, and the humidity was 70%—hot and oppressively humid, even in the shade—normal Dubai weather. This was Rub Al Khali coastal edge weather as it always has been. The weather made inside the only choice. From the buffet, we both took coffee and toast, then found a table with a view of the golf course.

Upon sitting down, I knew there was little time for small talk but I had to ask, "If this is an Abu Dhabi project, why are we meeting in Dubai?"

He responded abruptly, "Who wants to live in Abu Dhabi when Dubai is next door?!"

At the same time he handed me his business card.

Looking at Theuns' business card, I asked him, "What is it exactly that Sponsors, or Task Force Stream Sponsors, like you, do at CTF?"

Theuns, always impatient, summarized how the latest trends in business management, social justice, and environmental sustainability were all wrapped into a matrix system of job responsibility at CTF. He continued, "While there is no direct chain of command in this matrix system, I have the final project financial and schedule responsibility in front of the CEO and the Executive Board."

I said, "Okay, I like the clarity of one point of authority and communication, that should work well. But the matrix system? It sounds a bit awkward; though I'm sure you won't let it hinder my work, will you?" I didn't pause for a response. "Now, following our introductions, let's get to specifics. Please tell me the particulars you expect from me, and the appropriate details."

Theuns, always with a grudging tone, said, "What I expect? The best site finishes ever, on time, and on budget! Any questions there?"

"No—none, that's what I do; but give me background, please. How have you gotten into the last-minute problem that needs my help?"

Theuns continued, "On the landscape, we have no one internally with the proper field experience; and our project management team, our consultant and our general contractor cannot make the landscape happen. They are pretenders. They are not responsive—not effective—not efficient, we are not getting a 100% result! That is why we need you now. We do not have time to change horses. We have to get control in our own house!!!"

"I understand, I hear you. We have to work with the team you have in place; but that is surprising..."

Theuns interrupted, "CJ, I asked you because you know how things work around here. You need to fix both the quality and the timing of the landscape, now let me finish!

"This is CTF's first major built project. Our financial backers and our marketing, our branding people require it to be special. We expect Condé Nast to rank our Empty Quarter Project, Liwa Qsar, #1 in their list of "World's Best New Resort Destinations"; and we are over three months behind schedule, with only six months until the soft opening. JeanClaude Thibaut told me you're the guy and you are available. We have a major A-lister opening event, with all the leaders from all the Emirates. Since I am the Sponsor, I want to say this in words you Americans understand. My ass is on the line, and your ass, too, will be on the line! My position is 'no fail'! Your position is 'no fail'!"

On the job, Theuns was a machine, a 24/7 machine. This kept him from thinking about the loss of his family—he had a project cocoon just like mine. He drove for success. In that drive, there was no line he wouldn't cross—no line.

Theuns had found that at his high level of project management, as long as he provided what the owner, I learned a well-placed Emirati from the Royal family, needed, any legal setbacks or otherwise "impediments" would be, with the owner's deft hand, the shortest of temporary.

Theuns saw me as a white-collar mercenary, like himself. He was right. White-collar mercenaries are not hired to succeed at killing. They are hired to succeed at building projects. Why mercenaries?

There are places in the world where both salaries and threat of death to strangers are high. Traditional mercenaries of death work there. But at the perimeter of those areas, there is money for projects in places that may be either dangerous to live or just downright horribly unpleasant to live.

Only white-collar mercenaries go there because they know these are well paid, short term contractual situations—they are not family situations. The work is hard, intense, and the reward is high—paycheque, bonuses and a project well completed.

Theuns and I were both part of a Middle East stable of multi-cultural development and construction mercenaries, professionals of the hardest type, riding the huge cresting development wave in the Gulf Region. We went where the work was.

Theuns stayed on "a roll". He was pushing, he was hot, impatience on the boil, "This project is for only 200 keys, but we bring power and water from over 200 kilometres to the site. We have to be ethically responsible and environmentally responsible, no matter what the logic. We are building a fixed destination in a place where for centuries the few people ever passing through were... nomads! The challenges are many. We need that place first-class in six months. I will pay you US$15,000/month, and a 25% completion bonus. Now, I want to hear are you on board, or not?!"

Theuns hadn't touched his toast. His coffee was gone. His

Blackberry was buzzing every three minutes, and he couldn't put it down.

I said, "Look, I know this work and you're paying me fairly. I'll dig into it this week and meet you for an end of the day update this Thursday. I'll brief you on what I've found, and I'll outline an action plan to get CTF its finish and award quality, on schedule. But, Theuns, listen, please! You've got to understand that I'll need you to clear things for me–cut the red tape, give me line-level vetoes on all invoices, and no downtown meetings, do you follow?"

"CJ, I will do what is needed; but didn't you understand me the first time? It is you who must not fail! Are you in? When will you give me your action plan?"

I knew the game, I got Theuns' message. "That's clear enough. Just give me the contact details of the responsibles, and Thursday, I'll show you how it'll be accomplished."

Theuns pulled out a memorandum of understanding (MOU) for me–under agreement until hard opening (approx. 8 months), salary, housing allowance, 4WD transportation, completion bonus–straightforward. It was more than fair. He told me he'd have his transportation people deliver a fully insured, white, 4WD Mitsubishi SUV for my use for the duration of my agreement. I counter-signed my copy and his. "Okay, I'm with you," I said.

Theuns concluded our meeting, "Excellent, let us get this rolling. You know The Library at the Royal Mirage at the base of the Palm Jumeirah?" I nodded. "We'll meet at The Library, CJ, Thursday... say 9PM?"

We agreed.

Theuns texted me the CVs, backgrounds and contact details for the on-site CTF hospitality director, the general contractor, the project management team, the prime consultant, the landscape architecture consultant, the landscape contractor and all other applicable sub-contractors on my new Liwa Qsar project.

Theuns said, "See you Thursday," wrenched my hand again and left.

I remained. I reviewed my conversations with Theuns.

I could see Theuns' need for a result as both essential and pragmatic. I still had an uncertainty whether Theuns would be good for keeping his word. Would Theuns smooth the road for me—cut the bureaucracy—cut the "carpet office-blah blah-kumbaya" consensus meetings?

I knew that would be an ongoing challenge. There were so many pieces to this puzzle; and I was just starting. I sketched out who was who and set up a likely power structure. All of my key contacts were already on site deep in the Empty Quarter. Only the landscape architect consultant was here in town.

Then I set up my meetings. That same night I began with the landscape architecture consultant—a headache or an asset?

3-Dubai

Cultural Context

I'd been in and around Dubai on a couple projects—RAK and Sheeba; but I had always been too busy on their critical deadlines to relax and look see what normal daily life was really like in Dubai. And even though this new project was under that same kind of pressure, I had to go where I had to go. And well, that night I had my first chance to visit one of the regular "hot spots" in New Dubai, the Walk at Jumeirah Beach Residences (JBR.)

I arrived early for my appointment with the landscape architecture consultant for the Liwa Qsar Empty Quarter project, Geoffrey Tate, so I had some time to look around. At the Café di Roma, I sat down outside and ordered a hot chocolate. Chocolate soothed me. It had its own magic—working on the internal, soothing more and more until it calmed my entire body.

Nine PM, just getting dark, 35°C temperature with just a hint of cooling, light breezes off the Gulf. The evening crowd, the electricity of the paseo in early crank. The hot chocolate arrived. Turin hot chocolate—in a large-mouthed, open cup, almost a bowl. A real pleasure—chocolate pudding with a skin. Warm chocolate pudding—I liked it, winter or summer.

In New Dubai, The Walk where I sat was a linear pedestrian promenade, thirty metres wide, stretching along four, maybe five city blocks. One edge of the promenade comprised the entry level, narrow frontage cheek by jowl businesses including an exuberant variety of fashion shop hangouts, fast-food outlets, smallish cafés, and medium sized restaurants. And in front of them, the inner half of the promenade was chockablock filled with umbrella'd outdoor tables packed with customers.

The rest of the promenade was a palm-tree lined paseo show place. At the curbed outer edge was a one-lane, one-way, traffic-calmed road—talk about show and tell—the hottest cars in Dubai crawled it—Bentleys, Lamborghinis, and more. Beyond the crawl, the sand beaches of Jumeirah and the Gulf. It was all about see and be seen. This was not a *burka* and *niqab* dominated neighbourhood.

The Walk generated a vibrant, real-life, cultural mix—a front-page social tabloid, if you will, including a good sprinkling of Emiratis, loads of Middle East Arabs (the Egyptians, the Lebanese), some Magrebis (the North Africans), some sub-Saharan Africans, lots of Eastern and Western Europeans, and people from the old British Commonwealth... the South Africans, the Australians, the New Zealanders... some Bollywood sub-continentals... and a few North American expatriates, with their rambunctious pet dogs, barely kept on leashes.

What they all had in common? Work. This was not yet a tourist-dominated scene. These were workers and employers enjoying their time off. Maybe the time for tourism will come, but now? Contracted employees. Dubai is the geographic centre of Europe, Africa and Asia—a place with a future.

This was the public realm in first decades 21st century Dubai—clean, well-lighted, nicely designed, plenty of greenery, no rowdy gangs, no pushing, no shoving, no shouting, no screaming and no obvious petty crime. I couldn't complain.

***

Geoffrey and Tang

From this meeting I hoped to learn if the Liwa Qsar landscape architecture consultant had been already beaten to a useless pulp. Was the landscape architecture consultant still alive and "in the game"? And, if still "in the game", was the landscape architecture consultant committed to make Liwa Qsar gardens their best ever?

In challenging environments, large iconic projects, like Liwa Qsar, are built invariably in a fog of evolving problems and conflicts. Final solutions are ultimately discovered, not in advance in the air-conditioned, carpeted office, but in real-time, on the sweaty, noisy construction sites. I needed clear commitments from the landscape architecture consultant.

With my questions in hand and within this summary understanding of the project process, I was about to meet the landscape architecture consultant, Land Iterations and Derivatives—everybody knew them by their short name, LandID. LandID were an American landscape architecture company. Geoffrey Tate, a Brit, was their UAE and Mid East Regional Director.

On Liwa Qsar, LandID were the responsible consultant for all the site finishes—plants, irrigation, paving, walls, pergolas, cabanas, water features, plus oversight on way finding, signage, lighting, grading, drainage—the usual landscape architecture stuff.

Earlier in the day when I went through the documents Theuns made available to me, I reviewed Geoffrey's CV. Geoffrey? After his professional degrees from Greenwich and Edinburgh, he earned his Landscape Institute credential following a period with Ove Arup on a major international multi-consultancy project in the Middle East. During that project, he had worked closely for the first time with the famous master planning and design consultant, LandID. Afterwards, they offered him a position in their Los Angeles office.

He moved up quickly, becoming a Studio Leader, and then Partner. I concluded from his docs that, now the manager of the LandID presence in the region, his focus was clearly on his bonus-based, bottom-line office performance.

In their office of thirteen, he was the only Brit. His employees included his personal assistant and eleven technical specialists, five from the Philippines, four from India, and two Egyptians. He was very successful. I figured he was, in most respects, smart and focused enough to use his intense, yet often hidden emotions to business advantage.

On the evening, there was a bustling electricity all around me—an exciting mood: design was in the air, employment was in the air, improvement of family fortune was in the air. I felt a positivism that boded well for my success.

That setting on The Walk kept overwhelming me—captivating my thoughts. The buzz on the street was a multi-cultural buy-in to Western pop culture. Previously sports were the sole conduit. I could see design issues, couched in Western pop culture design jargon, becoming an easy entry for cross-cultural discussions. And I'd be having a bunch of these the next couple days.

And The Walk? It embodied that. The Walk had become a real-time mingling of Western pop culture with regional and local traditions...

The flip side was that there would always exist the possibility that local Emirati desire to protect their own heritage might overrule contemporary Western pop culture references. The blend of traditional Emirati culture with modern Western pop-culture... common roots—hard to define. It was a professional tightrope. I would have to make sure "who was who" among Emiratis on my project.

In addition to assessing cultural contexts, my head was

full of Liwa Qsar to-do items. I found momentary respite in a couple spoons of the warm chocolate pudding.

While I was gazing out to the street, absorbing the growing paseo, Geoffrey Tate arrived—along with a companion, a fashionable young Chinese lady, Wenli Tang, whom Geoffrey described as his office personal assistant. I stood to greet them.

I had not expected a threesome. Tang softly and confidently exuded such a blossoming aura of beauty that I felt a blur overcoming my professional focus. She had the studied, detached presence of a Parisian catwalk model, and a sexual magnetism intense enough to disable any man. Who would ride in a Lamborghini and emerge like a butterfly from one of those gull wing doors? She would.

She was the full package. Porcelain skin, soft make-up, short black... elegant, yet punk-styled hair with a vivid pink accent streak. She wore a Mao-collar silk chemise, in soft greys, luxuriantly hugging her subtly curvaceous body. Over the chemise, she had casually draped around her neck a finely woven black pashmina—one corner accented in vivid pink, by custom-embroidered, classic Lalique-themed artwork. Her chemise fell just to mid thigh. Loosely covering the tops of her black leotard which allowed her gracefully slender legs to be exclamation pointed by vivid pink, platform stiletto heels. Oh yeah, the full package.

I caught my breath, greeted her, and gradually regained composure, mentally reminding myself where my focus should be: the project, Liwa Qsar. Then I turned my attention for the first time to the landscape architecture consultant, Geoffrey Tate, the LandID Regional Director, the man responsible for design of all the site finishes at Liwa Qsar.

Geoffrey Tate was gracious and welcoming. He had brought a complete set of design documents, including bound A3-size landscape drawings, and a thumb drive, with the same, including specifications and bills of quantities. These he handed, with professional courtesy, to me.

It was easy for me to understand his character. I had worked with many Brit expatriate professionals. He had the look—he was on his game—no doubt about it. His hair was short, blond, cropped as is fashionable, with a bit of a... Rod Stewart... David Bowie... look. Geoffrey obviously had his fun.

Geoffrey Tate was in the prime of his consultancy career, forty, single, six feet tall, 175 pounds. He was like certain modern, yet old-fashioned public-school Brits, who imagine themselves landed aristocrats, carrying under the surface an envy and bitterness, regarding the "recent" American independence and their subsequent newcomer prominence in the world.

He, definitely a leg-over merchant, reminded me of the Guy Berger character, in a Dubai film I had seen at the MOE a couple nights ago... *City of Life*, written and directed by an Emirati, Ali Mostafa. The film inspected the lives of people in different contemporary Dubai subcultures. Geoffrey was the successful expat, Guy Berger party boy, taking what he could get from the inventory of Eastern European and East Asian girls here in Dubai—girls, trying to save their lives, just making a living like everyone else.

He epitomized the newly minted Western expat, interested in his own pleasures—not silk shirt, not hair shirt, but clubbing like there would be no tomorrow.

I was getting a feeling about Geoffrey. Nothing clear yet whether he would be an asset or a headache... but worries were swirling around the edges. Geoffrey had a strong design pedigree and mature site construction experience. On the other hand, his personal actions seemed to undermine his professional dependability. This enigmatic blend of party boy with consummate professional meant I had work to do.

***

Motives

In this meeting for project success, I sought an edge. I caught Geoffrey's eye and asked, "I wonder, Geoffrey, about our project; if LandID is an American company, why are no Americans working in your office?"

Geoffrey explained, "None of the recent American graduates, or any of the mid-level Americans, wanted to leave the US lifestyle for staffing this local office, even for limited three-month windows. Why? Either too comfortable at home, or too soft—either way, no problem for me. My staff is strong and dependable, the 'Ever Victorious Landscapers' is what we call them—good professionals, all.

"I set this office up to be a successful profit centre. As long as I keep finding capable landscape staff from other countries, which I have done so far with no problems, I am more than happy with the results. Most design is done back in the US; but all field work and project administration are done right here in our office."

I pressed for details about their design and its implementation, "Tell me then, what does LandID really want out of this project?"

Geoffrey was truthful. "We will be profitable. Our company is well known in the US, and the world, for its award-winning master planning and well-crafted design for resort destinations; but just as importantly we get the job done—dependably. And over the past four years in Dubai we have already built two wildly successful, international-award-winning projects. LandID has a look, a successful style built upon a practical, local flexibility on attention to detail, both in hard materials and plants. We have the basic things, the practical fundamentals in place for successful implementation in this region."

Geoffrey paused for a moment, sipped on his iced latte. When he noted my attention and eye contact, he must have sensed common professional ground. He continued, "It suits our objectives out here, where climate, work force, client whims, and a fickle and weakly developed local support industry altogether mean that the best of site construction detailing can never be achieved."

Listening to these words, I heard in Geoffrey's voice a veiled tone of fatalism—a weakness. I concluded that weakness was another reason I would be needed on this project. I kept these thoughts to myself and looked at Geoffrey with an uncertainty that thinly disguised my outright disapproval.

Geoffrey, without pause, leaned closer to me and more softly continued, "Examine it from any angle, but you must be realistic. You know as well as I, it's either a quality compromise to work out here or, it's our success just to get it built under these difficult circumstances. On each massive project, politics shape-shift personalities; and politics shape-shift project details—that's a given. Then the schedules, the deadlines, the planned openings—they're never delayed, never changed—even in the face of worldwide financial tremors like we saw in 2008-9."

I knew Geoffrey had a practical point. But I always strove to get the best craft, to get that superb beauty on opening day. I had learned that a successful project, an elegant result, finding a delicate balance with local practicality, would always be challenging. A consultant should never give up striving. Geoffrey's role in the project was becoming clearer. He would not be an asset. I would have to take over his site finishes design responsibilities myself.

I took a deep breath, relaxed, and gazed at the parade of automobiles slowly working their way down the traffic-calmed street—the $250K-plus automobiles. I saw in those autos the beauty, the craft, the art. They were a symbol, a symbol of human efforts to assure beauty—an inherent, an essential part of life... beautiful cars, beautiful girls, beautiful gardens. And I would achieve a beautiful solution at the Liwa Qsar Empty Quarter project.

About Geoffrey, I had concluded: Geoffrey's "practical fatalism" would likely not interfere. I could beat that, no problem.

I had found a trail, along which I was learning how Geoffrey looked at the LandID work in this region. I saw problems developing. I took a quick look at the drawings.

My fear for the worst was confirmed. Tonight's questions and answers had led me to understand that the LandID construction bid package for Liwa Qsar—their design documents—had been detailed using the "copy and paste" and "favourites" techniques from their earlier projects by young American graduates working in the US.

Those young professionals had never seen this part of the world, let alone ever built a project here. To them it was all desert, the coast of Dubai, and the Liwa Oasis, 300 kilometres inland—all the same. They had no understanding of micro-climate.

I recognized problems in that approach. I knew that the local Liwa reality, the inland desert site, its topography and climate were certainly more complex and significantly different from the coastal desert surrounding Dubai and Abu Dhabi.

Theuns had told me that it was too late to change any of the players. I would have to work with Geoffrey and his team. I needed to learn more and put a challenge to Geoffrey, "So, the way I hear it, LandID's site team has a non-productive landscape contractor and nothing is being done to change that? Right?"

I did not let Geoffrey answer, instead I pushed on, "LandID do not have a pro-active site team and you're leaving all the final touches to a contractor who's already not performing well?"

I looked Geoffrey straight in the eye, this time expecting a response. Geoffrey took a matter-of-fact defensive position, saying, "We, I and our site people, are going through the professional motions; and it isn't our responsibility to goose an unresponsive, poorly performing sub-contractor. We just push the paperwork."

I listened carefully. Geoffrey's words bristled with an undercurrent, a kind of static electricity noise. That was another warning, a sign for me to stay on my toes around Geoffrey.

Geoffrey again leaned over toward me and quietly revealed his cynicism for work in this region, maybe, once again, saying more than he should have, "Let's examine the background context a little more. Let's talk a second about sustainability. If you settled in an area, a region, such as this, where there has never been enough water, or enough food... and stayed here... you would have to be either A) stupid; or B) cursed. That is the baseline condition here.

"And furthermore, this place is a hell, a hell where naive, poorly educated people of all ages from everywhere come to work, and provide services for long hours, six days per week, via one, two or three layers of vampiric middlemen and scurrilous project managers whose only business is to make more money for themselves by cheating these poor souls!"

"Whoa," I interjected. I did not like these kinds of politics, so I staked out my ground, "What are we doing here, building a project or saving souls? I've been around enough consultants and contractors to know that truly ambitious people come to the Emirates from the East, from all over, to improve their lives, returning home after they've reached their objectives. They work hard here, live frugally, saving money to start a new business when they get back home—to build better lives for their families. There's nothing naive about that. You can't lump everyone together. And you, c'mon, you too, make a good living here—but now I'm wondering—as a consultant, or an activist?" I restrained myself from further questions and comments about how much Geoffrey paid his staff.

As Geoffrey watched the people of the paseo, his pupils dilated. He was silent. Tang was silent. I remained vigilant. I thought, I've stumbled into town... found a little Chinese love nest. I caught Tang's eye and she ever so softly whispered, "... shhhh-shhhh-shhhh..."

I had uncovered Geoffrey's real-life concerns. Liwa Qsar to Geoffrey was just another project number. In reality, Geoffrey was an activist gadfly—many of which try to gain notoriety by writing social justice articles about how awful life is in Dubai. Strange animal, this Geoffrey, I thought... on one hand he digs into the high-society culture of which Tang was truly a part... then back home on his computer he whines how hard life is for poor workers here. Wants it both ways, this guy.

In time, I came to know that Geoffrey and Tang epitomized, as it appeared on the night, the flash Dubai party scene that was clearly becoming an important cultural Dubai segment. I had no time for that. My professional career and my personal situation dictated I keep my nose—and all other body parts—clean.

I had to assure that I did not let my disagreement with Geoffrey's socio-political positions distract from the Liwa Qsar project objectives.

***

Consultant Contractor Connections

I had one more project area to explore with the landscape architecture consultant. Before I got started, I looked at my Turin hot chocolate. Completely ignored it during my discussions with Geoffrey. I spooned out the last remnants. Pushing my large bowl and spoon away, I took a deep breath.

My eyes and attention drifted into the unceasing paseo. It was impossible to ignore—such a great street scene—no drunken bums—no aggressive troublemakers—what a civilized pleasure it was, just sitting there talking. This was a clean public area.

Then I went back to work, refocused the discussion, and asked Geoffrey about the Liwa Qsar general contractor. I started, "Putting the LandID site role aside for the moment, usually I've found the general contractor can squeeze performance out of his sub-contractors, in our case the landscape sub..."

Geoffrey interrupted and explained, "This landscape sub-contractor, Green Tree, is new to the UAE. Their senior responsible people have twenty-five years' experience in Saudi Arabia. Their real strength is their Emirati sponsor, a high-ranking Sheik in the ruling family of Abu Dhabi, whose daughter married the ruling President of Dubai. With those contacts they were a—no questions asked—nominated sub-contractor; and, as such, the general contractor and we were forced to accept them. They do have well-experienced senior Lebanese managers, and a large nursery. But the people on site always say yes and produce neither according to the schedule, nor at the required quality. So... we do the paperwork—nonconformance reports, etc.—you know the drill."

I already knew the answer, but nevertheless asked, "Do you ever go out to site?"

Geoffrey unabashedly said, "No, and why should I!? One of the VE exercises deleted our senior site support, and replaced it with junior staff. That's it! We have two Pinoy graduate architects on site, and they're good fellows. They've both been working in the UAE doing site administration for me for the last three years. They know how to keep the paperwork prompt and flowing."

I had heard enough, I had it figured out. Changing the subject, I asked, "Geoffrey, I might need to visit you later, where is your office?"

"Right here in JBR. Just call, or text me, we can arrange a meeting on short notice."

One last time, out of professional courtesy, I told him I was planning to visit the site, and the Contractor's nursery, this week and would like to have Geoffrey there with me.

Geoffrey was clearly comfortable with his approach and staffing for Liwa Qsar. And, as he had already made clear to me, he was aware that his job was not to goose the contractor, rather to make sure the approved LandID design would get built as approved. He declined my request saying, "From tomorrow, I'll be out of town, busy on a new project in Qatar. You're welcome anytime to visit the site and the nursery, without my presence."

That, too, was much as I had expected. What he was really saying was he was sure his site people could take care of it; and he was more interested in a new project than walking around the Empty Quarter job site. Geoffrey trusted himself that if called to task he would have the answers to save his company's reputation.

In other words, this entire last exchange was but a superficial courtesy. I worked directly for CTF on this project and could go anywhere, anytime without Geoffrey's permission.

I had got the drift of Geoffrey's approach to this project. Geoffrey would stay on the sidelines, unless crossed. I also picked up an important fact—politics—the politics behind the landscape contractor's uncontested—and incontestable—appointment on the project. This could become serious big-time noise because this Green Tree Landscape Contractor had already been identified by Theuns as part of the on-site underperformance problem.

I saw Geoffrey's approach to be like any other consultant—hungry for change orders (contract change meaning additional income for LandID). If the landscape contractor underperformed and CTF wanted improvements, Geoffrey was in line for more money. He didn't want to go head-to-head with the landscape contractor, because of Green Tree's well placed Emirati owners. It was his gamble. CTF via Theuns wanted no part of that opening day gamble—that's why they hired me.

Geoffrey did courteously offer he would be glad to answer questions I might have. But my concerns had deepened. I had to make sure that Geoffrey's influence on the construction site was neutered. The last thing I needed on the short time frame of Liwa Qsar was head butting from the landscape architecture consultant. Through these discussions, I had gathered enough information to develop the groundwork for a possible path forward, free from Geoffrey's interference.

As I stood up to leave, I made a point to be cordial to Tang and Geoffrey. I thanked Geoffrey for his time and the contract documents he had delivered.

We shook hands and I left. Geoffrey and Tang stayed to hang out. The rest of my meetings would be 300 kilometres south from here, at the Liwa Qsar project site in the arid, super-heated heart of the inland Empty Quarter.

4-Entering The Beast

Linkage

My evening with Geoffrey and Tang had been long. I was worn out as I took a taxi back to my studio. I showered, made a tisane, put my feet up and, making notes in my diary, reviewed my conversations with Geoffrey. No more alcohol—I was deep into my project cocoon.

I was just about ready to take rest when my phone buzzed. It was JeanClaude.

"I thought you were just passing through on your way back to Papua New Guinea," I said.

"I was but I heard from Theuns van der Walt—a couple times. Today he told me you had agreed to do a project for him—in the Empty Quarter on the extreme east tip of the Liwa Oasis. Did I hear him correctly?"

"Exactly, and I am on board—he's sending a 4WD to me tomorrow and I am planning to visit the site the day after tomorrow to meet the key people and draw up a plan to get the landscape part of the project back on track—by the way, he said you recommended me to him, is that so?"

"What? You don't want to work out there?"

His question took my voice away. I didn't know what made him think that. And before I could respond he continued, "You've been pussy-footing around the edges of the Empty Quarter for I don't know how many years—15? You afraid? The *djini* got a hold of you?"

Finally sunk in—JeanClaude on his jokey thing—he liked taking things to the edge. Sometimes I didn't get it. This time... "A job is a job! I'm into it."

"You think I'm joking? Tell you what. I can reschedule my flight out of here and the two of us can ride together out to Liwa. Will that help? I've been in that inland region of the Empty Quarter quite often... I can point things out and answer any questions you have along the way. I'm staying at the Royal Mirage—pick me up there at the main entrance to the Palace at 8 AM and we can make that trip together the day after tomorrow, okay? Does that work for you, *mon ami*?"

His ethnobotanical background might be useful, I thought. But I could do without his silly joking.

"Sounds good. I have to finish my Liwa Qsar project planning and schedule my on-site meetings tomorrow. Are you calling from your room phone? If there is any change tomorrow, I will need to contact you. Otherwise, 8 AM day after tomorrow, main entrance Royal Mirage Palace."

***

Rub al Khali Coastal

The Rub al Khali, the Empty Quarter, what does empty mean?

Essentially... empty of water... empty of plants... empty of animals... empty of humans.

It is 500,000 square kilometres of sand dune emptiness, right up to and including the coastal edge of the Gulf... for millennia... empty.

But years ago in Yenbo, I met people knowledgeable about the Arabian Peninsular deserts. They were convinced there was something unusual and alive, though mysteriously hidden in those sands. What would I find here?

The nomads and the semi nomadic Bedu used the Empty Quarter coastal edge as part-time seasonal habitation to take advantage of fishing and pearling opportunities, but... never permanent settlement... until oil revenues.

And the rest is history up to today... 50 years of electricity and water fuelled desert development–Dubai, Abu Dhabi.

Following my Dubai meetings with Theuns van der Walt and Geoffrey Tate, I assessed the key people working at the Liwa Qsar project site. I organized my objectives. I made appointments to meet with them.

Then I coordinated with JeanClaude. Together we planned the 300km Dubai to Liwa Qsar trip to be a landscape transect through the Empty Quarter. I figured it to be an exploration to gather knowledge from JeanClaude while examining the difference between the Empty Quarter coastal edge and the Empty Quarter inland.

We would examine how the landscape modified as we moved from the urban coastal edge into the unpopulated inland core of the sand desert. This drive into the arid core of the Empty Quarter was a UAE drive I had never taken.

But first I would have to rein in JeanClaude's tendency to wander off subject. My goal and objective orientation would be tested. With JeanClaude, I might just have to find new lenses through which to examine the landscape.

My lenses—now that is interesting.

Despite the last-minute circumstances around which I normally received requests to fix projects, I've always endeavoured to understand the larger landscape context of those projects. To me, this included understanding the regional geography, both natural and cultural. Knowledge imparted strength.

From my previous international landscape experiences, I have been convinced that the local landscape always provides insight into the necessary features that make a project stand out, be spectacular. But how to uncover those features, how to identify those features, those landscape nuggets.

I had a technique to uncover nuggets. To broaden my understanding of the Rub al Khali, I would vary my perceptions of the subject as I had on other projects. I started through a variety of questions. With each question, I would consider a variety of options. I called each option, a lens. Each lens varied in its magnification. From each lens, I would sieve the varieties of information to discover nuggets, the landscape nuggets that could elevate project quality.

It all sounds a bit convoluted but it is simple. When something about a landscape catches my eye, my ear, my thoughts, my imagination, I explore it through lenses.

For example, I asked myself, exactly where does the Rub al Khali start and end? Do you measure it on a map of the world... a map of the Arabian Peninsula... a map of the United Arab Emirates... a map of the Abu Dhabi Emirate...a map of the Abu Dhabi Municipality? Or, on a map of oral history, as told by a Liwa Oasis resident? Is it a question of natural geography, or cultural geography? Is it a question of geographic space, or geologic time? It is a search for insight.

I used all resources to understand the landscape, to filter information, to gain knowledge, to enrich my projects. After all, I am a landscape architect.

Despite all my calculated lenses and such, I had a deep-down foreboding sense. It appeared this sand desert, around which over the last decades I had built many projects... this sand desert had immeasurable dimensions. That foreboding itself could be an important source of landscape design insight. And JeanClaude's role?

I hoped that JeanClaude's personal experiences in this one-of-a-kind sand desert landscape would open new portals. I hoped to find new insights. I was looking for nuggets, a unique desert edge, unique arrows for my design quiver to apply, if required, on the Liwa Qsar project.

***

Preparations

My kismet meeting at the Souk Madinat with my old friend, JeanClaude Thibaut, had been useful. He rearranged his schedule to free up a couple days to ride with me the three hours from Dubai to the Empty Quarter Liwa Qsar project and the three hours return.

I had known JeanClaude since my info-gathering in Yenbo, Saudi Arabia, almost two decades ago. Over time I got to know him quite well. On the surface, because of our similar landscape interests, JeanClaude was satisfied to share his knowledge and experience with me. But it was deeper than that for him. Years back, he had worked on a re-forestation project through the United Nations in Vrindavan, India.

Vrindavan was a place rich not only in ethnobotanical history, but also in timeless spiritual traditions. While there, he took up the study of yoga, for him a time of disciplined introspection that had helped his focus on his own personal life goals. Most fundamentally, he concluded his personal nature was best served by sharing his knowledge with others.

Additionally, JeanClaude found that this introspection helped him come to grips with his intellectual bullying, his superiority complex. He had always found it easy to have someone on, to wind someone up, to joke in a not-so-subtle way to belittle those around him. His time in Vrindavan taught him how he could control his darker side. He was intelligent by nature. His growth in personal and spiritual knowledge thus became a deep foundation. He used that solid spiritual framework to build his friendship with me.

JeanClaude once summarized to me his time in Vrindavan with a quote from the Vedic literature: "Just as sweetness is the immutable nature of sugar, service is the immutable nature of the soul." I understood that JeanClaude's soul was at its most comfortable when he performed service to others. That was the same lesson I took away from my talks with Vrndadevi in Ban Muang Thailand. But, in my experience, that was not a lesson that worked among white-collar mercenaries in the Arabian Peninsula.

Theuns' people delivered to me a CTF ID badge, the 4-wheel drive SUV, a white, v-6 Mitsubishi Outlander. It came equipped with wayfinding kit, a Garmin Nuvi with the most recent desert data.

Starting in Dubai, we would drive 120 kilometres along the Gulf coast to Abu Dhabi. Then we would continue along the coast another 30 kilometres to the Hameem turnoff, where we would head due south, inland for 150 kilometres, crossing the Tropic of Cancer, directly into the relentless, shifting, arid, sand desert, core of the Rub al Khali.

***

More Preparations

Early in the morning, I drove to the Royal Mirage to pick up JeanClaude. He was ready and waiting. He loaded his things and climbed right in.

I had to lay out the ground rules. I had to be alert because I had seen JeanClaude at his worst when nobody knew whether JeanClaude was telling a good joke or the truth. I was already experiencing that this new project was working well as a cocoon to shelter me from the death of Bree. And now we were on my job, on my time. I wanted to keep my job focus steady.

"JeanClaude, let's keep it straight today–no more jokes about desert fear or *djinns* or anything like that. My life is getting back on track with this project and I don't want to be sidetracked. Do you follow me? Can we agree on the no joking or sidetracking?"

JeanClaude replied, "*Mon ami*, you act like I was trying to undermine you?! Wasn't I the one who helped you package yourself for this kind of work? Wasn't I the one who put Theuns van der Walt in touch with you? You know I am not trying to undermine you. Let's focus on our commonalities. Too many professionals do not want to see, or even just hear about, the 'unclean' reality of human relationships with the landscape. Modern memes oversimplify everything... there's definitely a trend toward a technology-driven, atheistic secularism... that commoditizes the landscape... when in reality, just under the surface is a richness of understanding and diversity of explanations between humans and plants, humans and the landscape... why ignore it... why sweep it under the rug?

Besides, isn't sharing this richness what you and I have been doing together, the last couple decades... seems like longer? Heh, heh, your shallow American roots—they show."

"Yeah, yeah, hey, my roots may be shallow but they are very broad spreading—they give me stability and focus; and you, your roots may be deep; but they are not attached! And you get so far over the edge, so often..."

JeanClaude interrupted with a smirk and asked, "Do you have it out of your system, yet, *mon cher ami*?"

"Yeah, yeah, I'm fine, let's get on the road, eh? The sun's already risen. The weather's windy... and dusty."

JeanClaude said, "Windy and dusty? That's for sure—you've seen this before, haven't you? It's a *shamal*—a wind out of the northwest, often turns into a windstorm, a nasty windstorm—and if that happens—if it gets any worse—we won't see anything today. How do you say it... let's keep our fingers crossed for better weather."

***

Historical Landscape Transect-01

It was pedal to the metal as we began our 300km drive through the Empty Quarter to the Liwa Qsar project site.

Departing Dubai, we took the Sheik Zayed Road toward Abu Dhabi. But upon entering Sheik Zayed Road, we found it in total gridlock.

I said, "What a start!!! We have both—shamal and gridlock!"

In our comfortably air-conditioned 4WD SUV, JeanClaude relaxed in his seat, and smiling, said, "We'll work through it.

"*Alors*, let's begin this way... you asked how I got involved with Liwa? Well with this gridlock, it's easy to talk. A few years back I gave a short course at Harvard. In that course I had a student, an Emirati—a person whose family originally came from the Liwa Oasis. He asked me to assist in setting up the structure for his research on historical relationships between human culture and plants in extremely arid environments—a guy with Bedouin roots asked me to help him study the landscape—*bien sur*, without question!"

Trying to focus conversation on my project, I quickly added, "I'm sure—I'm looking forward to hearing all about it. But let's focus—we're heading to Hameem on the east end of the Liwa Oasis. It's the last place on any map where we have to turn onto an unmapped route into the deep desert. Did you ever visit this place before? If so, what was it like? Did you visit it regularly, or just once, or twice?"

"*Sans doute*, I know Hameem. It was maybe five years ago... then for over nine months—almost a year, I drove the road from Abu Dhabi to Hameem three or four times a week out and back. I used to pass through Hameem and go further, another twenty-five kilometres, about halfway to Mazaira. You should know that Mazaira is a town in the exact centre of that 100 kilometre long, linear strip of dune valleys known forever and by all as the Liwa Oasis."

I said, "Then you saw Hameem regularly, eh? That's great! Now, it's happening!" I thought if I could keep JeanClaude focused then this was where best value could be found in his always rambling and colourful approach.

JeanClaude continued, "The Hameem Road was paved the entire way. It was literally a long, slow ride out of and past the edge of civilization into another world... starved of water, starved of contemporary cultural landmarks. I felt like I was going back in time as I drove. It didn't even have kilometre post markings. I liked to call it a drought-attenuated connection to modern life.

"With each kilometre I drove further south, the desert dominated more and more. The deeper I drove into the Empty Quarter, the more and more I felt *isolé*, isolated. The Empty Quarter had a strangely conflicting feeling."

JeanClaude paused... Liwa memories or something else flowing through his head, I figured.

I was eager for detail and pressed, "What do you mean the Empty Quarter was strangely conflicting?"

He answered, "...an uncomfortable effect... there was something inherently uncomfortable sitting somewhere, beneath the seductive beauty of the sand—beneath the mesmerizing motion of the dunes..." JeanClaude got lost again in his thoughts.

Some people, like JeanClaude, who are into meditation, like the feeling of isolation. But the kind of isolation that JeanClaude troubled to describe was not peaceful; instead it was edged with the threat of danger—a danger for humans that was like a thirsty, hungry fly on the edge of a venus fly trap. Enter in and it will snap shut. It is not a question of if, but when.

That uncertainty fed hidden fears; and, when JeanClaude inwardly examined those hidden fears... despite all his worldly landscape experience... he struggled. The struggle suffocated his thoughts, stopped his words. I wondered if it was similar to what I had felt during my walkabout in the Great Sand Sea, the Egyptian Sahara, or what Bree had felt on the Moroccan edge of the Sahara.

I sensed the rare hesitation from JeanClaude. Then, figuring he was about to tumble over the edge again, I pushed him on the shoulder and said, "Oy, wake up!!!"

JeanClaude came back to reality, chuckled a bit, and said, "I'm okay. Sometimes it was like I might as well have been watching the desert on the television, at home... maybe it was my car, the air-conditioned metal box that gave me such a protected feeling...

"...as alluring as the dunes were, day in, day out... there was something that pushed me away... I could not fully define the breadth of that feeling. But a large part of it was the *luminosité*, the brightness. There are two things about brightness here, the sun itself... but more so the brightness of the sun reflections off the sand. We are on the Tropic of Cancer—the sun is always overhead and its reflections have a special intensity.

"The brightness forced me to look away—not like this strange shamal, dull, dusty, dreary yellow we've seen today... but an ever-so-strong clear sky brightness that forced my eyes to desire shelter... and there was no shelter. It was an aggressive brightness... and that was as seen from the protection and shelter of my car, my 'AC box'!"

I said, "Okay, okay... I'm not sure where this is headed... somewhere useful, I hope—it is intriguing, the 'AC box'—an interesting choice of words..."

Speaking over me, JeanClaude continued, "My AC box had tinted windows, and I had polarized-lens sunglasses... but the brightness... where does what you see gradually become so bright to be injurious to your eye, and not far from blinding? CJ, there was this section of desert on the way to Hameem, where I recall, the colour of the sand... it was a blend that either by light reflection in the colours themselves... or light refraction because of heat waves... the sand was a blend, a vibrating mix of a hot pink and a psychedelic orange. In the mid-day sun, I could see these colours vibrating... impossible to focus... the heat... the brightness... the colour... my eyes hurt like I'd never experienced... I was seeing movement, change that my sense of sight could not compute... I wasn't looking at the sun, but the sand!"

I observed, "I'd call that some kind of natural warning, wouldn't you?"

"Give me a break, *mon ami*, this stuff is not your normal linear engineering textbook stuff! It's weird science. Because we are on the Tropic of Cancer... mid-day, most of the year, there are no shadows. No shadows!!! Sunshine and no shadow means our standard place and time, sun-based visual reference points are missing... *disparu*, disappeared, absent. The most fundamental visual signpost with which we have all grown up, shadow, has disappeared... the sun is out, the sky is clear, but there are no shadows. They had been replaced with optical illusions... with a sort of visual imbalance... I don't know, I never really came to grips with it... all these things added up... but then, they didn't add up."

I had to take over, "Time out, time out... now, we are officially over the edge."

"Patience, patience, there's more," JeanClaude added. "Late in the afternoon, with the sun lower in the sky, the shadows returned to transform the entire landscape. It is not a *cliché*, it was a reality... I could have sworn I was at sea... felt movement... rolling swells... choppy waves as far as I could see in any direction. Those were the dunes, the sand and the dunes... the sands... the sands... the sands..."

I interrupted, smiling, "I guess I can imagine that; but I'll have to see it to believe it. I suppose you are also going to tell me you felt sea sickness while driving?"

"Of course not, but..." The Sheik Zayed tailback had broken and we were moving nicely; but JeanClaude was totally caught up reliving his Empty Quarter memories.

We arrived at Gweifat. JeanClaude said we'd better stop here for gas and supplies.

***

Gweifat Gas Station

We pulled into the gas station. JeanClaude said, "This is the end of the Abu Dhabi municipality. The beginning of the Gweifat Road. If my memory serves me, this is the last gas station before Hameem in the Liwa Oasis. We can't take a chance. We have to stop."

We filled up, paid at the pump, then parked and went into the immediately adjacent "7-11" type snack shop. The shop and its toilets were built as an integral part of the gas station, very modern-America in layout and style... heavily used and clean. Here, they were run by government gas companies, and open 24/7/365. Inside the shop we bought a bunch of half-litre bottles of drinking water for our trip deep into the desert.

At the checkout cash register, next to the chewing gum, there was a small box of individually shrink-wrapped sticks. The box was labelled in Arabic only. Each stick was thick as a fat pencil, a bit irregular though, not straight as an arrow, and about fifteen centimetres long.

I asked JeanClaude, "What're these? I've never seen them in Carrefour, or any of the other food stores in Dubai. Now don't get onto any ethnobotanical STD, sexually transmitted diseases stuff, eh, just give me a straight answer!"

"They're *mishwak, mon ami*–toothbrushes, from twigs or roots of the *Salvadora persica.* That's about as exotic as it gets. Though not a native to the UAE, this good size shrub is endemic, tolerates drifting sand like a champ–you'd like it in the landscape–it's fresh green year-round. And as a tooth cleaner, *mishwak* have a tradition in the Arabian Peninsula back at least as far as the coming of Islam. And they're widely used both in Africa and in the Indian sub-continent."

I chuckled and asked, "But, do those roots and stems work? And, if they do, for five dirhams each, they might well be worth it."

"Do they work? As you might figure, some alternative scientists and herbalists encourage their use—instead of toothbrushes—but, do they work? Try them out yourself... make sure to visit your dentist in six months for a proper cleaning!"

Before we left, we checked tire pressure, engine oil and water and charged our mobiles. We had only a short thirty kilometres along the coast on the Gweifat Road until the Hameem turnoff. At that turnoff, we were about to enter the area where JeanClaude explained we would lose all touch with civilization.

Fortunately the shamal was weakening. That meant we could see the expansive strength, the unlimited breadth of the huge monster of a sand desert.

According to the Google Earth images, I had figured that after the Hameem turnoff, we would see no more coastal scrub, no more sabka, just Empty Quarter dunes. From the coast to Hameem, I had calculated a straight shot south—about 130 kilometres of pure sand dune landscape. About halfway there, we would cross the Tropic of Cancer.

***

Historical Landscape Transect-02

We got back on the road. The *shamal* had definitely lessened. Visibility was good. Traffic was light to say the least—damn near non-existent. We sped down the asphalted road to Hameem. This was it. Straight into the beast.

"What else do you recall? Anything traditional, any standard landmarks at all?" I asked.

Answering my question, JeanClaude got back on a roll. "Well, let me see... I remember what looked like a huge international communications station just off the road, and a signpost here or there for oil rigs. I'm sure you can relate to that. Most days, I'd see only two or three other vehicles the entire trip. Sometimes I did see super-sized vehicles, the tires themselves as tall as an SUV, crawling ever so slowly along the road edge... 20kph or so... they were oil rig, soft sand vehicles, with tires, cab and trailer three times larger than anything normally seen on the road."

With impatience and a little bit of humour, I took over, "So, let me summarize, you had vehicles three times as large as normal, traveling 1/5 normal speed, no shadows, psychedelic orange sand—what was going on? Something strange with you, maybe? Getting into the plants, again? Definitely over the edge! This is just the way you always take a ride on the landscape. You suspend your logic and let the landscape take you for the ride. Listening to you is like reading a Kerouac novel. I've got to turn my filters on high. You're making me pay for this info!"

"No, no, not at all! Listen, you've got to broaden your view.

What I meant when I said the road was a tenuous extension of human civilization into an area not accustomed to human civilization is that a paved road has a lot of civilized implications that the adjacent sand desert landscape challenged—those cultural implications were stripped away! Except for my AC box on wheels... *et mon ami*, there weren't even any radio stations."

"Animals, what about animals, wildlife, fauna, anything like that?"

What JeanClaude didn't say was there couldn't be any animals because there weren't any plants. The tropical ecosystem of the Empty Quarter sat right at the extreme end of any environmentalist's continuum of natural diversity. How does a landscape come to be called the... empty... quarter? No water. No soil. No plants. No insects. No animals. No reptiles. No birds. Been that way for millennia. Only geologists speculate. There is no record. There is no consensus. There is no water. Lack of water means lack of life. JeanClaude and I were in a little box that was a self-contained life support system... and that was all we had.

JeanClaude said, "There were camels being herded along the roadside, and the inevitable camel roadkill. Once a month or so, I'd see a *rigor mortis* camel just off the shoulder... never saw one being hauled away... never saw one decomposing... someone must have cleaned up.

"The camels... the camels were absolute magic! This is camel country. I would see hundreds of them at a time, walking just off the roadside, herded by guys on four-wheel ATVs, four wheeled all-terrain vehicles, powered by motorcycle engines. The camels moved over the sands as if they carried no weight at all... and you know how hard it is for humans to walk through soft sand. The camels had a resolute gait... a presence that said... they belonged here. These were not circus or tourist camels. These were camels being taken care of, being bred... bred for racing. They looked strong, proud, at home."

JeanClaude recalled further, "There were no highway lights, no lights anywhere. Driving at night was like being in a tunnel by yourself continuously for 150 kilometres. Sometimes I wanted to do the night drive without headlights... using only moonlight. It was eerie... no plants... no water... no vehicles... no nothing... a huge sand desert... a strip of asphalt... my vehicle... and me... eerie, eerie, indeed. I'd stop for a moment and turn the engine off... dead silence... often it was still, the still of infinity; but I could see what, who knows, gazillions of stars... I felt as if I had been dropped into obscurity... silence... isolation... extreme emptiness... extreme distance... no point of reference for human civilization... CJ, I have seen lots of strange landscapes in my life, and stranger human interactions with plants, landscapes... but out there... sometimes... if I say otherworldly, the connotations get in the way... I often felt like the desert was driving me out of it... I often felt an urgency to be free of it... get out of it... to see the lights of Abu Dhabi... the signs of human civilization."

JeanClaude had just hinted at a life force inherent to this desert, inimical to humans and human civilization. This kind of ethereal vision of nature was all but eradicated from humans by the scientific revolution that ended the Middle Ages... and all scientific "progress" since. Even for me, this was uncomfortable territory.

I jumped in, "Right, you always take me to some existential stepping-off point. I have work to do. What do you remember about Hameem, that's the last town before my project. Do you have any memories from there?"

"Special for Hameem? Well... it had the only gas station on the east end of Liwa... a typical, how do you say it... one horse town... stop for gas... listen... you could hear a car coming from more than a kilometre away. A car passing... following it with your eyes through its entire time of visibility—that was a big event. Then, it was quiet again, back to normal."

"Did you see people? What kind? Who were they?"

"Ha-hah, people?! Contract farm workers. They looked like they had spent their entire lives out there... a bit like ocean-going seamen who have been at sea an eternity... they had a certain, hardened look... the look of people outside the rules of civilized law... the look of survivors who had faced down serious duress... men, carrying that experience, scoured into their souls and etched into their faces. They looked as if hopelessly imprisoned for life; but they were proud survivors in a landscape that defied any contemporary concept of modern life material sustainability. They knew there was no compromise with this beast of a sand desert. They took the suffering it gave... and feebly, feebly they recovered, slowly what they could.

"Real-time hell, that's what it often felt like... every day for months at a time... you had to shrink away from it to survive. People who lived there did not fight it. It is unique, a daily core reality... this huge, arid, sand desert in a tropic zone... it is something fundamentally opposite from temperate zones... it's in your face 24/7/365... the heat kills... the sun kills... the lack of water kills... the lack of arable land depresses... the blowing sand ravages... maybe those, maybe those are the uncomfortable threats, just barely hidden beneath the slyly seductive, surface sands?"

JeanClaude fell silent. Those were strong words about our destination. Made me think... I questioned myself... and I am going to build a five-star garden resort destination out there? Doubts crept in.

***

Hameem

An oasis without romance, Hameem was barely an agricultural town. Hameem was hardly a farm village. Everything looked rough. Sitting in a sabka valley, Hameem, surrounded by dunes, had a sole purpose—agriculture. Agriculture? Nothing more than scruffy-looking date palm orchards protected by beaten up windbreaks of dried out reeds.

And for humans, Hameem had about twenty single storey, recently constructed, simple flat top, white box houses. Supporting the residents... a small grocery store with small restaurant, a mosque, a feed store and a gas station. That was it. That was all. We filled up at the gas station.

The gas station... no fancy 7-11 out here, no snacks, toilet out back. We were no longer in some modern 21st century new urbanist landscape. Rather, we had just gone back sixty years in time... returned to the southwest American boondocks, early 1950s style.

I asked JeanClaude, "What about this place? Remember anything noteworthy? Anything to recommend?"

"*Rien de tout*, just about like I remember it... and all the other date palm village oases along this road—just like it, all the way to Mazaira. In the sixty kilometres or so to Mazaira, there might be ten or twelve of these farm village oases scattered along the way—all in individual sabka valleys—all looking just like this one. How do you guys say...what you see is what you get."

Not far from the gas station, on the roadside, a hundred

metres away, we found the large CTF Liwa Qsar project construction panel sign which marked the final turn to access the project. According to JeanClaude, the parade of trucks that kept this entry busy all came from Mazaira.

"Well," I started, "we're in new territory now... a road that neither of us have ever seen..."

"Not only that, *mon ami,*" JeanClaude added, as we turned off the main road, "but the road looks like it will no longer be paved." I slowed down, shifted the SUV into four-wheel drive, and began our new direction on our last leg—due south into the Empty Quarter.

To reach the Liwa Qsar project destination, we still had to go another fifteen or so kilometres. But from now on, it would be via a compacted, soft, gatch (locally available limestone fines) construction haul road—a very heavily used dusty road constantly being wetted down by large construction water tankers and re-compacted by large earthworks graders and rollers.

Aside from this haul road, all we could see and as far as we could see was that brooding sand desert, the Empty Quarter.

In the first 500 metres, we passed a huge pumping station and its auxiliary buildings, certainly for potable water. The pumping station was bustling with excavation, construction... supply deliveries. Further along the haul road we found an ongoing continuous roadside excavation. Being fed from huge wooden spools sitting on flat bed trailers, this was the installation of underground electrical supply cable... cable thick as your arm. This was the permanent main electrical supply cable for the project. Construction happening everywhere.

Slowly, carefully, we pushed on. The construction haul road was barely wide enough for two vehicles to pass. Heavy road graders were working behind the water trucks to make sure the road had no ruts, to make sure the sand dunes did not reclaim the road. Progress forward was slow. The gatch construction road wound around huge dunes, separated by undeveloped dune sabka valleys. The roadside dunes were so steep, all vehicles had to stay on the gatch construction haul road.

In all the twisting and turning through these larger dunes, their seductive visual attractiveness worked its magic on us. Winding around and through yet one more series of dunes, JeanClaude noticed, "What's down in that valley on the left?"

I looked. "That looks like a labour camp—looks like forty-foot containers—maybe a couple hundred of them—each has windows in the sides and each window has an air conditioner—no additional shade at all—yeah, that's a labour camp."

Once we passed the project labour camp and rounded one more huge dune, we reached the project security gate.

At the gate there was a barrier across the road, a pull off for parking, a temporary hut, and what looked like a team of four or five uniformed security guards, opening and closing the barrier.

There was a scrum of trucks of all sizes and purposes. The roadside was temporary parking anarchy. Both entering and leaving, every vehicle's driver had to stop, get out of the vehicle and go inside the hut to exchange passes and IDs.

There was a swarm of men outside the door to the hut trying to get in—rustling with others trying to get out—aside from JeanClaude and I, there wasn't a white man to be seen. The security guards did not have control on this day.

Theuns had given me a CTF Construction Site Pass. The gate guard looked at it, noted our license plate number, BKV 974, then waved us through. JeanClaude and I had escaped that mashup.

We continued on, passing around another two large dunes before we finally saw the Liwa Qsar construction site. By all observations, we had left modern civilization. We might as well have been on the Moon or, more appropriately, Mars.

I felt relief about finally being at our destination; but I wondered why JeanClaude was so negative about this desert. I actually found the dunes to be quite visually attractive, both in their individual forms and their overall unpredictability. Their landscape beauty was strong, dominant—I thought briefly of the three dominant Grindelwald mountains, but their presence was bathed in plants and water. Here there was no water, no plants. So what was this arid landscape dominance surrounding me? Those thoughts left my mind as I focused on the bustling, massive construction site appearing straight ahead. Suddenly I felt the tension of the job site. I was well into my project cocoon.

***

Destination Five Star

JeanClaude and I had made it. We'd finally arrived. And it was a shock after seeing so few vehicles, so few people over the past 150 kilometres. An endurance test for sure. It had been a very long haul. And as I observed, not a great ride for potential guests.

I thought, this is the place where I'm supposed to build luxurious courtyard gardens?! Hah! My conviction still wavered. But as I took a moment to look around, it became clearer why someone was convinced that this endeavour was going to succeed.

Well! It might as well have been a big-budget movie set—way out here in the middle of "empty", the middle of nowhere... and the site? Swarming with activity! The Liwa Qsar buildings were situated on the east end of a long and narrow valley with its edges defined by tall and long dunes.

Sitting well above the valley floor, the horseshoe-shaped arrangement of buildings tucked into and stepped up the lower dune side slopes, opening out widely to the west. At the end of the buildings, on the right, the north side, and dominating this end of the valley, a huge dune rose steeply, 300 metres up from the sabka valley floor. A world class vista!

The vista made me pull over to the side and stop. Amazing landscape! And for me... the adrenaline had started to flow... my project obsession was being fed... big time! We both felt this destination was worth the price of admission.

This Empty Quarter landscape setting and well blended buildings reminded me of southern Morocco. Where the Draa and Todra rivers descended from the Atlas mountains into the Sahara desert. In the Moroccan town of Ouarzazate, the Taourirt Casbah has been the most often photographed Atlas qsar town.

Both the Ouarzazate Qsar and this Liwa Qsar, by their form and substantial ramparts, provided protection for humans. But here, unlike southern Morocco, there were no adjacent snow-covered mountains and no rivers in the valleys. Here, there was complete absence of surface water, absence of palms, absence of trees, absence of any noticeable green.

With what looked like thousands of labourers at work, the 150-room hotel and fifty villas were in the peak of construction activity, yet without finishes. In a small section of the taller construction, a specialist theming plaster sub-contractor was putting on samples of the final finish, capturing the hue, the value and the texture of the surrounding sands. They had completed a large enough sample to enable JeanClaude and me to imagine the final look. The sample definitely blended well with the desert sand.

The hotel main entry was obvious because it was the most enormously protected, the only four- and five-storey structure. It gently stepped down into attached three stories and down again to two stories. The hotel and all villas were surrounded and protected by qsar walls. Massive ramparts clearly defined outside, the desert, from inside, the residences and the, yet to be built, courtyard gardens. Overall the visual image and details were traditional qsar fashion. Walls buttressing the lowest levels, stepping up the side slopes of the dunes, and finishing on top with crenelated edges.

By now, the *shamal* had totally relented. We found a place free from the hubbub of site construction activities to pull over and step outside—to look out over and down the valley—and for the first time see with detail into the expansive dune landscape.

During the construction process, this stunning natural valley had been protected. It was clear why the site was chosen, and why the buildings had been placed where they were. The composition and grandeur of this large landscape of valley, dunes and sky, could only be done justice by a photographer with the vision and skills of Ansel Adams, or a cinematographer like David Lean's Freddie Young. That was the view being protected for all guests.

The valley stretched out before us. It wriggled out for what might be kilometres. The huge dunes in front of us stretched further than we could see. On closer inspection of the foreground, forty to fifty metres below us, we could see sinuously sweeping over the sabka valley floor, small, graceful, long and thin, micro or mini-dunes. Each seemingly only a metre or two high.

The micro dunes or dune fingerlettes had been aligned fundamentally by the prevailing NW and SE winds. There was no creek, no wadi, no flow line on the valley floor... just random depressions, shifting hollows, created by those ever moving, slowly evolving, serpentine dune fingerlettes.

Upon more careful examination, JeanClaude and I, straining, could see on the gentle undulations of these red desert sand dune fingerlettes, and in their hollows, growing randomly, fine textured green mounds, small shrubs. Most likely, according to JeanClaude, *Zygophyllum mandavillei*... never more than fifty centimetres high... scattered... discrete... very sparsely distributed.

They could be seen in various ages from young to juvenile, to mature, to senile. Their entire life cycle was there to view, in one careful look. JeanClaude added, "No matter the shifting red sands, their tap roots take advantage of the groundwater often only three metres below the valley floor. Five years ago, I saw plenty of them."

Both of us were captivated by the miniature—the sinuous red dune fingerlettes snaking along the valley floor. JeanClaude said, "Down in that whiter valley bottom—that's the sabka sand filled with fines and a pH level just like on the salty coast. The sand up above in the dunes... that's the good stuff... the sand preferred by horticulturists."

JeanClaude wanted to walk the valley. He wanted to go among those shape-shifting red sand fingerlettes. He was looking for mineral desert roses and fire plants, *Leptodenia pyrotechnica.* Two metre tall, loosely branched shrub clumps, known to shelter desert gazelles.

And me, I was late. I had to get started with my meetings. We found the Site Construction Offices. We parked our SUV under a car park shade structure in a spot reserved for "CTF Guest". We climbed out for a moment—oh yeah, it was hot.

We climbed back into the air-conditioned SUV. I had a couple last minute preparations to finish. JeanClaude had his own agenda. He was going off on foot. As he parted, JeanClaude said to me, "Life is simple: eat, sleep, hike. See you later, *mon ami.*" And after tucking a couple water bottles into his ruck sack, he walked down into the valley.

***

Liwa Qsar

What was Rudyard Kipling saying when he described the social landscape of southwest Asia as a world of danger to honest men?

With just 15 minutes before my first scheduled appointment, I took the time, sitting in my air-conditioned vehicle, to write some of my observations and thoughts. This was a desert like none I had ever seen. There were no mountains in the distance—just sweeping dunes. The Great Sand Sea in the Egyptian Sahara? The context was different. There—a functioning sand-surfer tourist destination. Not comparable. Here...

The dream is the mirage. For the people of the Western world, the Empty Quarter has always been an elusive froth.

It has always been an ambiguous froth... a strangely arid yet attractive froth. Whispering mystery and romance, the Empty Quarter provides odd enticements from its rarely found plants... evanescent bouquets full of ethereal promise.

Fragrances have a surprising emotional strength anywhere... but here in the Arabian Peninsula and The Empty Quarter? They have an unusual intensity that can be off-putting... but there is a subtle sweetness that attracts. Myself, I don't wear any fragrance; but the regional plants have a sweetness underneath a mystical pungency.

Every Empty Quarter visitor discovers a personal connection to a mirage. It is unseen yet it lodges and takes root. Every visitor reaches out for a spectacular red sunset, trying to grasp something. But carrying away nothing. Only uncertainty as dark descends. Uncertainty with threads of hope.

While writing, I got a text from JeanClaude that had only an Empty Quarter quote from Wilfred Thesiger,

"It was very still with the silence which we have driven from our world."

I concluded JeanClaude was describing how he was making his own personal link with that desert.

Looking for landscape nuggets, I sifted wispy images from JeanClaude's descriptions from our ride into the Empty Quarter. Mirage-like stories. I hoped that my efforts at Liwa Qsar would be no mirage. I was there to make beautiful garden courtyards. Nothing more.

The ride out to the Liwa Qsar project with JeanClaude contained too many inexplicable encounters. I had to put those aside. At least, that was the conclusion from the project management side of me. But my design roots kept bubbling on a mental back burner that maybe there was something important in those wispy mirage images.

The project site was chosen to give the guests a luxury room looking west at a view framed by the largest and steepest red sand dunes in the Empty Quarter. The project intended to provide shelter, a comfortable, elegant shelter, to protect from the uncertainties, from the threats in this stunning landscape.

The workday never ends on these types of high-visibility, fast-tracked projects. For what was left of today, I had a handful of white-collar mercenaries to meet. I had to figure out who were the movers and shakers and who were the wasters. I began with the key players, living and working and constructing this hoped-to-be iconic resort in this sweaty 50°C world, in the arid inland core of the Empty Quarter.

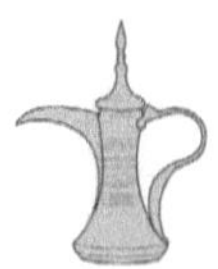

5-The Work

Kelvin Isley

I normally had little problem distinguishing between mirages, dreams, imagination and the real-time requirements of building large, complex projects. But the *shamal* and the 300km trip coupled with the arid +40°C temperatures had troubled me.

I had concerns in the back of my mind about the practicality of luxurious gardens in the core of the Empty Quarter. The morning's gruelling trip had only heightened those concerns. The drive to the project had loosened my focus; and there was an awkward aura underlying the attractiveness of this dune landscape.

But, I was glad to be finally on the job site. I took shelter of the familiar, embedding myself in the reality of the construction process—an essential component of my project cocoon—it had been a long while since I had felt that project cocoon comfort. It felt good. I was fully engaged in the game, my landscape architecture game.

My first appointment on site was with Kelvin Isley, the CTF Hospitality Director. Kelvin was the final responsible, as CTF representative on site, to make sure that construction happened to technical standard, to quality expectations and on time.

Over the course of the project, I came to know Kelvin well. He was from New Zealand. He followed in the footsteps of his grandfather and great uncle, who had spent much of their professional careers in the Middle East and North Africa. Kelvin stood a tallish six foot two and weighed a fit 185 pounds.

He had a friendly face. He was a direct man who succeeded by knowing how to listen and how to command and control to get the required results for successful complex, hospitality projects in challenging locations.

Kelvin, in his late 40s, had sun sensitive skin with a ruddy, splotchy complexion. His blondish hair looked like the sun was bleaching it, burning it off. But despite those sensitivities, he had an ingrained natural fitness. His natural fitness resulted from a childhood hiking in the New Zealand countryside, which built his life-long capacity for endurance.

His father had been Research Director in the New Zealand Department of Conservation, Southland Region. Kelvin grew up in Invercargill. His father made sure Kelvin was at home on the Routeburn and Milford Tracks, like his own back yard. And his father always took him to Maori meetings where Kelvin absorbed the traditional insights these men had learned from the landscape.

He was a well-organized Type-A personality, and made good intuitive reads on other people's personalities, especially their issues in relation to the goals and objectives of the project. He worked twelve to fourteen hours a day at Liwa, and still had time, every weekend, for his wife and two growing kids in Abu Dhabi.

During his two years in the Empty Quarter, he had set out to know, by firsthand experience, this awkward sand desert landscape. He hiked down into the sabka valleys and up along the dune ridges whenever he found free time.

He channelled the right side of his brain, listened to the Empty Quarter, heard the Empty Quarter, and in the most unusual of ways, became one with it. Over his time on site, this had enabled him insightful observations on the life forces in the desert, few as there were. He had come to know the *rimal* rhythm, the sands rhythm of the heat. And he had become an amateur of traditional Arabic desert poetry in the form known as *nabati.*

On the day, I found him outdoors in the midst of an impromptu on-site construction meeting. I introduced myself. Kelvin asked for a couple minutes to finish up his meeting and then walked with me to CTF's site office.

The site construction offices were arranged in a large, clustered grid with many two-storey, double-width, prefab modules. Kelvin's office was upstairs, at the edge of the grid, overlooking project construction.

Inside, Kelvin offered a chair. I sat down and observed two noteworthy things on the walls: first, a series of large satellite images of the site, labelled, taken monthly; and second, a set of A0 size schedules of program versus actual–bar charts, depicting all site construction and material procurement activities, updated weekly and heavily marked up in colour with notes.

As Kelvin sat down at his desk and reached into his mini fridge, I noticed a carved piece of rough wood, displayed like a name plate plaque on the desk. It looked like an old, gnarly piece of *Prosopis cineraria* trunk that had one side cut, smoothly planed and engraved:

'...the desert slipped in,
through wall, and ceiling,
rising from beneath,
settling about us,
...listening, pressing, waiting...'

Unsettling but not different from the gist of JeanClaude's input during the ride out here. It was an Algernon Blackwood quotation.

***

Down to Business

I knew that quote from my time in Cairo years ago; but before I could say anything, Kelvin handed me a cooled, half-litre plastic bottle of water, asking, "How can I help you?"

I thanked Kelvin for his time, and explained, "Theuns asked me to get this landscape consultant and landscape contractor team together, have you been briefed?"

"I certainly have, and I'd be glad to help if you need anything. We've only six months to soft opening and no softscape action at all."

"Yup, that's my task, Kelvin. I do have two questions. First, I'm going to be working directly with the landscape contractor and the landscape consultant. Time being so short, I don't need or want to spend time with your contracted Project Management Team, unless you see essential value here on site. What do you say?"

"CJ, they're paper pushers so just stop in and see me with updates as appropriate, okay? Listen, I've just hired a new guy, Gary Dolford, as my right-hand man. He'll be in-processing and settling-in over the next couple weeks. He's a Yank like you. Used to play in the National Football League. Anyhow, he's an infrastructure engineer, electrical specialist. He'll be handling all site infrastructure and finishes. As your first point of contact if you need anything, his office will be across the hall. Most of the time he'll be on site, I'll give you his cell number as soon as he gets here. Now, make no mistake, on the landscaping we need action, not talk."

"I got it. Next, I need to get with the general contractor's construction manager (CM) to get some details. Then I'll work on down the chain of command. I told Theuns I'd have an action plan by close of business this Thursday. So, can you point me toward the CM's office?"

"The general contractor's CM? That would be Bob Rosenwinkel. His office is in the prefab construction module next door, upstairs. And CJ, please keep Gary Dolford and me in the picture with the same info you share with Theuns."

Then, pointing to some bright red highlighted bars on the bar chart schedule behind his desk, Kelvin emphasized, "This landscaping is way behind. I'm sure you'll fix that!"

Kelvin stood up as he finished speaking, turned and looked out his window, southwest into the mid-afternoon hazy sun and dune landscape. Without turning back, he asked, "By the way, I was just wondering... have you ever worked in these sand deserts before? Do you know what you're up against, CJ?"

I blinked a couple times as what seemed a rhetorical question settled in. I waited for Kelvin to turn around.

Then I answered, "There's nothing that compares to the Empty Quarter, anywhere in the world. I am sure we can agree on that. I've built a couple very large projects here in the UAE and worked on the edges of the Eastern and Western Sahara before; and there's one rule that guides me—I can always learn more. So if you will, please take a minute and share the observations that help drive you to succeed in this landscape."

After I finished speaking, Kelvin said nothing and turned back toward the window again. I thought Kelvin's question was quite normal to be asked—actually the most fundamental of qualification questions—had I worked in a sand desert before? Kelvin remained still, and quiet, looking out the window at the resort construction in the Empty Quarter landscape. He let silence control the room.

Then finally looking back at me, he shared, "There are 3,235 humans working out there today. They're housed and fully supplied with water and power, food, shelter and air conditioning. This we've done, we're doing in a landscape that for centuries, no, for millennia, likely never had even twenty-five humans pass through it in a single year. Do you sense any kind of disconnect?"

I once again had my worries about the practicality of this project ratcheted up even further. I wondered if Kelvin knew more than he was telling. Little did I know that he was on the edge of a landscape portal the likes of which even Algernon Blackwood, the seer of all things landscape, had not imagined.

***

Morphogenetics

Kelvin Isley had briefed me with landscape context. He had given me a complete introduction to the Liwa Qsar project landscape. Kelvin was a landscape man.

With an addictive energy, he then decanted details of his own experiences. He spoke as if he had had a taste of the "spice". I thought of "spice" as an indefinable but powerful presence. Kelvin's words changed tone. They carried a ruffled discomfort, an awkward uncertainty. He displayed a conflict wherein, although there was that discomfort, he could not hide his undertone of wanting more—more of that beast, the Empty Quarter, the Rub al Khali.

I listened, his mood and words almost putting me in a daze.

Kelvin explained landscape disconnects, "Contrary to the fine artwork, the craft of Western photographers and journalists, this landscape is, first and foremost, not about beauty. It's about death, and the daily battle for survival. Survival of the fittest. He who adapts, survives."

I had heard something similar from JeanClaude during our drive to Liwa. But when I looked Kelvin in the eye, and felt his energy for the desert, I picked up the thread and said, "I like the way you think. Historically, I understand this huge sand desert as a landscape of death; but in a contemporary sense, I'm not so sure."

"I'm not surprised," Kelvin said. "If you have another moment, I'll tell you what happened to me."

"What do you mean, Kelvin?"

"Listen, this desert has some kind of invisible electromagnetic forces hidden within. At least, that is how I see it. I've been out on it, in it, virtually every day for two years. I live out here in a trailer cabin. We have a Management Oasis Camp (MOC) in an old date palm orchard two kilometres from here. There are 75 cabins. And, oh, by the way, if, as I imagine, you plan on being out here every day, I can arrange a cabin for you, too. No rush, we can do that later. You'll be able to check with Gary."

"Thanks for the offer; I will be out here every day. And about the cabin, I'd like to finish my meetings first and check back with Thuens before I commit. Now, what were you saying about this desert of death?"

"CJ, I've made it a point to confront this desert landscape head on. You need only walk across two dune ridges and you might as well be 200 kilometres away from the nearest human. The nearest water. Except for a compass, which sometimes even loses its accuracy, and modern electronic way finding, which has its own unique shortcomings–there's 100% visual disorientation."

His words... jogged a personal familiarity... made me recall my Great Sand Sea desert days in Egypt. Showing interest in the story, I looked inquisitively at Kelvin.

Kelvin continued, "I carry a GPS beacon. It's as important as water. I notify Security in advance when I explore on foot. I have an established check-in protocol, every two hours. That was my security... but that's not the story."

I listened intently. I was learning about the landscape, this sand desert landscape, my home for the next eight months.

"As I said, I'm convinced the desert is alive with some kind of continuously modulating, subtle energy. Anyone who has visited and carefully observed can easily 'see' its restlessness, its subtle rhythm. Photographs belie it. They invariably portray a dune as a stable, seductively shaped form, with which contemporary humans positively identify. It's the very still day that reveals, oh so subtly, its inherent energy... its own story. For me, it's very personal, very intimidating... very... I've concluded... otherworldly... yet, I'm not really sure."

Kelvin continued, "You know, I walk these dunes night, day,

sunrise, sunset, mid-day... it was the mid-day...

"The 'restlessness' of the sands creeps out very slowly and very subtly on still days. Maybe like a ground-hugging mist, on the moors, in northern England. You never see it actually emerge or any signs of it until its fingers are slowly wriggling along the surface. With purpose, or, without purpose... always unknown and unforeseen.

"Scientists have made attempts to measure the subtlest changes in temperature–isotherms–and humidity–pressure isobars–to try to understand the subtle changes in conditions that immediately precede the visual presence of these smallest, serpentine, mist fingers..."

I interrupted, "The science is interesting, but I am late and I do have to go..."

***

Too Much

Kelvin wanted to tell more.

"Now, hang on, please, give me another minute. I was out at mid-day, a still day, climbing up and down the dunes on foot. I paused over the edge of a dune hollow. The heat in mid-day does not come solely from the sun above. It feels even more intense reflected up, off the sand. That's normal any day.

"But on that day, I was completely engulfed by the extreme dry heat from all directions... I could feel it, not just on my bare skin but especially even through my boots... I could feel it like the smallest tentacles had emerged from, and swept over the sand to explore... they touched lightly at first... touching the soles of my feet... a pins-and-needles-like feeling... then reaching, grasping, tickling, tingling, seemingly searching at my ankles... my feet were anchored in the sand... in the midst of trying to think through and analyze this feeling, I felt the pins-and-needles from those tentacles, reaching up my calves, exploring, grasping the sides of my knees... each touch... each tickle felt like a probe for an open door, a probe for an entry. Each place touched became hotter and hotter through gradients... not just that medicinal dry heat that many enjoy when they step outside of an air-conditioned building into the desert heat... but a growing, a consuming heat that begs, at what point, does too hot become a burn?!

"I felt the pins-and-needles at my knee joints and ligaments, many pinpoints, many tickles... many picks... many probes... time escaped me then... so many sensations consumed my senses... the next thing I knew, the increasing number of elongated tentacles and their searching, leading pins-and-needles points were grasping my thigh, and then at the inside of my thigh, toward where the leg meets the internal hip socket. It all was happening too fast. At the same time the pins-and-needles tentacles, the tingles, their grasp quickly found, wrapped and tightened on my scrotum... then my urethra, my anus... both simultaneously invaded... entry had been found... gates had been breached... my overloaded brain crashed... I collapsed.

"I must have lain in the sand for an hour because the next I remembered was Security, their ATVs, the shade netting, the IV—helping me recover from heat prostration, that's what they called it, heat prostration, right in the hollow where I fell.

"What I sensed, and what I felt prior to losing consciousness, left no bodily marks on me—was it some kind of primitive morphogenetic process in action? I don't know. But, while I still take my walks, the fear of an unknown now accompanies me out there—every time.

"CJ, you're a landscape man, let me suggest, before you finish this project, read from pre-Islamic sources, the *mu'allaqat,* about desert *djinni,* non-human life forms told about for millennia. See what you can learn from Liwa inhabitants about their interpretations of the *mu'allaqat,* and these strange sands. And the next time you see softly swirling sands in a gentle breeze, remember what has happened to me—remember these softly swirling sands may be bringing you more than beauty."

I did not know what to believe from this well-anchored and surely dependable Kiwi. Kelvin had apparently been through some kind of macabre destabilization... some kind of surreal twilight zone, some kind of, what... landscape experience... and returned? I shuddered.

As if I needed more convincing, my conversation with Kelvin had got me thinking—there are mysteries in this landscape—mysteries that distract, unsettle—mysteries that sometimes only reveal themselves over longer stretches of time. I had no time for this now. I had to re-focus on the project.

"I'd like to explore this further with you, Kelvin, but right now, I need to see that CM, Rosenwinkel."

I said goodbye to Kelvin and headed for the CM's office.

As I left Kelvin's office, I had to put aside what I had just heard. I was not sure that Kelvin's story was sun-fuelled imagination. If it was, it would not impact my work. But if it was real...? I put it aside.

***

Bob Rosenwinkel

I was champing at the bit to meet the construction manager. It was time to get this site construction situation into a proper project perspective.

The general contractor's top man, the Construction Manager, was an American, Bob Rosenwinkel. His office was upstairs in one of the two-storey, stacked, prefab construction modules. His Kerala Indian male secretary, seeing that I was with CTF, said, "The door is open, go on in, no one else is with him now."

I looked into the large room. It was five or six times larger than Kelvin's standard site construction office.

Bob Rosenwinkel was preoccupied, staring out a large window at the construction site. Standing behind his executive size desk, he was dressed in a colourful golf shirt and contrasting golf trousers, looking all ready for the first tee. He had his back to the door, his head enveloped in a lazy maze of cigarette smoke.

I took the quiet moment to observe the office. The front half of the room had a large, rectangular meeting table with nine carefully arranged chairs, four on each side and one at the head. Against one side wall was casual seating, with two sofas and a generous size coffee table. Displayed on the coffee table were a selection of large-format books, on Sanaa, on Persia, and, on the Arabian Peninsula. In front of his desk were three straight-back chairs.

With the presence of construction samples, mock ups, and models. With a just-beneath-the-surface electric tension. And with the smell of tobacco and working men in the desert, the office looked and felt like a construction manager's site office. He was the man in charge.

In time, I learned his details—they were tricky. Rosenwinkel, his was a sad story. Bob Rosenwinkel was a Midwest American. But, nearly five years ago, as his wife and two teenage daughters were on their way to visit him for the grand opening of a five-star resort destination at Anguilla in the Caribbean, they disappeared. They were never found. They were presumed dead, when their private flight, without any notice or communication, apparently crashed in the Caribbean. There were no survivors, no black box, no aircraft, no bodies, no nothing. He carried on.

At five foot ten, 260 pounds, he had the look and build of a bull, a nearly immovable offensive centre on an American football team. His brown hair, kept in a short, pompadour style, was now age- and stress-flecked with grey. He had successfully built famous skyscrapers in New York City and in the London Docklands before he began his international, five-star resort destination career.

And the Liwa Qsar Project was his sixth resort destination, all massive, complex, uniquely themed and honoured by Condé Nast, for both quality and success. He knew how to put a job together and how to finish it; and he, too, knew people. He used intimidation and anger as tools to motivate people who didn't motivate themselves.

In his mid-fifties, Bob Rosenwinkel had a puffy face, not grossly but definitely tainted red from chronic high blood pressure. That complexion, coupled with his weight and three packs of cigarettes a day, suggested his early retirement, and soon.

I introduced myself, "Excuse me, Mr. Rosenwinkel, my name's CJ, I'm here from CTF, to talk about external site finishes."

Bob Rosenwinkel turned around and with a welcoming, an infectiously warm smile, reached out, shook my hand and said, "Call me Bob. I heard you were coming. Nice to meet a fellow American. C'mon in, CJ, sit down."

I sat down in front of Bob's desk and said, "You seemed a bit distracted when I looked in..."

Bob answered in his down-home, Midwest American finest, as he sat down. "Yeah, I'm a fuckin' short-timer—I've been here in the desert for eighteen months now—seven days a week with no time off. My dick is pointing to the DXB exit gate. I'll be in Bangkok this Sunday for a good hose down; and who knows after that."

Bob's smooth, blade-shaven face had a thin, strong, Jackie Gleason pencil-moustache. Then, with Jackie Gleason over-the-top drama in his voice, he began, "Now, what can I do for you?"

I opened, "I've been told that the landscape consultant and the landscape contractor are getting nowhere, what's going on?"

I had walked into Bob's game. "It's real simple, your landscape consultant is a cunt, and your landscape contractor team are nothing but a bunch of fuckin' assholes."

"What do you mean?" I asked.

I could read the situation. Bob lit a new cigarette and took a deep, long, drag. He looked sternly at me. I could tell he was analyzing me—the usual questions. Could this guy do the job or was he just another linguini-spined landscape architect that had fly shit for balls? While Bob held the smoke in his lungs, he rolled the cigarette between his fingers, dramatically examining it while deciding about me.

Bob slowly let the smoke out of his lungs into the air above him, watched it dissipate, and looked back again at the cigarette in his hand. He opened his eyes so wide they bulged. Then he turned, focussed on me, and laid it out. "Look, when it comes to this work, there're only three kinds of people. Dicks, who get the work done. Cunts, who get it done to them. And assholes, who just get in the way... and there's only one kind of person I need here in this worn out, fuck-hole of a desert!"

I saw what was going on. Bob Rosenwinkel had special vision, acute enough to see on these very large and complex projects how all the pieces and people fit together. He had seen many landscape architects over the years and he needed to get a result from me. If I didn't show the right stuff in the first two weeks, I'd be out on my ass before I knew what hit me!

Steel-grey eyes sparkling, Bob looked directly into my eyes and got to the meat. "Now, I'm going to have these buildings built, serviced, their 200 keys delivered; and they will be sitting in nothing but a pile of fuckin' sand. You CTF guys forced this consultant and contractor on us, now, you guys better fix it! You've got six months, CJ! Am I clear? Do you follow me? Are you ready to meet your fuckin' maker?!"

Not for the first time, I felt the heat. I stood up, looked my countryman square in the eye, shook his hand, and finished, with just one more question, "Yeah, I hear you, and I know what needs to be done. We are in agreement I've got work to chase right now! Where's that landscape contractor's site office?"

Before we finished, Rosenwinkel gave me the contact details of his site superintendent and site scheduler, telling me I must attend their weekly progress meetings while making myself available 24/7 to their calls and texts.

On my way out from Rosenwinkel's office, I thought this bullying man I just met knew how to do the work so well that he had probably found the means to more than well enough support a lavish international jet-set lifestyle for his wife and two daughters before their tragic disappearance. And now, I thought Rosenwinkel had become even more so, one mean and selfish son of a bitch. I had seen this type before. I knew what I had to do.

***

Marwan Abourachid

Things were shaping up now. The personalities were strange; but with white-collar mercenaries in the middle of this desert, I expected that. The good news—in a project process sense—I saw nothing unusual in what I heard from either Kelvin Isley or Bob Rosenwinkel.

I concluded that on site I would have a free hand—be free from their interference, as long as I could assure improved adherence to schedule and, above all, steady progress toward a stunning opening-day experience.

Two construction prefab modules over, I entered on the ground floor and found a narrow central corridor having doors to eight rooms, a kitchen and a toilet. Looking for the landscape contractor, I walked down the corridor. The corridor office location signs were A4 size paper printouts taped on each door. I found two doors with the signs, Green Tree Landscape. I stuck my head into one of the two landscaper rooms and asked for the project manager. They said, "Next door."

Before I left, I looked around. This landscaper room was about four metres by four metres, normal for site contractor offices. The room was stuffed with four desks, chairs, a refrigerator, computers, cables, routers, bookcases with shelves of files, reports messily scattered on all desktops, a plotter in one corner, a printer tucked into another corner, plans and papers everywhere on the floor—too much stuff—but all necessary. In that single office four or five people, no women, all men, squeezed into a space sized for two—low budget all the way—poor working conditions for sure. Nevertheless, the office was AC shelter from the outside beast of 50°C and blowing sand.

Entering the office next door, I introduced myself and politely asked to meet the project manager. This office was all men and jam-packed like the first one I saw. If this was a typical hard and soft landscape construction office for a high-profile Arabian Peninsula project, it would have Lebanese in charge, with a handful of Syrians and Egyptians in support. That was the case. Mr. Marwan stood up, introduced himself as the Green Tree Project Manager and asked one of his people to give up his chair and make tea for me.

Marwan Abourachid was a grizzled Lebanese, in his mid-fifties, five foot eight, 195 heavy pounds, and more than a bit paunchy from all those years of great Lebanese food. His greying, ruffled hair and stubble beard looked like he had just rolled out of bed after a two-day binge. He was friendly and gentlemanly to meet, but he carried the underlying bitterness of a Lebanese who had had his country taken away from him by Western powers—by other outside powers—by regional politics. He had lost his homeland. He was of the diaspora. He was a Lebanese with no way home... except in his dreams.

So, with his agricultural engineering degree, from the American University of Beirut, he made his expatriate living building gardens and landscapes for rich clients—Saudis and Emiratis. Among friends, Marwan long ago concluded that these clients were for the most part all just crude and tasteless Bedouins, without the culture and the class of the worldly, cosmopolitan Lebanese—the Lebanese, who for millennia, starting with the Phoenicians, had been the keepers of culture in the Eastern Mediterranean Basin.

Marwan was happy to make as much money as possible by skimping and skimming on every aspect of the job to plump up his own retirement. His own retirement? He hoped it would be a peaceful place in the foothills of the cedar forest mountains of Lebanon, just a short drive outside of Beirut. He always dreamt of that new home—a dream—a mirage.

While the tea was brewing, Marwan, from the office refrigerator, offered me a plastic half-litre bottle of cooled water. We sat down to talk while the office continued around us.

For one of the most prestigious contracting firms in Riyadh and throughout Saudi Arabia, Marwan had worked for twenty-five years building landscapes and gardens. He was proud that the Liwa Qsar hardscape was close to being on schedule. He was also proud that all the requisite India-quarried sandstone was on site already or en-route. But on the subject of softscape, the plants, he was defensive, evasive.

He and I talked about the climate here in the Empty Quarter versus Riyadh, and the Red Sea. We talked about site water availability and quality. It was the local season to be planting date palms. Marwan had 1,000 date palms to plant, and none of them had been planted yet. Marwan complained that the general contractor had not made any areas available to him.

I told him that was no surprise, every job site was that way.

"Marwan, in all the years you've worked in Saudi Arabia, I'm sure you have worked with lots of Brits, Aussies, South Africans... right?" Marwan nodded. I continued, "Then you know the sport, rugby... right?" Marwan nodded again.

Turning the pressure up, I said to Marwan, "Possession of site areas among subcontractors is like a rugby scrum: if you do not grab the ball, the other side will not hand it to you. It's your job to win or lose! Grab it, Marwan! You've got to make this happen!"

Marwan looked distracted. I continued, "So, have you sourced the date palms? Have they been approved for quality?"

Marwan, in an encouraging and confident way, replied, "Not to worry, there are plenty. I've planted tens of thousands in Saudi Arabia, and I will do a first-class job here."

Despite hearing a gentlemanly tone, I heard the evasion and sensed a growing dissonance. Distasteful noise that I did not want to hear. This was a warning.

We did some quick math and found that Marwan would need to be planting 200 date palms per week right now to finish the planting before the hottest of the summer arrived.

"Marwan, let me ask you again, have you had the sources for these date palms approved?"

Marwan said, "I will bring as many palms and people as required." I had been through this before. The words meant nothing. I would have to push and cajole this one home. The bottom line was that Marwan might get everything in the ground—the night before opening day—but it would be straggly, messy, under stress. For a five-star, A-lister party opening with all leading Emiratis in attendance, it would never pass—worse, big time fail!

I asked, "Date palms aside, what about the 200,000 other trees, shrubs and ground covers for the project? Have the shop drawings been submitted and approved? Have the plants been procured? Have they been approved? Are they in a hardening off program already, so they will be ready for planting at the end of the hottest season?"

Marwan, confident and gentlemanly in tone as before, replied with no specificity, "Not to worry, the plants are at the nursery." It was easy for me to conclude he was low-balling costs on this part of the project to feather his mountain retirement. The project would look hopeless on opening day. This was unacceptable.

I knew that the plant nursery was the key to opening day success for the gardens. And I saw zero preparation, zero concern on the level necessary for a world class opening day—and zero attitude for success by the landscape contractor's project manager. Big problem.

Continuing to apply the pressure, I said, "You say everything is at the nursery? Okay, how about we meet at the nursery tomorrow, with your horticultural specialist, and look at samples, check quantities, for all the required plants? Can you make that happen?"

Feeling the pressure, Marwan, with his gentlemanly overtone replete with a growing insolence, said, "Okay, we can meet there tomorrow at 10AM. The nursery is just outside Abu Dhabi. I'll tell our nursery manager."

We agreed and I took the nursery manager's contact details to confirm the route to the nursery. Then I shook hands with Marwan, thanking him for his hospitality, and said goodbye.

My meetings were finished for the day. I thought about

Marwan Abourachid, an obvious obstacle. I thought about the Green Tree Landscape Contractor and its owner, a prominent member of an Emirati ruling family. I took a deep breath. The solution was not obvious. Worse still, Marwan epitomized the personalities in this region that prompted Bree to once remark they are unpredictably-striking-snakes not worth the time of involvement—a dangerous work and life environment.

I had found no shelter out there on the day. Amongst the people, their personalities and the desert itself, it was complex as had been every other project in this region. I now had both feet stuck in. I was knee deep into the mashup. This was the work.

When I arrived at our SUV in the shaded car park, I found that JeanClaude had not yet returned. I tried his cell. JeanClaude was out of range.

I walked to the edge of the car park. I looked down the long and twisting dune and sabka valley below me—no humans. The afternoon heat had not yet broken. I thought about the missing JeanClaude and humans in general—wanting to belong to something. Doesn't belonging imply something that does not change? Something that does not change—isn't that eternal? So what is this longing for something eternal—for something that is without time? Everything with JeanClaude always ended up beyond the mirage of real life.

The late afternoon heat bore down into my head and shoulders as I walked back to the SUV. That whole existential dead end of thinking about JeanClaude took me... nowhere. I easily changed directions thinking, yeah, building gardens, I can touch that, I can measure that, I can achieve that! I can get my hands around that! But the earlier *shamal*, and this afternoon heat... achieving gardens here in this desert? The desert was strong, the landscape contractor was weak, and behind—bad odds. I'd have to earn my money on this project.

I climbed into the SUV, started the engine and turned on the AC. Then I thoroughly reviewed and summarized my meeting notes. JeanClaude still had not returned, his cell still unavailable. So, I drove about two kilometres over to the on-site Management Oasis Camp—to take a look around. The oasis was nothing more than a derelict grove of scraggly, poorly maintained date palm trees under insufficient irrigation. But this could likely become my home for the project duration.

Small, temporary construction office trailers had been "remodelled" to serve as cabins, I thought of them as studio "flats" supported by an outdoor swimming pool, a cafeteria/ restaurant, a recreation room with pool table and a big flat screen TV room.

Hmm, I thought–austere but close to the work–useful. I asked myself if I really wanted to live out here–after just having heard Kelvin Isley's "morphogenetic" story. Then I chuckled–something was odd about that story... but, in short order, I convinced myself that story had nothing at all to do with this project.

I drove back to the shaded parking spot, the original JeanClaude drop-off point. I reviewed my notes again, and set up an action plan for my Green Tree nursery visit. Then, as the blazing red sun began to set on the far west end of the dune valley, I patiently awaited JeanClaude's return.

Today... deep in the Empty Quarter... the sands had "welcomed" me.

***

Return to Dubai

Ahead of us, we had a long ride back to Dubai. JeanClaude had returned and had questions. He asked, "Now that you have spoken with your key colleagues at Liwa Qsar, what has caught your attention?"

I thought for a moment, then answered, "They were all types I have seen before. I know what I have to do on this job... but wait... one funny thing that might be right up your alley..."

"*Comment*?" he interrupted.

"Sorry—one exchange I had with a guy that might interest you," I continued, "... a Kiwi, a New Zealander... the head CTF guy on site... seemed like a level-headed guy. Well, he told me the strangest story about his experiences on foot in the sands. I threw it away as the result of a job too intense; but what he told me did have a ring of verity—a ring of my Great Sand Sea experiences in Egypt."

"Well, can you please get on with it!" JeanClaude was interested.

"Okay, he said he was possessed by something in the sands—something that invaded his body and captured his consciousness—and he was intense about it—like it had opened a door through which he must pass—he must explore. Me, I have a job to do; but I thought it might interest you."

"I suppose," JeanClaude said.

Then he added, "That is not the first time I have heard that kind of story from people in the sands."

JeanClaude had known me a long time. I looked at him.

He seemed to have ignored what I just told him; but then he started.

"On our way out here, we talked about how this Empty Quarter desert landscape is filled with unexplained anomalies. These 'anomalies' have been observed by humans for centuries, even millennia."

Millennia, I thought, here goes JeanClaude... maybe he needs to talk to keep awake. It was dark and there were no other cars. I was pushing. We were doing 120kph. I should be glad he was talking, keeping me alert. Anyhow, he kept on talking, only from time to time asking, "Don't you see?"

I was half asleep the whole way, until we stopped for snacks at the Howeteen Restaurant. The only crossroad on the trip. It was a hole-in-the-wall place—a truck stop. Just had sped right by it on the way in—hardly noticeable—bunker-like in simplicity. We got some chewables and drinkables and took off again.

JeanClaude kept talking. He was on about the Indian "Hindu" books, the Vedas, the Puranas and their perspective on human history. I wondered what this had to do with the Empty Quarter; but JeanClaude was so into it, I just kept quiet.

He said, "According to the Vedic scriptures, time moves in cycles. If we study our clocks we can observe this. One full circle of the second hand takes one minute; one complete rotation of the minute hand takes an hour; one full sweep of the hour hand represents daytime, another sweep represents night. The solar system itself is like a gigantic clock where time is measured according to the positions of the planets. By the movements of the earth, moon and sun, we can understand days, months and years. The Vedas also say that one planet controls each day of the week. They also mention very long periods of time. For example, there is a cycle lasting over four million years!

"In each of these cycles, all of the God's ten incarnations appear on schedule. Each of these periods consists of four ages. Sanskrit, the language of ancient India, calls these yugas. There are four yugas, which rotate endlessly, just like the four seasons of the year. The first Yuga is the golden age, the second is the silver age, the next the copper age and finally the iron age. They are called Satya-yuga, Treta-yuga, Dwarapa-yuga and Kali-yuga respectively.

"At the moment we live in Kali-Yuga, the iron age, also called the Age of Quarrel. It began five thousand years ago. At that time, a great sage called Vyas wrote down the Vedas. He was a very wise man, able to see into the future, and he predicted what would happen in this Kali-Yuga. He wrote some interesting things.

"Mon ami, if you will allow me to paraphrase:

- '...religion, truthfulness, cleanliness, tolerance, mercifulness, bodily strength, memory and the duration of life will diminish day-by-day.
- ...to be successful in business, one will be forced to cheat.
- ...men and women will marry simply by verbal agreement.
- ...just by being rich a person will be considered respectable, even if his habits are beastly.'

"Are you listening, CJ?"

I nodded and smiled.

He went on, same vein,

- "'...people will think that simply by wearing the clothes of a priest one becomes religious.
- ...if a speaker is expert in juggling words, people will consider them very intelligent, even if no one understands what they are saying.
- ...the leaders of countries will be little better than thieves.
- ...the main goal of life will be to fill the belly.
- ...people will think that beauty depends on one's hairstyle.
- ...people will often go to a church, temple or mosque merely for the sake of their reputation.'

"Don't you agree that is what we are seeing these days?"

I nodded my head. Then it got really weird.

He continued,

- "'...the Golden Age, as the cycle begins once more.'"

In the end, I finally had to ask him, "What does all this have to do with the Empty Quarter?"

He said, "The Empty Quarter is like the oceans. So deep, and under the surface, it is so dark and so expansive. Things are buried. Unknowns flourish. What your colleague uncovered may be threatening. Who knows? You, *mon ami*, must be alert. How do you guys say it? Stay on your toes during your work out there.

"And if that guy has more strange stories that get in your way, we can talk more."

I just wanted to get back—back to the city—back to my studio. I had a critical meeting first thing in the morning.

***

Pirates

The next morning found me on my way to the Green Tree Nursery. This nursery, part of the landscape construction contract, was dedicated to supply the 200,000 plus plants for the Liwa Qsar project. These would be the plants for the first ever five-star resort destination gardens deep in the Empty Quarter.

Nurseries had to be right for any project because if the plants were bad—if the plants were not healthy, the project would fail. I had been doing this work a long time—I knew the critical pinch points. Unfortunately, I had lots of bad memories from previous projects in this region. Over decades. But my early career work with nurseries in Southern California set an amazing standard. A standard for which I still strove.

A quarter of a century ago, maybe longer if I really tried to count, in Southern California, nurseries like Monrovia, Keeline Wilcox and ValleyCrest had rows upon rows of trees, shrubs and ground covers. Each plant in each row properly pruned and grown to near perfection. Seemingly unlimited quantities in any size you wanted. Healthy plants all. And those nurseries were clean, beautifully clean. And each plant was labelled with its Latin name—its scientifically correct name.

Selecting plants then was the same as going down the breakfast cereal aisle in a large American grocery store. Clean shelves, clean aisles, huge selections, multiple sizes of each, in massive quantities. Just like cereal boxes, the plants in these nurseries were labelled, well displayed, and neatly set out.

That sophistication and mastery of horticultural and

logistics processes integral to plant growth was a spectacular achievement. An achievement that I had never fully appreciated, until I worked with the pirate landscape contractors in the Middle East.

In the Western Region of Saudi Arabia, my Yenbo project. The large new town. Street trees were part of the infrastructure work. That was the first time I had seen on a competitively bid, huge project scale, plants being grown in the used empty tin cans normally thrown out from labour camp kitchens. Always rusting, the cans were lucky to have drainage holes. They were always stacked cheek-by-jowl to save on land rental costs. Plants were hand-watered seemingly by chance. And pruning equipment? Just never around.

The captain of these pirate landscape operations was invariably a French, Belgian or Afrikaner character, meanness carved all over his face—*un kepi blanc*, French Foreign Legion escapee at best, or at least suitable for a starring role in a Werner Herzog movie, men of neither scruples nor fear. Everyone who worked for the captain was a day labourer at the cheapest rate. If the day labourers would have come from farm backgrounds in Bangladesh, or Sri Lanka—eh, never such luck.

But today on my way to the Green Tree nursery, I was consumed by one question alone: could these guys do the Liwa Qsar job? More questions followed and they, too, needed answers. Could they provide the right plants, the correct size, the health? Could they provide the necessary support logistics that would enable the gardens to sparkle? And could they provide the maintenance to keep things healthy and clean at five-star quality?

And if they couldn't?

***

Nursery Entry

During my professional career of Arabian Peninsula landscape work, I had visited many landscape contractors. In every visit I inspected their offices and interviewed their staff. I walked and analyzed their nurseries and their projects. How many? There were so many I couldn't count them. And how many would make my short list of preferred bidding contractors? I could not name three. But each country was different. Each project was different. Each team was different. I always started with hope. And so, on that day, I began with hope.

I left particularly early in the morning, even for me. The weather was better. Yesterday's *shamal* had blown itself out.

I needed extra time because, in my experience, large commercial nurseries were usually far off the beaten path. My assumption proved correct. I had to call the nursery manager a couple times. No GPS coordinates. The desert between Abu Dhabi and Al Ain had roads; but it was weak on signage. And landmarks? Ever try to use sand dunes as landmarks in a sand dune landscape?

Despite the mobile calls to the nursery manager, it was non-stop guesswork. The turn off from the main road—no signs—uncertainty. Then I drove the better part of two or three kilometres down an unmarked, unpaved, soft sand and gatch access road. I thought I must be on the right track when for the last kilometre I noted along the roadside a continuous two-metre-high chainlink fence, covered with shade cloth and further protected inside by a single hedgerow of closely spaced, large, full *Conocarpus erectus*, the standard evergreen nursery windbreak in this region. Finally, there was a sign at the front gate, Green Tree: yup, that's the Landscape Contractor's nursery. This was the place.

The front gate itself sat about ten metres from the sand and gatch access road. I turned my SUV into the entry drive, itself also of sand and gatch. On either side of the entry drive, I saw, sitting on the raked desert sand, a rather showy display of cloth-bag-containerized specimen plants. It was a display, not really a design—not exactly mirrored on both sides of the gate.

As I turned into the entry drive and faced toward the gate, I observed eight columnar plants, four on each side. They were three metres tall, *Bougainvillea spp.*, hybrids, cultivars, all tip-pruned into columnar submission, all in flower—dark red, rose, magenta, orange—like coloured, candy columns.

Around them at their feet, on both sides of the entry, were loads of heavy, multi-trunk *Chamaerops humilis*, six to eight natural trunks in each bag—Mediterranean fan palms, an overall height of one and a half to two metres—fifteen or more on each side.

Behind all in the background were large *Olea europea*, three on each side. These olive trees had beautifully furrowed, mature trunks, with sixty centimetres average diameter—lots of character, low branched—overall heights around four metres—broad spreads. But these olives had had their mature secondary branching structure amputated—more than half of their amazing mature character amputated before being shipped from wherever... Spain, Italy, Lebanon. The new juvenile growth didn't quite hide the ugly scars, but, that new growth promised a renewed and healthy future—testimony of olive trees' enduring strength.

I didn't see anyone, so I beeped my horn and waited for someone to open the gate. While waiting, I thought that this display of mature specimens represented a substantial financial commitment—there to impress the *Sheiks*, and *Sheikas* no doubt—most likely to end up in their private gardens.

Meanwhile, from a cheap white plastic armchair partially hidden in the deep shade, under an olive tree, a relaxed, non-uniformed guard emerged. He greeted me with a smile, and on a clipboard, wrote down my vehicle details. Formalities complete, he opened the gate and pointed me to the visitor car park and the office entry.

As I drove in, I saw the forecourt was empty, quiet—no other cars, no customers, no staff vehicles. The main office was of lesser quality than the prefab modules used for construction offices at the Liwa Qsar job site. But to welcome visitors, in front of the office door they had built an attractive modular set of seven translucent, tensile shade structures. Four of the translucent shade structure modules covered four guest parking spaces. Three more translucent modules functioned as a porte-cochere entry to the office.

I paused my vehicle under the porte-cochere to look at the focal point of the office entry, a recirculating water fountain. I opened the SUV driver's side window and examined the fountain—pre-cast manufactured stone, creamy limestone look, three-tier, generic Mediterranean style. The fountain's central stem was three metres tall, and the lowest tier had a four-metre diameter.

As the water moved slowly through its three tiers, it provided a refreshing sight, a subtle sound, and even an aura of sustainability. There was nothing flash about it—detail in the casting was weak. But there were treats!

Around the fountain on the paving and stacked on the broad edge of the lowest basin were decorative pots, a profusion of them. So many pots, I could not count them. I saw a jumble of all sizes, shapes and colours. They were filled with every imaginable small and medium size *Aloe spp*, and *Agave spp.* Those in turn were underplanted with many succulent ground covers. Sprinkled throughout the aloes, agaves and succulent groundcovers were *Echinocactus grusonii*, golden barrel cacti. More than a dozen, in varied sizes, most quite large.

I parked my vehicle under one of the modular shade structures. Checking the time, I still had nearly an hour until my scheduled meeting. I got out of my vehicle. Before entering the nursery office, I paused to look again at the cacti and succulent display.

This jostling confusion of succulents and cacti more than made up for the cheap detail in the fountain. These drought-tolerant plants and the dribbling water fountain were pleasant and fun for my eyes. I noted the rare sight of exotic plants looking healthy in this hot, arid Empty Quarter sand desert.

Even though all the plants were healthy—a good sign—I thought I must be careful not to be swayed by a couple of show plants. In this forecourt, I sadly noted that the lack of crisp detailing on the generic three-tier Mediterranean water fountain reached nowhere near the high quality required by LandID drawings and specifications. The Green Tree nursery did not, on first view, exhibit the required high standard for the Hollywood to Bollywood grand opening. Today's meeting would tell the complete tale.

There might be fireworks.

***

Thomas George

Yesterday's meeting on the Liwa Qsar project site with the Green Tree Landscape Contractor had disappointed. Their project manager, Marwan Abourachid, stonewalled. He protected his lack of performance. He had been obstinate. Despite that difficult introduction, I was still hopeful about visiting their nursery.

Hopeful I was, not just because of a couple nice show plants at the nursery entry. Rather, I had found that many people working in nurseries were sensitive about plants. Workers in nurseries often felt the special things plants offer people—but not always if day labourers.

A nursery in the Empty Quarter meant there had to be water. A nursery this size meant the landowner would likely be a member of the ruling family. Just as I had been told by Geoffrey Tate. I focused on the important evaluation issues. Nursery quality. Nursery logistics. Overall landscape project process management.

I lingered by the shaded fountain, enjoying this little distraction, trying to identify all the aloes and agaves when the nursery manager came out and introduced himself.

"Welcome, Mr. CJ. Glad to see you found us."

"Thank you for your directions, Mr. Thomas."

Thomas George, from India. Maharashtra to be exact. He offered to take me for a quick trip around the expansive nursery. To give me general familiarity before our 10AM meeting with Marwan. The game was on. First thing I learned: Liwa Qsar was only one of twenty or so large Green Tree projects.

And Thomas, he was not shy to talk about his background. Loquacious he was.

Thomas George, in his mid-forties, was a second-generation Christian from outside Bombay, not far from Goa. His father was a farmer and Thomas, as a youngster, had won a local scholarship to a technical school where he studied agriculture. He completed those studies with honours and was invited to study at the College of Agriculture, Pune, where he, after developing his horticultural focus, received his Bachelor and Masters degrees. At five foot eight, 160 pounds, Thomas was clean shaven, with a full head of thick, black, coconut-oiled hair, combed straight back. He was a family man with a son aged nine, and two daughters aged five and seven.

I came to learn that he had been nursery manager for the contractor for a dozen years. While he had Christian humility, his pride in his work and his lack of exposure to the standard nursery practices of the modern West sometimes blinded him to the reality of the lower quality of his standards. Some Lebanese categorized his work as according to "Indian Nursery Standards"—sticks in pots, as I saw it. But the Lebanese, as his managers, were happy to be making money from it, earlier in Saudi Arabia, and now in the UAE.

I jumped into Thomas' golf cart. We sped through large, high-clearance shade houses with mature palms and trees, ten-metre shade houses, five-metre shade houses, then three-metre shade house after three-metre shade house of shrubs and ground covers, all protected top and sides by 50% shade cloth. I then saw the open field inventory with rows of containerized trees... intensely stacked cheek-by-jowl with containerized shrubs underneath... they, too, jammed cheek-by-jowl. It didn't take long for me to realize that the 200,000 plants needed for Liwa Qsar were less than 5% of what this nursery held.

Thomas took me through the propagation and potting up areas. To say Thomas was quick with numbers was an understatement. He was expert in the art and science of mensuration.

He rattled off how many projects they had in addition to Liwa Qsar, how many species, how many numbers, how many cubic metres of water per day, how many plants going to this job, to that job, how many coming in by container this week from Thailand, from Egypt, from Italy–how many plants overland from Oman.

Talking with him was like riding along a one-way street, he kept talking and talking–a fast talker filled with facts and numbers, numbers and facts. As if he didn't want to let anyone ask questions.

Thomas' English and horticultural knowledge were so quick and fluent, I was reminded of the "Slumdog Millionaire" film, particularly the older brother of Jamal Malik, the fast-talking and streetwise Saleem.

How was I to know that Thomas, as a youngster, didn't ride the Maharashtra Special south out of Bombay, making a "Saleem-like" teenage living off the Western tourist marks!? After all, Thomas has been successfully doing just that. Employed for a dozen years operating huge nurseries, here and in Saudi Arabia. Providing plants to the marks, the Western consultants, the Western landscape architects.

I chuckled at the speculation. My quick nursery tour had been useful. I had been pleased to see standardized plastic pots instead of rusting tin cans. I noted the timed automatic drip and spray irrigation everywhere. The nursery drew its water from wells and had its own treatment facilities to assure neutral pH.

The nursery was diverse with palms, trees, shrubs, and ground covers, intensively cultivated and highly active. But I was blown away that I was still seeing the cheek-by-jowl storage of every plant, especially the tightly packed plants under dust-laden shade cloth. I hoped those weren't scheduled for our open-to-the-desert sun Liwa Qsar project site.

Thomas brought me back to the office. We were relieved to be again in an air-conditioned shelter. He took small plastic bottles of cooled water from his mini-fridge and handed me two. We refreshed ourselves.

What had I learned from my look-see? I had seen too many, very poor conditions undermining successful production of strong, healthy plants.

***

Digging In

Thomas and I had just returned into the cool of Thomas George's office when Marwan Abourachid arrived. Greetings were cordial; but I felt a frigid coolness between Marwan and Thomas. And like yesterday, Marwan emanated a sour aura that covered his gentlemanly words.

With the thinnest modicum of collegiality, Marwan hardly acknowledged Thomas' presence. I was not surprised. Often while working in this region, I had seen certain Arabs treat most Indians, most sub-continentals as less than servants. Especially those of Hindu beliefs.

I knew this friction between Indians and Arabs had long historical roots–religious and business. The Brits, for practicality in the nineteenth century, had installed the rupee as currency in this Gulf region. At the same time the rest of the Arabian Peninsula, including Lebanon, was under Ottoman control. In the realm of contemporary Arabian Peninsula business management, Lebanese and Indians competed, head-to-head.

Because of the rupee currency in the Gulf region, many Indians had long come to this region and been in middle and upper management positions, establishing their own business networks to support their Arab business owners. In 2009, according to the local newspapers, Indian expatriates sent home to India for deposit, US$50 billion. Another UAE local business survey noted that a full 20% of expatriates in the UAE earning more than US$250,000 a year were Indians.

They knew how to run a business, make money, and

network—an Indian mafia, if you will—born out of their English education obsession with careful bookkeeping, and their own home-country-based real life "slumdog-eat-slumdog" competition. This Lebanese-Indian friction was hopefully just a sideshow. If it was more, I would have to correct it.

Thomas George's office cum meeting room was spare and crowded—organized, but barely adequate. Nothing was hidden.

A carefully arranged furniture combination filled the centre of Thomas' office. His desk sat at the end of the meeting table that could accommodate five guests. Tightly squeezed in along the edges of the room were at least three more nursery office support people, including his finance manager, all in one open-plan, unpartitioned room. The support staff continued their work in the periphery as I ran the meeting. The people in the room, in fact, all the people working in the nursery were sub-continentals... Marwan and I, the only people not of dark skin.

With only six months till Liwa Qsar soft opening, I asked Marwan and Thomas to show me the Liwa Qsar plants. I learned the project plants had not been consolidated at a single location in the nursery yet. When I asked why, Thomas said he was awaiting instructions from Marwan. Marwan, staring dream-like out the window, said nothing.

Neither Marwan nor Thomas had a contract project plant list. So, I, taking my plant list from the set the LandID Consultant had given me earlier, laid it on the table for their review and discussion. Marwan looked at it, quickly flipped through it, and said, "This is not the list we bid, the plants are different, and the total numbers are all wrong."

I saw this for what it was, a belligerent contractor's stock response—anything to set up a context for an extra funds change-order. In the meantime, one of Thomas' helpers dug out an old fax with a project plant list. I proceeded then to take them through the list, plant by plant. It turned out, upon careful review, only about 10% of the plants were different, and the numbers were not too dissimilar. Marwan's obstructionism was obvious.

But Marwan knew how this game was played and obstruction was a central part of the plan. The way Marwan figured it, every change I wanted would be more money in his retirement package. With money involved, obstructionism was Marwan's strategy.

I sensed the game. How? The night before, as I had become impatient waiting for JeanClaude, I went back to Marwan's office—his guys were all gone. He was alone scribbling some figures. Marwan, at his gentlemanly best, was cordial and invited me in to sit down. He offered me Lebanese coffee. He made it himself, called it his family recipe—the way his father used to make it. The aromas of cardamom and strong coffee filled the small office. We talked for at least 15 minutes. He told me about his life and I shared details of mine.

This was not my first Middle East rodeo. Marwan's strategy was not new; and Marwan... Marwan had concluded that nobody and nothing would upset his retirement. Marwan was proud how Lebanese had chased American Marines out of Beirut before. No way this one American, me, would quash his carefully organized retirement plans.

***

Golf Cart Caravan

I asked which plant list had been used to procure the Liwa Qsar plants. After listening to a confusing discussion between Marwan, Thomas and his staff, I finally gleaned that the nursery inventory of plants for Liwa Qsar came from the fax list.

I said, "Right, for today, that fax list of plants will be the basis of our work. Let's go out to the nursery for inspection. Make copies of that fax for all of us, please; and then we will visit them plant by plant."

While the office copying was done, Thomas called his two right-hand men, long-term employees from his homeland, Vishnu and Padma, from the nursery. They brought two golf carts, and then, after all climbed in, drove everyone around the nursery as we worked through the Liwa Qsar plant list.

It was a disaster. The nursery had the plants, and the quantities, but over 90% of the shrubs and ground covers were in shade houses that effectively, because of heavy dust on the external shade cloth surface, provided 70% shade. All the plants had been purchased young. And due to the combination of crowding and lower light, none was well formed, well branched or naturally structured.

Of the broad-leaved trees, maybe about 25% at most, had, by chance, any properly developed secondary branch structure. The balance suffered from being grown too close together, for too long, with too little light. And even though these had to be planted in the next six months, there was no dedicated hardening-off area. They were all tender from too much nursery protection and tight cheek-by-jowl stacking.

However, I was heartened to see that most of the plants were healthy, as far as their leaf condition was concerned—so watering, soil pH, fertilizer, pest and disease control were acceptable. But this was not enough. I had to make a point while we were in a shrub and ground cover shade house.

I asked them to stop the carts. I got out, politely asked for their attention, and said, "Look down this shade house, block after block of healthy-looking masses of shrubs; but excuse me if I call this as I see it. It is a big 'shell game'—a cheat—with the bad plants hidden!

"As we look from this central aisle, they all look good. Each three-metre by ten-metre mass of potted plants looks excellent. Let me show you how false that is, in this case with a block of red *Hibiscus rosa-sinensis* cultivar. Of these cheek-by-jowl stacked pots, let me choose any three or four plants at random, from the edges, and the centre.

"Look. Set them here in the aisle, by themselves, where we can easily see and examine them. Take a good look at these plants, individually. What do we have? Stems like weak soda straws, tall and thin, single stems, sixty centimetres tall, with only two or three healthy leaves on top—soda straws, so weak, they can hardly stand upright by themselves—soda straws, straining for light—soda straws, having none of the natural branching structure of the species! And in six months they have to be in the ground growing at Liwa Qsar!!

"Not one of these plants is acceptable now. They are all losers. And none should be sent to site like this!" The demonstration was clear. For a moment, nobody offered opposing arguments.

Then Marwan pointed out, "The consultant's specifications asked for seventy-five centimetre height; those hibiscus meet that specification."

"Just a minute, Mr. Marwan, the specifications are for a plant of natural form. These hibiscus are abnormal, poorly formed due to the conditions of growth here in the nursery."

Marwan rebutted, "When we plant these on site, we will cut them back, and they will branch out with natural growth that will be adapted to the site. Isn't that what you want?"

"No! The plants must be of natural form, natural structure, adapted, hardened off, before they are delivered to the site. C'mon guys, you know this climate! It's first-degree-murder to take an exotic plant from this 70% shade and plant it in the middle of the inland desert without protection. I will not let that happen!

"In front of us, is the shell game. Nobody can find the moneymaker. Nobody can find the good plant! The plants as a mass of green leaves, all looked acceptable; but not one individual plant is acceptable! You guys have serious work to do.

"Your softscape work on site is already behind and you know, as well as I, there is only one way to recover! We need improvements in manpower and quality. We will make this project the best you have ever built, but in order for that to happen, I need your cooperation and we have to work as a team. We must improve, now! We must improve here, in this nursery!

"Are we all clear on that? Do you understand this is a problem? Unsatisfactory conditions that must be fixed? When we get back in the office, we'll set up a recovery pruning and hardening off program. Let's move on."

Leaving one shade cloth area, back outdoors again, and rounding the corner, I spotted, directly in full sun, a couple rows of surprisingly well-structured young trees, about three metres tall—with an appropriate trunk diameter, good branching, healthy foliage throughout—well balanced specimens—unusual for this nursery. They caught my attention.

I directed, "Stop here! What are these, Mr. Thomas?"

Everyone piled out of the golf carts. Thomas, for once, was struggling for the name. I thought they looked familiar, but I was not sure. Vishnu, from India and Padma, a Hindu from Bangladesh, pulled one sample tree out of the line and placed it in the middle of the aisle so all could look at it. I saw no butchery, but a good 360° distribution of healthy, undisturbed secondary branches—a beautiful, a graceful natural form, and no stretching for sunlight.

Marwan recalled, "These come from Pakistan... I am sure."

Vishnu and Padma agreed. Then Thomas said, "Right, we received them two months ago." But no one could remember the name.

Then Marwan said, "I know them—Asam. The Pakistanis make tea and poultices from them to help their young girls grow big breasts." He used both hands to demonstrate larger breasts.

Thomas translated this into Hindi. Vishnu and Padma looked closely at the leaves on the trees, made similar motions with their hands, demonstrating larger breasts, and agreed the same thing happened in their countries—India, and Bangladesh.

Now, it was "men's club time", and all were smiling, some sheepishly, some lustfully, at the thought of women's larger breasts. I smiled, even chuckled to myself as I remembered Eddie Murphy in the movie, *Beverly Hills Cop*, when, as Axel Foley, he took Detective Billy Rosewood for his first visit to an LAX strip club, and said, "Don't worry, Billy, everybody likes big titties!"

As cooler heads returned, more discussion ensued and the tree in question turned out to be a tamarind, *Tamarindus indica.* I made a mental note of these good-looking, well structured, healthy young trees if substitutions would be needed at Liwa. But then we all got back to project business.

We discussed the shade cloth reduction of open sun outdoor air temperatures. I verified the temperatures with my hand-held Kestrel environmental device. Open sky 45-50°C. Under shade cloth 40°C.

I made one more point. The Liwa Qsar garden courtyards had no nursery shade cloth. Daytime air temperatures would regularly be 50-55°C in June, July, August and September. And because this project was just south of the Tropic of Cancer with the sun directly overhead during the months of peak summer heat, there would be no shade at all from buildings.

Guaranteed. Every year. Four months. Every day. Intense heat. The arid tropics.

***

Realities

Every plant in the nursery was exotic. Like every worker, every plant was from a foreign land. There was not in this nursery one plant native or indigenous to this Empty Quarter landscape. That was the nature of landscape practice, the landscape industry in the Arabian Peninsula. And the nature of the Empty Quarter landscape itself.

The desert was too hard. The entire native plant endeavour was at best in its infancy. Too young for the seed germination, cutting selection and propagation efforts including tissue culture to have evolved and matured into a commercial tool. That takes decades of scientific and commercial attention. The goal to yield plants that can stretch reliably into different hardiness zones and have them available in commercial landscape nurseries requires serious effort and long-term commitment.

I understood the need for environmental protection as afforded in the nursery by shade cloth overhead and side nettings. These were all new plants, either via propagation or having been brought from other more protected coastal areas. All exotic—a rare few durable enough to become endemic. Even an endemic like *mishwak, Salvadora persica,* needs irrigation! Among plants, only the strong, only the adaptable, could survive the relentless, aggressive, blended imposition of blistering sun, scathing wind, low humidity. This project was in the heart of the inland Rub al Khali where there is no mercy.

The golf cart caravan site tour complete, Marwan, Thomas and I returned to the office. Back inside air-conditioned shelter, we sat down again around Thomas' meeting table. Before we got to work, we refreshed ourselves courtesy of Thomas' staff with quarter-litre boxes of cooled juice and half-litre plastic bottles of cooled water.

I was internally reviewing everything I had seen and heard. I had to make a call whether this nursery could be successful on this difficult, very technical horticultural job. And could I build a successful team with the guys at the table? I needed to make further analysis.

I spread the faxed plant list out on the centre of the meeting table. One more time we worked through it, carefully, plant by plant, quantity by quantity. Thomas, Marwan and I reviewed the plant list for which plants could harden off without struggle—that is, looking good and healthy on opening day in the courtyards of Liwa Qsar. And which ones would struggle, not look healthy and likely fail.

And the results? A full 40% of the plants were unanimously agreed not survivable under those site conditions. A 40% failure rate?! Unacceptable!! Just unacceptable!

I was wary. I really did not want to fuss around changing the approved design. Even though I enjoyed planting design that inspired me, my years of commercial experience had taught me that there was a large range of definitions for "beauty". And I had learned some lessons from Bree—lessons about the time frame of learning with plants and I had concluded what is important about plant neighbours—the criterion that matters year-round—when young, when old. But here, plants were going to die in the first exposure to Tropic of Cancer Empty Quarter sun, heat and dryness.

I knew that changes in the plant list were fertile grounds for the contractor to request extra costs. I laid out ground rules, saying, "Mr. Marwan and Mr. Thomas, please listen very carefully. You bid this project with this plant list and made no condition on their survivability. So you have contractual responsibility for the health and success of every plant on this Liwa Qsar project list. Finished. Understand?"

Marwan and Thomas said nothing.

I continued, "This is how it will play out. You have told me that 40% of the plants on the list will fail on the desert site. Now, if that is the truth, if 40% fail, you will have failed. You will have embarrassed yourselves. You will have embarrassed the Sheik—the Sheik who owns Green Tree! Embarrassment and failure on a huge, first-of-its-kind, high visibility, Emirati project in the Empty Quarter? Not good, agreed?"

Marwan and Thomas said nothing; but the squirm began.

I followed quickly, "On top of that, we just toured the nursery and found all the Liwa Qsar plants in horrible condition, not at all ready for installation! And Mr. Marwan, you yourself suggested to plant them at Liwa Qsar to see if they settle in—what, in some kind of scientific research experiment? That is an unacceptable horticultural logistic that guarantees an opening day failure.

"Now, you can either work with me or suffer a number of embarrassments and financial penalties. Think about that for a moment; because we are going to correct these issues today, right here at this table. Decide what is it going to be. We work together as a team for success, or you fail on your own and I make sure you lose money.

"And one last thing. I know you have read the contract clause that enables us to cancel any part of the work from you if there is repetitive failure to perform in the best interest of the owner/developer—and to make things crystal clear—in these meetings, I, Mr. CJ, am the owner/developer!"

***

Making It Work

Under my breath, I swore at the consultants, and at the bevy of CTF design managers and project managers who had let this "guaranteed failure" be approved. Too many managers without horticulture nous. Dead or weak plants on opening day? This was not about fault finding—it was about finding a solution for a first-class opening day experience—on time and on budget!

Marwan and Thomas both agreed to work with me under my conditions. We reviewed the unsuitable plants again, this time listing proven and practical replacements available without overseas importation. We worked through the list of the "too-weak-to-survive" plants one more time to confirm that the substitutions for each would be available at local UAE nurseries. I emphasized LandID's natural height, spread and structure specification as requirements for the replacements. There was precious little time for any new failures now.

I told Thomas and Marwan that due to the obviously unacceptable quality of their current project plant inventory, I would have to substantially reduce payment to them on their monthly invoice for nursery progress. However, I added, if—if they submitted acceptable samples for my approval next week, and if they delivered to the nursery the following week all substitution quantities of that same quality, then I might not reduce that payment.

To clarify the breadth of the potential paymaster penalty, I emphasized that without exception, anything short of 100% sample submittal and approval, as well as all quantities, of the approved quality, here on site within 14 days, would be met with financial penalties, retroactive and continuing monthly until project plant quality was acceptable. Both Marwan and Thomas said they understood and agreed.

After a bit of multi-cultural souk and legal contract arm-twist to-ing and fro-ing, I tasked Marwan to mark up the shop drawings with the agreed, "no-cost" plant substitutions. I tasked Thomas to set up a project specific hardening off area at the nursery—to begin the plants' acclimatization to sun and wind exposure.

"Now, who is responsible for the date palms, Mr. Marwan or Mr. Thomas?"

Thomas looked at Marwan. Marwan nodded his head yes.

"Good, now here is what must be done, Mr. Marwan. I need date palm plantation starting in ten days. So first thing next week I want to see your sources for 1,000 date palms. Bring samples from your suppliers, heel them in next to your construction office in Liwa and tell me how many you are getting from each source, right? Then I need a work programme for labour, equipment, materials and watering to get all 1,000 date palms planted on the project site in the next seven weeks. And I need you to get an area work plan signed off by the CM showing which areas you will work in, week by week—all that in my hands next Wednesday, right?"

Marwan was dazed. He was not taking notes... he was beyond argument... he wearily nodded his agreement. I could see what was going through Marwan's mind.

He could not keep his focus on the meeting, on the nursery outside or on the Liwa Qsar project. His thoughts had drifted. He was too close to retirement. He could feel the cool, *Cedrus libani* forests near Al Shouf in the mountains above Beirut. He could see the heavy, new fallen snow sitting gracefully on the cedar trees... he could smell the fragrant cedar wood fire burning in the fireplace of his new retirement villa. Marwan was in another landscape—one that soothed his soul, that sheltered him—sheltered him from the Bedu—from the Hindu—from the "argy bargy" Mr. CJ.

I addressed Marwan and Thomas directly and forcefully, "Let

me make clear what I, as Owner/Developer Representative, expect from you on this project. The owner/developer is paying you to deliver healthy plants to the project site—healthy plants with natural form and structure that meet the specifications. This nursery is where that improvement must occur.

"The project site shall not be a scientific research centre or plant hospital. No weak or injured plants shall be delivered to, or planted on, the project site. Is that clear? These are the basic Owner/Developer quality expectations on all plants. Do you both understand this?" Marwan and Thomas both agreed, confirmed they understood the instruction.

I explained the plant spacing and pruning that would be necessary in the nursery before any of the stock could be shipped to site. No one had pruning tools. And no one from Green Tree could seriously discuss techniques to bring these plants to a healthy, natural form.

For now, I instructed Thomas to use the same area dedicated to hardening off for the improvement pruning. And put all Liwa Qsar project trees, shrubs and groundcovers there. This week's tasks were agreed and next week's meeting time was set. Upgrading and training became primary on the next week's agenda.

I was reeling. I left the nursery feeling like I had just been beating my head against the wall. Counting Thomas, his staff, and Marwan, altogether, this landscape contractor had over fifty years of landscape and nursery experience in the Arabian Peninsula.

Yet Marwan's project management logistics were verging on negligent. And in Thomas' nursery, many of their standard practices regarding plant structure were woeful at best, if existent at all... but fixable. This part of the project was a disaster in progress. And while not entirely hopeless, it needed immediate and massive attention. Theuns had already said no changing horses here... so...

I needed someone with mature, first-class horticultural skills, plus the nous and the nerve, to oversee the logistics, pruning and hardening off in this nursery to get the plants and their installation to five-star quality standard.

It was white-collar mercenary network time. I knew another American who had been managing landscape contractors in Saudi Arabia for years—but he was in Russia now on an oil and gas project—but maybe he was at the end of that work. Then I wondered, maybe... maybe Theuns has a South African connection, I'll ask him—because this Green Tree Landscape Contractor has no one.

This had been one of those days—started with hope—ended with downside.

The battle for the plants had begun. Thomas and his staff could, under proper control, be counted on to do the horticultural work. But regarding Marwan, I had no idea where Marwan would take it. Marwan was a stubborn cuss. I would give Marwan two weeks to prove his logistical skills and his willingness to make this project become world class. And then what...?

On my way back to Dubai, I contacted JeanClaude by phone. JeanClaude had local contacts at the highest level. I gave him the background of the Green Tree Project Manager, Marwan Abourachid and asked what might be the implications of a "push-comes-to-shove" project manager removal strategy. JeanClaude said he would look into the business context of the Emirati owner and Green Tree. We agreed to meet early Thursday night at The Library before my make-it-or-break-it meeting with Theuns.

If this Marwan thing did not turn into a festering boil of a problem, and if I could get a horticulturist on the team who knew five-star standards, then I could see my way toward getting a doable project path to success for Theuns. A couple very big ifs.

***

Library Majlis

I had less than a week to get it all together. I contacted UAE landscape colleagues from my earlier projects—Sheeba and RAK—to make sure of costs and accessibility of plants. I was getting close to a solution, but...

It was Thursday. I was on my way to meet with Theuns van der Walt. The purpose was to lay out for him my program to get his Liwa Qsar courtyard gardens first class and ready for grand opening in 8 months. I had to finish one more touch on my program. My plan was to meet with JeanClaude in The Library an hour before my scheduled meeting with Theuns.

On my walk from the parking lot to The Library, I had lingered, to say the least, as I walked through the Royal Mirage hotel gardens. The gardens had enchanted me. I called them Tamarind gardens—because of the bittersweet Bree memories they elicited from me.

In those Tamarind gardens, I had discovered portals and thresholds... architectural and otherwise. I had found design inspirations.

I was late as I entered The Library. I was immediately calmed by the mingling fragrances of agar wood, sandalwood and amber. Blended in a *bukhoor*, an incense. The blend lightly infused the cool, dry and comfortable library air. I inhaled deeply two, three times, then felt simultaneously relaxed and focussed. JeanClaude, sitting, reading the local newspapers, saw me enter. He arose. "*Comment* ça *va, mon ami?*"

"Glad to see you," I responded as we shook hands.

After sitting down, we discussed what to drink. Since

JeanClaude had learned that fresh mint was grown locally in The Library gardens, we agreed the best drink would be Moroccan fresh mint tea, prepared in front of us. Massive amounts of fresh mint leaves and a pinch of black tea for steeping. Refined white sugar chipped from large blocks for sweetening. The final presentation should include a seasonably available layer of fresh orange blossoms, floating on the top.

Proper Moroccan mint tea preparation was always theatre. The drama arrived as the waiter poured the tea from the pot to the small tea glasses. With effortless grace, he poured an elongating threadlike stream of tea, almost a metre in length. Then, smooth as silk and with consummate ease, he closed the stream of tea down so that not a drop was spilled during the pouring.

As it was poured, the smell of the steaming, fresh mint tea captivated. After the pouring ceremony, a cloth was removed from a small, colourfully hand-painted, Moorish style earthen bowl. Inside the bowl were pure white, fresh orange blossoms, along with freshly picked, young green mint sprigs. The waiter gently tonged them into the tea. The orange blossom fragrance overlapped the mint, nearly to sweet intoxication.

Even after sampling the hot tea and quietly appreciating the fulsome, blended aromas, I still had my journey through the Tamarind garden in my head. I brought this up to JeanClaude. "I've just spent the last hour walking through the gardens and courtyards here... I call them Tamarind gardens... amazing they are!"

"How so amazing?"

"I was enchanted... you know... when something that my senses observed caused me to lose consciousness of where I was?"

Then JeanClaude said, "Teleportation, *mon ami.* You are describing teleportation..."

I interrupted, "Teleportation? What? I never left the garden. Or I should say my body never left the garden." But as I thought about it, I recalled all my portal and transcendent effulgence experiences with plants and landscapes. I wondered if my "teleportation" was the result of the design or my emotional memories of Bree. I added, "But my consciousness did detach from the garden. Are you calling that teleportation?"

"Indeed I am. It shouldn't scare you. It has been around as a concept, as a study for, how do you say, donkeys' years. Let me elaborate, in your Tamarind gardens you have had some kind of Fortean experience. That is an experience explored by Franz Hartmann and written over 200 years ago. In fact, even today as scientists are exploring events that are faster than the speed of light, they have entered into the spooky realm of quantum teleportation. It is truly activity at the speed of mind. All in its early years, except for Einstein..."

At the end, I had to turn this train of thought back to a reality I could understand. Interrupting, I said, "What I really learned in the Tamarind gardens was that their quality, design, materials... they have the full range of great landscape architecture... they were beautiful. I was fully captivated by them." I didn't want to share with JeanClaude my alternative Tamarind garden explanation as generated by my still-aching emotional attachment to Bree—we had business to get to. But JeanClaude was being his loquacious self. He kept on.

"Sounds like an Atlantis sort of suspension of disbelief to me—which reminds me... *un moment.* I have something for you. Yesterday, I was in Abu Dhabi. They do have something going there. The best bookstore in the UAE, Magrudy's. And I picked up this present for you. Let me get it from my rucksack. It's a wonderful compendium of UAE native flowering plants. From both coasts up to the Hajar mountains. Across all the inland deserts and oases. Great reference material. Put together over a period of twenty years by a Dutch Indonesian lady who worked here as a doctor. General practitioner, if you know what I mean."

JeanClaude pulled the book out of his pack and handed it to me, saying, "Marijke Jongbloed wandered this landscape in the mood of an ethnobotanist. An old-fashioned alchemist, more interested in how humans used plants. For each plant, and there are over 500, she has included ethnobotanical notes and a distribution map. I hope you find it useful in your work here."

The book was thick and heavy. I flipped through it—easy to read—great photos for every plant. But it took me away from project design issues, the purpose of tonight. I said, "JeanClaude, my walk through those gardens was important. The installation looked about five or so years old and you know what it told me?"

JeanClaude said nothing because he knew I had the next sentence on the way.

"It told me that there are knowledgeable plant people here, with first-class skills—at least on the maintenance end. I need first-class horticultural and logistics skills people on the landscape contractor's team. Speaking of the landscape contractor, did you get a chance to look into the Green Tree connections with their Emirati partner? I need Green Tree managers committed to first class quality. Their project manager is not in the game. Did you come up with anything helpful?"

JeanClaude said, "As a matter of fact I learned that the Green Tree Managing Director is a good man. An old-timer, Lebanese Druze, well known among the Emiratis as both knowledgeable and trustworthy. He has written a book about ornamental plants of Saudi Arabia. I was also told that he and Marwan Abourachid are close and long-time friends. Green Tree has many large projects, so I'm sure if you speak with their Managing Director about quality, he could likely move Marwan Abourachid to another project. It's up to you now. I wish you the best on that, *mon ami.*"

I smiled and thanked JeanClaude—a big load off my mind. I sipped again the mint tea and relaxed. My ears now delighting in the background music of a lute solo. Great sound system, crisp yet soft, perfect character for The Library.

***

Cultural Forefront

JeanClaude was examining the wall across from him, the large botanical drawings, fruits, fronds, flowers, etc. of *Phoenix dactylifera.* For a rare moment, I knew what he was thinking about—the simple beauty of date palms. He looked in my direction. I could read his eyes.

JeanClaude said, "*Mon ami,* you are a dedicated landscape specialist who, in your own way, also loves the beauty of plants. But you are also an international fortune hunter. Or a storm chaser if you will. But what you are here to do is good, as I see it... to bring more plants to the lives of Emiratis. You are above all else, good hearted, always been that way."

I just listened.

JeanClaude took another drink of mint tea and continued, "Look at those date palm botanical drawings—those date palms have so many uses in a transient oasis-based culture. Uses both simple and complex. They have a reverential position in an austere Emirati culture."

He let that sink in, before he explained further to me, "Ècoute, *mon ami,* the success of the Emirati tribes, enduring and working through the climatic hardships and the shortage of water, has built a unique strength of human character.

"Based upon these strengths, the Emiratis have an internal pride that is rarely examined by the world's mainstream media. You can find references to it in books written by authors like Wilfred Thesiger and Frauke Heard-Bey. But most mainstream writers, expat workers and businessmen alike choose the easy way—accepting the centuries-old, negative stereotypes of the

Bedu character and overlaying them onto all contemporary business and workplace relationships. That's good to know, but it will not get you to the core of people's motivations here, *mon ami.*"

JeanClaude always spoke in a soft voice in public. I had to strain to hear his next point.

"In public, the Emiratis do not talk about it; but they have a self-consciousness about this modern world, its communications, and its values."

JeanClaude, sitting up in his chair and drawing closer to me, continued, "Emiratis think that modern, Western world values are not based on the strength of austerity, but rather, based on the relativity of excesses."

I thought about cultural understandings and the ambiguities of cultural differences, then added, "This kind of cultural gap is a fundamental challenge in all work out here, at least that's how I've found it. For me, a three-stage process has always worked: inform myself, then trust... but verify." We both sat back, taking another sip of our mint tea.

The conversation paused. The air was cool and calm. We were, too.

Cultural gaps? Most people use the catch-all terms multicultural or cross-cultural. But in real life in this part of the world, they were ambiguities that could upset any conversation, any work process. I hoped that these kinds of issues would not become a major visibility on this project.

The local managers relied on the white-collar mercenaries to make technical and design decisions. As long as the project was ready as scheduled for the public opening, rarely were there problems. But these cultural issues were uncertainties that could erupt anytime, anywhere, on any project.

Culture and religion were inseparable, or maybe only divided by the thinnest of threads. Sometimes, most of the time, I had what I myself acknowledged as a bit of a "head-in-the-sand" approach. Ignore it because it rarely erupts. Rarely raises its head. And that head, what is it? That head is the core essence of Islam as defined by the Prophet Mohamed in the Koran. When that head rises, the white-collar mercenaries leave; and the real mercenaries arrive. I saw no warning signs in the UAE.

A sudden quietness startled my thinking. The background instrumental music had stopped. The *bukhoor* was still in the air—strange perfumes. The Library was silent. The lute began again. I drew a deep, long breath—amazing how fragrances from plants can calm and refresh. How wonderfully the delicate lute music complimented the light plant fragrances in the air.

I wondered whether Theuns might show up early tonight like he had at our last meeting at Emirates Golf Club.

***

Occam's Razor

Enjoying our pot of mint tea and the incensed air, Jean-Claude and I sat comfortably in near silence. Only the delicate strings of a lute solo, the *oud*, modulated the background. Its music was everything that the Empty Quarter wasn't: gentle, controlled by humans. Riding amidst the delicately fluid currents of *oud* music, we absorbed the cultured atmosphere of the high-ceilinged library. Its mood was gentle, with indirect lighting. Emirati artifacts and art covered the softly coloured walls.

The artifacts were from the sands. Displayed on the near wall between those drawings were colourful hangings of old, handwoven cloth. This was the cloth used in and around a life of camels, sheep and temporary shelters as were common in the sands. Complementing the handwoven cloth was a selection of large format, black and white photographs, featuring *barasti* shelters. *Barastis* are built and woven with parts from the date palm, *Phoenix dactylifera*, and the mangrove, *Avicennia marina.*

The photographs included a wide variety of *barastis* from the island Abu Al Abiad, others from Al Ain, Abu Dhabi and Liwa. The *barasti* shelter photos demonstrated the need for shade and ventilation. It might arguably still be deduced, even with plentiful electricity and air conditioning in the country, these *barastis* revealed a fundamental core for understanding a practical local approach to sustainability. But sustainability of what? The hellishly impossible climate/environmental reality of the Rub al Khali? A discussion for another time and place.

On the far walls were exhibitions from two regional artists.

One exhibit included the works of an Emirati lady, Najat Makki. Her colourful, emotion-driven paintings were inspired by sand, sea and sky. The second exhibit included the works of another Emirati artist of world renown, Abdul Qader Al Rais. His paintings featured doors and windows. These emphasized pervasive regional issues of the unique and complex social, physical and metaphysical challenges of inside and outside—can't get away from cultural differences.

While I was enjoying these, I questioned Jean-Claude, "Abdul Qader Al Rais, those paintings, about shelter, about inside/outside. Such a metaphor for the cross-cultural boundary Western non-believers encounter here. First it was sports that bridged the cross-cultural boundary. Now another bridge is opening for crossing that boundary. Certain facets of the arts and design are becoming here in the UAE, at least in Dubai and Abu Dhabi, a sharable path to allow more movement across the boundary... inside/outside/inside.

"Sometimes it is so confusing... for example the ongoing senseless murder of Muslims by other Muslims in Iraq and Afghanistan this past decade, or for how long—how many hundreds of thousands were killed in the 1980s' Iraq-Iran border war? How can anyone balance that heartless disregard for human life with the beauty, the sensitivity of this library—the arts and crafts on display here?"

JeanClaude observed, "It does uncover a basic human condition, *n'est-ce pas*, no matter which culture, which religion. Focus on your work... the background is deep... and murky... dark... everywhere... but there are some good people, for example, what I shared with you about the managing director of Green Tree and the Emiratis."

JeanClaude had a knack to get on the inside. This was no small benefit for me; and it was inside info like this that enabled me to tolerate some of JeanClaude's foibles.

JeanClaude said, "These historical, austere desert relationships are never clearly obvious to many of the businesspeople and workers here in the Emirates. Look behind the scenes and you will find these are the relationships that keep everything ticking over. These relationships with roots deep into Bedu history guide the morals and ethics of this Emirate and the UAE."

There was a difference between superficial Western "understanding" of Bedu behavioural history and the deep roots of Bedu social history that JeanClaude referenced. There are familial behaviour expectations and duties despite an unbelievably aggressive climate, weather and overall environment. There is a civilized behaviour that has assured longevity among so-called nomads.

JeanClaude continued, "CJ, I'm sure you've read this before; but on this kind of high-visibility project it is good to remember how this place works. The unification of the Emirates started in the nineteenth century with Sheik Zayed bin Khalifa bin Nahyan the First. It was consolidated in the twentieth century by his great grandson, Sheik Zayed bin Sultan bin Nahyan. In the late 1960s, to be exact, he successfully coordinated the unification of the seven Emirates.

"*Alors*, leadership by the Nahyan family still continues today. These are the rulers of Abu Dhabi. And these are the rulers of the UAE. The leaders of the other six Emirates and the Nahyans interact through *majlis*, open informal discussion by concerned groups, as has always been the tradition. Of course, national government institutions and administrative procedures have been overlaid. But look underneath and you will find the strong, fundamental bond of the evolving Bedu *majlis* tradition born from shared long-term hardships."

We sat quietly for a moment. I wondered out loud, "JeanClaude, I've had something nagging at me during my last projects here. Maybe you have heard something. Tell me what you think... could this modern UAE development of Westerner attracting tourism—Atlantis, the Louvre, the Guggenheim—be nothing more than a peaceful exercise intended to spread Islam? Might that be?"

"*Da'wah*, right?"

"That's right."

JeanClaude recounted a similar conversation he had had a couple years back wherein a young Emirati said, "'*Jihad* and *da'wah* are simply both sides of the same coin—if one is convinced in his belief, he uses his natural abilities to convince others—thus *jihad* and *da'wah* exist, side by side.' So, it might be as you said."

JeanClaude suggested to me, "*Da'wah, taqqiyah, muruna, kitman, tawriya*—as an infidel, a *kafir*, you can never be sure. What is it that keeps people from sharing trust, from sharing 100% trust? I think you're right, CJ, in this kind of cross-cultural business climate. Inform yourself first, then trust... but verify. Or, as others might say today—you just have to be able to compartmentalize."

I thought this could be said differently. Know your enemy. I followed on wondering: is everyone I work with here my friend, or my enemy? Business is not warfare: or is it? If I dug into this too deeply I could get lost in the dark side of my work. I paused and thought. With an inward smile, I saw that sometimes cynicism and common sense mingle as uncomfortable friends.

With wry humour I said to JeanClaude, "The Emiratis, they make it easy to come here to do business. The only thing they confiscate from you on entry is Occam's Razor." We had a jolly laugh and finished our mint tea. Theuns was due any minute. When the Servant came by, we asked him for a fresh pot of mint tea. While we waited, we listened to the *oud* and became quiet again.

The lives of white-collar mercenaries, on the edge. Things may appear normal, business as usual for days, weeks, months, even years. Then boom. It is one huge package of uncertainty. Is it not strange, this expansive Dubai development? Curiously, massive sensual, attractive resort destinations, every bit in the Western style have escaped the eyes of the terrorists who focus their destruction on the Western capitalistic and irreligious way of life? How does the UAE remain free of these masters of destruction?

***

Theuns is in the House

I whispered to JeanClaude, "I heard a strange story from one of my new colleagues while we were out at Liwa Qsar the other day; and I've been thinking about the weirdness and fear around it..." But before this topic went further, my mobile vibrated. I reached for it, but before I could read the text message, Theuns van der Walt had found me and was in my face, asking, "Well, CJ, are we fixed?"

"Good evening, Theuns, before we get into business, I'd like you to meet a colleague of mine."

I introduced JeanClaude to Theuns, explaining JeanClaude's historical work in Liwa. Theuns interrupted, "Yes, we have met before. He recommended you to me. Now, in front of your colleague, you'd better not let me down." I tried to lighten up the conversation, observing and remarking that for this Thursday evening, the end of the normal local work week, Theuns was looking fresh and unusually relaxed.

Theuns pulled up a chair, moved slightly closer to us and privately shared, "Once a month like this evening, I come to this spa for a gentleman's facial. Most spas offer gentleman's facials and Thai massage, but most of them are done by Filipina girls. Here the girls are all Thai; and here, the gentleman's facials are special." Theuns smiled, just short of a leer, and winked, saying, "These girls have all the skills." Then, without a pause he concluded, "So you asked me about my relaxed state, now you know."

JeanClaude said nothing. I had to speak up, "C'mon Theuns, that story is so old. Here in Dubai that was an urban legend years ago."

"Enough with that urban legend crock, CJ. It's just because you haven't been there. These hotels have more options than most people ever guess. Hotels are discreet about these options for preferred clients. I have a South African friend, working as a pastry chef in this hotel. He makes special creations for the spa."

Theuns winked, smiled and said, "He makes zatar croissants to order—not just any variety of wild Eastern Mediterranean herbs, but his own special mix, a traditional, Lebanese Gold Zatar—mmm-mmm-mmm—I'm feeling good just talking about them."

I interrupted, "Ahhh, you're starting your own urban legend! Let's get down to business."

JeanClaude had something to add, "*Za'atar* is as varied in this part of the world as the chefs are—you never know what you will get—it is a chef's art—so Theuns may be right on target."

I said, "Enough. I have to get to an important business issue. Let me start with this question.

"Theuns, you have a great network of South African friends everywhere; and I'm looking for a can-do horticulture specialist—a real pusher—you know anybody—South Africans—here in the Gulf?"

"Why? You already got problems?"

Theuns continued, "Now, CJ, I do not want to hear your problems! I want to hear you tell me how you are doing with the fix. I am counting on you. What have you found this week, regarding Liwa Qsar? You are in the game—we will have the result, right?"

I took a sip from my mint tea and lingered over the fragrance of the floating orange blossoms, making Theuns wait for it, then carefully explained, "It's possible; but it will be eight months of hard and dedicated work by a team."

"A team?!! I don't want to hire a team, that's why I hired you!!"

"Let me finish, please. Some of the landscape contractor's people, obstructing impediments, may need replacing—

and that's where I need your help. And, secondly, if I am to succeed on such short notice, my interaction with any internal CTF consensus-based management structure will have to be 'suspended'."

Theuns was not satisfied. He was impatient, he wanted for an answer only "yes we can". And despite his recent refreshed relaxation, he had no time for any details. Theuns' agitation set my teeth on edge.

I remained focused and emphatic, "Listen, Theuns, you must keep your design managers and commercial bean counters away from me—and give me line-item signoff on all landscape contractor invoices..."

Theuns interrupted and pushed, "Yes or no? You can fix it or not?"

I squared up to Theuns, and looking him directly in the eye, said, "Yes, definitely, it will happen! But please listen carefully! It will cost you for my full-time presence over eight months—six months to soft opening plus two more months to hard opening, eight months in all. It will also cost you for extra work by the contractor; but not a significant add for them—just enough to make up under-specified and improper consultant plants, plus, of course, the essential special touches to get the 'wow' for the opening day reveal. I'll keep the costs down by using only locally available materials, a maximum 12-15% cost add to the softscape, okay—and none of that team-review time wasting, agreed? Do we have a deal?"

Theuns looked into my eyes, and then without comment nodded agreement. Quickly moving on, Theuns recommended to all a special "energy" drink, available only at The Library.

I persisted, "Theuns, if you've got a South African bully who knows five-star horticulture and landscaping backwards and forwards—text me his details, I'll contact him directly."

Theuns nodded his head again and then busied himself ordering the "energy" drink. I looked across at JeanClaude. JeanClaude raised his eyebrows in question. I smiled back at JeanClaude, took a sip of mint tea and savoured that mint aroma to the very end.

I understood that the cultural challenges working with

white-collar mercenaries often had nothing to do with local populations. I chuckled to myself—I knew this part of the job. I had just gotten the okay from Theuns to make these Empty Quarter gardens happen. The job was on!

***

Emiratis

The largest unknown factors on this project, as always in Arabian Peninsula work, were the locals. Here, the Emiratis. Sedate. Well dressed. Dedicated family people; but, but... More and more of the younger Emiratis have had education in established Western academic institutions. And Western academic institutions were undergoing strange diversity and inclusivity socialist restructuring times.

These young Emiratis, as any other young, educated people, were anxious to show their skills. They were eager to take on professional decision-making responsibility. The unknown and the uncertain were always close. And so it was on this Liwa Qsar project.

Theuns' electro-green energy drink arrived. As he drank the strange potion, two Emiratis walked in. Judging from Theuns' reaction, they were acquaintances. Behind them came a third Emirati. They were a group—a group of friends.

All three of them wore traditional Emirati clothes. I looked carefully. The three Emiratis wore white *kandouras.* Two of them, Theuns' acquaintances, wore traditional white *gutras* with black *aqals* as headgear. And the third, whom Theuns had never met, wore a simple brown *hamdaneyah* as headgear.

Introductions began. From their names it was clear that all three were immediate nephews and cousins of the ruling Abu Dhabi Nahyan family. One of them, Fairuz, in the brown hamdaneyah, when he saw JeanClaude, treated him like old friends. They shared a light nose-to-nose-touch greeting and spoke closely at length.

JeanClaude introduced me as his old friend to Fairuz. Fairuz was the person from Liwa, the student whom JeanClaude had advised and helped structure local ethnobotanical research. JeanClaude said that no one knew the people, the plants and the sands of Liwa like Fairuz.

I learned that Theuns' two Emirati acquaintances had been showing a special interest in the Liwa Qsar project. They introduced Theuns to Fairuz. Fairuz and Theuns shook hands and exchanged greetings. The five of them engaged in a brief discussion about CTF's Liwa Qsar project, my role and Fairuz' personal interest in any high-visibility project in the Liwa Oasis.

Theuns, recognizing the position of Fairuz and his close relationship with JeanClaude, began to show JeanClaude increased respect. But when Fairuz' acquaintances started about local football, Theuns became more interested in talking football with them.

The football guys had sat down in front of a small bank of 11" colour LCD touch screen displays at one end of The Library—out of the way, in a large bay window nook. Each display had its own individual wireless Bluetooth headset. All three displays had the same football match. The men were animated, talking local football, the UAE President's Cup Final. And because one team had a South African trainer, Theuns was especially cranked up.

Meanwhile JeanClaude, Fairuz and I carried on in quiet conversation. I learned that Fairuz had returned recently from the US. He had completed both his Masters and PhD at Harvard University, focusing on overlap shared in the domains of business management and ethnobotany. Then for a year he served a post-doctorate internship with Booz-Allen.

He had just turned thirty. At five foot ten and 165 pounds, he was trim and fit. His black beard and moustache were neatly cropped, short, in a style becoming his family and their position of power. He spoke softly, like the well-educated gentlemen he was. His presence radiated command and control as often seen in a person groomed for leadership, and appropriately confident to accept it.

Now he was finding his way forward to a proper position in the Abu Dhabi Emirati hierarchy. To marriage, and to fulfil his destiny to improve his country and its way of life. He was diligent, patient. And he was fond, youthfully fond of flash cars. And driving them hard.

I was pleased to meet Fairuz. Though I was curious that JeanClaude had not earlier mentioned Fairuz' connection to the Abu Dhabi ruling family, I made little of it, because it was not the "style" of JeanClaude to vest himself in self-aggrandizement.

I now saw this gathering in The Library as an interesting dynamic. Theuns meeting Fairuz the first time. Both with a stake in the Liwa Qsar project. And I wondered, how did Fairuz' two friends get involved with Theuns in the first place? And why did Fairuz just now enter the picture?

Was some kind of subtle power play about to be exerted on the Liwa Qsar project? Was it only an aside to the main show? Or was it simply Theuns and his two Emirati friends having their fun in just another "boys-will-be-boys" sports night out?

***

Sustainable Rimal

What happens when popular jargon meets a larger than life, a larger than time landscape? What is sustainable about something that is "always shifting"? Or, rather, is "always shifting" the most fundamental component of sustainability? Is sustainable larger than time, is it larger than eternity? Ha!! The more attention paid to popular jargon, the more folly suffered!

Fairuz, JeanClaude and I had much in common. We shared interest, yet with varied perspectives, on the sands, *rimal*, and on the Bedu lifestyle.

We sat down together. Fairuz asked for dates and *kaouwa*, Arabic coffee. As was normal in The Library, the Servant brought beans which he then roasted, ground and prepared on a side table. Preparing coffee for guests—a traditional task for men. Fairuz invited JeanClaude and me to join him—we did.

Traditionally taken in restrained amount, the dates and *kaouwa* were a pleasureful tastebud chess match between bitter and sweet. Between hot and room temperature. Dates—sweet, soft, tender, buttery, room temperature. *Kaouwa*—a thimble full of the hottest, bitterest, freshly brewed, cardamom and clove flavoured coffee. There was something medieval or alchemical, certainly medicinal about that combination of tastes.

I had no idea where this would go; but that night I had the opportunity to ask an Emirati, a landscape amateur, sand desert questions. My chance to find a rare nugget or two to build up the cultural content quality of the courtyard gardens?

At least, strengthen support for the Liwa Qsar project.

Following the *kaouwa*, I decided to explore the weird topic brought up the other day in Kelvin Isley's office. Kelvin described his experience of an almost unearthly, powerful rhythm of the heat emanating from the sands. I drew on Wilfred Thesiger's recognition of the exceptionally strong power of the sands. Thesiger had observed the Bedu were a people intensely occupied with the sands. To Thesiger's surprise, Bedu never commented on the beauty of the sands, the sky, the night, or the sunset.

I asked, "In books from both before and since the coming of Islam, I have read that *djinni*, spirits, have resided as unusual forces in the sands. Fairuz, I'm curious. Is there anything about the *djinni* in the sands that could be a good ethnobotanical reference for landscape architects? Or instruction toward a path of sustainability?"

JeanClaude listened carefully to my question and spoke first, putting sustainability into a larger context. He said, "I could see the need among certain social groups for sustainability as a desire for secular eternality—as a contemporary replacement for the stability traditionally supplied by religions. As far as I am concerned, it is short-sighted. A fad. Ignorant of powers greater than the human mind and intelligence. Ignorant of the powers that moved the sands, that put the sands in place. But, at the same time I value these social efforts—opportunities to bring more people in touch with their ethnobotanical roots."

Fairuz and I listened.

JeanClaude re-focused and interjected some facts. "If I may, *mes amis*, on the sustainability part, for centuries, it can be concluded that without oil and electricity, this Abu Dhabi Emirate region sustains at most 25,000 humans, but with significant, serious hardships."

"Interesting, this concept of sustainability," Fairuz started. "I agree with your numbers; but the quality of their life, the tenuous nature of the supply of food and water, made life here almost like a... a penal colony."

Fairuz suggested, "Current environmentalists, mostly from the temperate Western world, romanticize a simpler lifestyle.

Pre-oil. Pre-industrial. Life here was hell. Even fifty years ago. A day-in-day-out major struggle for existence. Not unlike pre-industrial agriculture, but worse... without arable soil."

I was not sure whether Fairuz was trotting out a "poor-me-chitchat story" just to fill time, or sharing an insightful, accurate picture of life before oil. I quickly found out it was the latter.

JeanClaude added, "Along the same line, I recently read a novel written by an Emirati lady, born in the 1940s. *The Sand Fish* was the title and the lady's name was Maha Gargash. She described her life as a youth with their small herd of goats in the foothills of the Hajar mountains. She went on, writing that after marriage, her move to the Dubai region brought impossible hardships. Dependence on pearling made hardship of her entire life."

I speculated, "But don't people always find some small pleasures even with hardships all around them? Life among a free people is never all hardship, correct?"

Fairuz replied, "If your pleasure is finding uncertain brackish water sources for survival! That is the simple pleasure that kept people, as Thesiger observed, from enjoying the sunset, from seeing beauty in the sands. The Empty Quarter meant death was in your face, using an American idiom, 24/7/365."

Fairuz then rhetorically asked, "Now that we have technology to produce water for health, for cleanliness, for fresh fruits and vegetables, for healthier animals, for pleasure gardens, who... who in their definition of sustainability will deny us these?"

JeanClaude suggested, "Your question, if I may, is it not, *mon ami*, similar to those asked by many other developing countries currently chafing at the developed world? Chafing at the 'one-world' impositions from those same 'textbook environmentalists'? Asking broad-reaching austerities of developing countries?"

Careful not to touch political subjects directly with Fairuz, I then offered, "Couldn't what you say, JeanClaude, be reworded into some kind of post-modern imperialism? Or maybe... maybe... maybe it is just good old-fashioned totalitarianism—we know what is good for you, now just take it!?"

Fairuz spoke with a gentleman's clarity, evenness and measured passion. He paused, first looking deeply into JeanClaude's eyes and then he turned to me, looking deeply into my eyes, and said, "I will not speak for others now. But personally, I find it offensive that engineers and planners from the temperate climate West bring their standards, their self-serving bases of calculations, their romantic fantasies to our country, and demand us, in their own polite and politically correct language to, for example, cut our water use by 50%. Let them come and live in the sands, the old way, for only two months."

Then he made his point clear, "Before self-righteously engaging in discussion about how much water Emiratis should or should not use, let them arrive at Liwa, traveling overland on foot, on camel from Salalah, instead of stepping off an Etihad 767, and taking a BMW 7-series to a five-star hotel!"

Normally, the world saw the impeccable, gentlemanly public face of the Emiratis. They make an international attempt to be seen as part of the worldwide push for sustainability. But here, sitting calmly in The Library, ensconced in a beautiful garden, in this intimate private discussion, Fairuz had clearly just revealed an educated, though usually unspoken, local reality. He had contrasted it with the politically correct, popular sustainability soundbites.

Fairuz then asked, "What is sustainability in a 67,000 square kilometre Emirate that is 100% sand desert? Never in history has it sustained more than 25,000 people. There is no such thing as desertification when we are—when we start with 100% desert!"

He continued, "Is it not a symptom of strength and significant affluence, if one can detach from the realities of the sands? If one can abstractly view them as beauty, as an object of enjoyment? In this respect, Sheik Mohammed of Dubai uses beauties and strengths of nature often in his *Nabati* poems."

Fairuz sat quietly, deep in thought. He focused his eyes on JeanClaude and me, saying, "You guys... you guys must understand there is a 'special tapestry' of the sands that can never be known by consultants, or amateurs, or tourists to and in the UAE."

He concluded, "That tapestry is woven into our souls by our ancestry. Its weave is not easily revealed, except among brothers. And most outsiders cannot see it, even if laid before them."

My jaw may have dropped if I had not been expert in hiding surprise in these cross-cultural discussions. But internally, I saw in Fairuz, I had found a kindred spirit. Fairuz might be the Emirati necessary for support as the Liwa Qsar project moved into and through the critical stage of construction.

I had Theuns' approval. Now I might have found an Emirati project champion. Fairuz was a landscape man, erudite in his advocacy and understanding of the larger landscape issues.

***

Early Months

Pilgrimage is about undertaking an austerity in travel where the ultimate objective is an improvement in a human's wellbeing: spiritual, emotional, intellectual, physical.

I had Theuns' approval. I had to hit the ground running. I needed to be on site every day, meeting with the key people. I could not waste a week.

I arranged for a cabin at "The Oasis", the MOC (Management Oasis Cabins). A word about "The Oasis". Here's how it was and how it worked now. It was an ancient date palm orchard that had depended on ground water for irrigation in a small sabka valley about two kilometres from the work site. The underground water table clearly no longer satisfied the date palms.

At the very beginning of the project work, about fifty prefab studios were laid out along three edges of the smallish oasis orchard. Each studio, about the size of a 20foot Maersk overseas shipping container, was nicely fitted out with daily necessities for each-short term bachelor occupant.

In addition, to service the management bachelors, white- and blue-collar mercenaries, they also built a prefab community centre. The recreation-cum-restaurant building served three meals a day and off-hours snacks. An outdoor swimming pool, under the palm trees, was the only place smoking was allowed. And for AC recreation they had an indoor large flat screen TV and a separate room for snooker. No alcohol was served.

Potable water was trucked in daily. Sewage tank water was pumped out and taken off site daily. These were an upgrade from the labour camps JeanClaude and I had seen on our way here. The MOC was air-conditioned studios in a date palm oasis with swimming pool. That sounded like a tourist holiday resort. As it turned out, I didn't spend much time there except for meals and sleep—my work was so demanding.

The MOC cabins were for management types who didn't want to make the 300km commute every day to Abu Dhabi or the 500km daily commute to Dubai. Our cabins were minimal but they did have AC, toilets, showers, bed, desk, chairs and mini-fridge. They came with curtains and bedding. There was a laundry room with a bank of washers and dryers. Cleaning and laundry were on us, the individual occupants. Rules were no cooking and no smoking in the cabins.

In the beginning, there were no landline phones—everyone had a mobile serviced by wireless Etisalat towers—landline high-speed connections would arrive as the project infrastructure was completed. For personal/private entertainment, you had to buy, back in Abu Dhabi or Dubai, your own flat screen and DVD player. Though we did have internet access at our project management offices, there was no internet access provided to the MOC. Most of the white-collar mercenaries had their own work arounds for internet access.

It was time to get truly stuck in to this Liwa Qsar animal. Theuns had his hands full with infrastructure, architecture and operations. He expected me to solve all external site finish issues. Theuns described the dangerously lagging site finishes under the landscape contractor as FUBAR—FUBAR, that's what Theuns had called it. I had my work cut out on a short time frame. This was the cocoon I needed after Bree's death in the Mannlichen debacle.

I was getting accustomed to the project and the people—where were the weak points and where were the strong points. I uncovered these as I reviewed contract documents, measurement and payment clauses, shop drawings, material submittals and invoices. At the same time, I extensively visited, walking through the on-site works in progress, comparing the progress with the drawings.

The first thing I had to fix needed a sit down with Marwan Abourachid. He brought nothing to the table. No date palm information and no plant reorganization at the Green Tree nursery. Marwan unfortunately never changed, he did not know when to stop obstructing.

From the beginning he was a stubborn cuss who masqueraded as a gentleman. After three weeks of him saying yes to me without producing improvements—without noteworthy cooperation—I had to take action.

There was but five months till soft opening, when everything had to be ready, and seven months until the hard opening when the press, the public and the VVIPs would arrive.

I did two things. I went to Kelvin, briefed him and got info on which Quantity Surveyor to see to halt the Green Tree nursery progress payments. Did that and then made arrangements to meet privately with the Green Tree Managing Director (MD).

I met with Marwan's boss, the Green Tree MD, the Lebanese Druze, a good man according to JeanClaude's research. The Green Tree MD unquestionably wanted this work. He wanted the prestige of this landmark five-star resort destination, the first ever in the Rub al Khali.

I explained to him what we had done in the plant list modification for drought, wind and sun tolerance, at no cost to CTF. On these additional plants to replace those certain to fail in the inland Empty Quarter, the MD was nervous. Then, I explained the new material for an opening day upgrade that would be a change order add, more money in his pocket. The MD understood the larger picture, saw the direction, and was on board.

I told him why we needed to reorganize the plants at Thomas George's nursery. The MD found that sensible, too.

Then lastly, I came to the issue of his Project Manager, Marwan Abourachid and his inexcusable tardiness, lack of logistic preparation and weak project process organization. The MD shifted in his seat; but I think I already had him working with me.

I told him I needed "can-do" people in key positions. The

MD suggested that perhaps he could reassign Marwan to another project just getting underway. That was just what I wanted to hear. I figured that would be the key to progress everything on site well.

In an effort to strengthen his Liwa Qsar team, the MD reviewed with me resumés for potential placement and then committed to bring immediately three new people to our project: 1) a new Lebanese project manager; 2) an Australian consultant botanist/horticulturist; and 3) a Syrian field logistics specialist. I liked the way the MD was supporting the project; but until the new personnel would arrive and get stuck in, nerves would be with me.

But as far as the plants aspect of the landscaping was concerned, everything had moved to better starting positions. I felt some brief relief. I went back to planning my work for the next day.

After Marwan left the project, I found new life in Thomas George and his team. What would happen when the new project manager, horticulturist and logistics people joined? I'd have to see. In the meantime, Thomas and his guys brought all the project plants plus the new ones into one dedicated area in the nursery. Then they set up their horticultural improvement through structure revitalization and hardening off.

As those changes were settling in, I heard from Geoffrey Tate of LandID. It was about a month into my time on the project. He had learned that the shop drawing planting plans had plant selection changes. He started to make noise about modifications to the LandID approved design drawings. I cut him off, saying he had one of two choices: 1) Either noisily and with high visibility maintain his original design, then watch in the first six months, 40% of his plants die in the desert; or, 2) Just be quiet and let me finish it properly, without additional plant costs back charged to LandID.

In his own way, Geoffrey knew how these projects worked; that is, he knew when he had to make noise and when he had to back off, to be quiet. On this project he kept quiet. And that is how he kept his regional workload growing, how he made his regional office a financial success.

After that, things began progressing smoothly with his Pinoy guys on site. We had to move some manholes out of pedestrian/golf cart hard pavement junctions into adjacent ground cover beds. Working with the quantity surveyors, I showed them how the adjustments could be made without additional material or labour costs. Each change had been a pain in the neck until all concerned had learned from me neither manholes in paving nor manholes in lawns were going to happen.

***

The GDawg

On-site problems were solvable, but off-site? Do not forget that the off site was a huge sand desert, subject to incredible windstorms. Our site was protected by qsar walls. These were like medieval embattlements. These protected us from the sands. There was no noticeable vegetation. There were no larger drainage patterns. And the sand dune topography was mobile. Needed protection was for our lives. Believe it or not, we had to bring water from 300 km. We recycled water. Sewage treatment enabled an organic mulch programme. That was all the off-site/on-site relationships. Humans came to the site for protection. And the larger landscape issues from off-site could be simply summarized as danger to human life.

I was glad to be working within the protection of the already built outer walls. It was fun to be working on a series of inner courtyards. I dreamt that this was a 21st century Alhambra project. But I was missing Theuns—his mobile disconnected. I asked around and then I got a call from an Emirati board member at CTF who asked me to come into his office. This was a trip to Abu Dhabi. This was an example of off-site problems—off-site human problems. He quietly told me Theuns' story—an embarrassing matter about drugs and sex, which, shortly thereafter, came out discreetly in the press.

Theuns was off the project; and CTF was looking for a replacement. He told me to carry on in the meantime. But it wasn't over; I worried about who might replace Theuns, because he and I had had an understanding about how I would get the job done. That was precious. I couldn't lose that.

While I did not agree with Theuns in many of his personal predilections, I did like his handling of job items. He knew how to put the right resources in the right place to keep the project on and ahead of schedule.

Unfortunately, he had little tolerance for Emirati interference in project matters—maybe that was a clue. While his standard retort for people who didn't like his argy-bargy management style was, "too bad, that's why the Emiratis hired me", I never did figure out what motivated him on that fateful "boys will be boys" night with the Emiratis in the desert. Maybe it was a cross-culturally misunderstood "who killed cock robin" pride and envy thing.

Anyhow, in an evening of bad decision-making, bad choices, Theuns tried to practical joke, but it ended up embarrassing the Emiratis; and he paid the price. Off the job, in prison; justice was swift in this country. This was just the kind of happening that Bree always feared could happen to me. Well, I always keep my nose clean. But, for Theuns, after six weeks' trial and prison, his government arranged to have him freed on the condition that he stay out of the country forever. So, he played no further part in Liwa Qsar.

It boiled down to me and Kelvin. As a key person in the site project process, Kelvin was a logistics and management wizard. Inside the first month, I went in and told him how much the extra cost would be for the opening day special planting upgrade—and he pushed it through without a squawk from the quantity surveyors, the cost, schedule or contract people—the number crunchers—the bean counters or the upper management in the Abu Dhabi carpeted offices.

But, by my second month on site, I found it harder and harder to keep in touch with Kelvin, my go-to guy to get things done. Somewhat mysterious for such a key player to be inaccessible.

Fortunately, parallel to that, Gary Dolford had turned up on site. Dolford had also moved into the MOC at The Oasis.

Both of us being American, we easily became friends. Dolford wasn't the typical American football player. We found it easy to talk under the date palms in the evenings at the MOC. He was an interesting guy. He reminded me of StoneSteve from Tangier. Both of them had two distinct personalities in their speech. Steve could be a furry freak dope head or a consummate technocrat. Dolford could be a sharp engineer or a brother from the hood.

Relaxing in the plastic arm chairs under the ancient date palms, next to the MOC rec centre, I asked, "What's going on with Kelvin? He's never in his office and doesn't answer my texts."

"Can't say; but he has shovelled everything into my inbox. Gave me full responsibility. I'm good with that; but I hear you, he does disappear. But that can't stop this project—sometimes you got to play injured—we can do that."

"How long since you've been out of professional football, and what got you here?"

"Four years ago I did my shoulder real bad after two years a starter. Fell back on my university studies—got a job on the Palm Jumeirah, Dubai. Atlantis project. Worked with Rosenwinkel and the site super there. Not much of a jump to get here."

In summary, I learned he double-majored in architecture and civil engineering during his six years at university. He knew how to handle all utilities interfaces with not only architecture but also the landscape. As a defensive half-back and safety he was sharp in the interpretation of passing routes—reading people within process patterns—he knew how to recover quickly when the field was redefined—that was how he earned his nickname—the GDawg. Kelvin's right-hand man, he became my key, my go-to CTF contact.

We solved a lot of daily site construction and administrative problems as we adjusted hardscape paths and courtyards without extra costs or delays. Like me, he was on site every day, on foot solving problems as they arose. That was how white-collar mercenaries achieved tight schedule success on these huge international projects.

We established communication on professional, cultural and personal channels. As days and weeks moved us closer to opening, the GDawg and I were making the project happen.

***

Water Is Life

As the calendar moved through April into May, Thomas George brought samples of date palms from many different farms. Most of the date palms would be used in "natural" clusters with a variety of trunk heights. There were a couple more formal courtyards that required matching heights and, as I emphasized, matching trunk diameters.

Overall, I told him to stick with the height requirements from the design drawings but the health of the trees must be excellent and the trunks should be thick though some variation would be acceptable in the "natural" groves. I told him I wanted to see the palms in the on-site holding area no sooner than a week before planting. And the planting of the palms had to be coordinated, agreed and signed off with Rosenwinkel's scheduler in advance.

This was work that had to be done immediately without waiting on the arrival of Green Tree's new project manager, horticulturist and logistics people. Thomas was good. I hoped his yes meant yes. Time would tell. He turned up with Rosenwinkel's scheduler and marked up plans showing the 1,000 palms would be in the ground by the end of June. That was cutting it tight.

I was particularly pleased with Thomas George's date palm pruning, digging and transplanting techniques so that at soft and hard openings we would have reasonably sized date palm frond crowns. Nothing better than the feel of a fully crowned date palm on opening day!

Shortly thereafter, Green Tree's new personnel arrived,

agreed the program and things started happening—equipment, more people on site prepping and installing. I was fully engaged in the project, just starting to feel like finally I had it in hand.

Then came the issues of water. A thousand palm trees? In the world's largest contiguous sand desert, an arid beast? And the irrigation system had not been installed beyond pressure lines to remote controlled valves. But more so—provision of water to the holding tanks for permanent irrigation had no permanent hook up. One environmental thing kept impressing itself on me. I couldn't ignore it. It was the lack of water, humidity, moisture—always. I kept thinking about it.

The reality of the black and white. Presence and absence of water meant presence and absence of life.

This was not a trite subject.

It was easy to say "there is no water".

It was not easy to live if there was no water.

At the outset of the project, I had to get this right... without water, there was no life. I needed to support plant life, ergo I needed to understand the water situation. I had discussions with different managers, water resources officials and key members of the project team to understand in detail both the context and program of water provision at the Liwa Qsar site.

The underground water table local wells were essentially brackish. The trend was increasing brackishness. Projected Liwa Qsar project use exceeded any recharge calculation.

Domestic and amenity water came primarily from the desalination plant at Mirfa, hundreds of kilometres distant on the Gulf. To improve capacity, we also drew water from a recently built treatment plant at Jbel Dhana. Their re-mineralized water matched international potable water standards. Potable water pipelines were being extended from Mazaira to supply the necessary volumes to the Liwa Qsar/Hakeem region. These lines provided for the project and for anticipated future growth.

Measuring the run of pipes from the furthest water plants to the drip emitters in the Liwa Qsar plant beds, the treated potable water travelled approximately 300 kilometres.

On site, the tertiary sewage treatment plant recycled its effluent into the irrigation system storage tanks. For all irrigation water supplies, the projected quality standards showed no issues with total dissolved solids. These waters also were free from any other materials or chemicals deleterious to plants or humans.

The water had to be right; and by the grace of God and a lot of hard work by many people, we got it right. This work was my cocoon—so many issues, so many collaborations—I was up to my eyeballs. Totally engaged.

***

Mid Months

We were down to less than five months till soft opening. We were still catching up. Water. We needed water. And the hottest and driest of the summer was upon us. The next months were all about water.

I went to see Rosenwinkel and his scheduler. The mainline from our site to Mazaira had been upgraded and completed, but a new supply from the Gulf desalination plant was still under construction.

According to contract documents, responsibility for adequate supply of suitable quality water was split 50/50 between the infrastructure contractor and the landscape contractor. They both had to pay for the 10s of tanker trucks each and every day until the permanent irrigation water supply was in place. And until the irrigation tertiary system was in place and approved, the landscape contractor had to hand-water all. Talk about danger of losing newly planted palms. I felt like the father of 1,000 newborn babies. Sleep much at night?

I managed some relief as Green Tree's new project manager worked closely with the General Contractor to facilitate tanker access to the date palms. He also peopled the site with many more workers to assure that no palms were without water.

The new logistics guy at the nursery worked well with Thomas George. For the date palms, uniformity of trunk thickness and good health became the rule. Where we needed matched heights, we got them. The date palms were being planted and watered. Many and fast. Where did they come from? There were no date palm nurseries—so where did we get them? Carefully selected from regional farms that had date palms no longer in favour. No longer in favour?

The date palms "no longer in favour" we could acquire were usually no longer qualifying for government subsidy or, believe it or not—certain varieties had popular fashion so some types were in favour and others out of favour. From individual privately owned farms, we got the best of those date palms no longer in favour, or in other words—throwaways. That had happened to me before when I had to oversee international procurement of hundreds of coconut palms from small farms in Thailand and Malaysia; but that was another job, Sheeba.

And Rosenwinkel? When he saw progress, he was happy.

At Liwa Qsar, he used to find me out on the site, about twice a month. He would drive up in his big white G-class Mercedes SUV with special oversized soft sand tires, roll down the window and ask me a question.

He always had a question. His questions always showed his thorough understanding of the construction process as it related to the landscape, drainage, water quality, water proofing, etc. And he always pushed the other trades to clear their inventory and debris off the site areas, making them ready for landscaper access.

I sat in regularly with his site supervisor and scheduler, whose meeting with the sub-contractors' superintendents was extremely short, simple and direct. There always was a large site plan laid out on the meeting table. Each site work area had been outlined in red and annotated in red when the last trade was to finish and the landscaper was to start. Excuses were neither heard, hinted nor tolerated at the meetings. Items for coordination were listed. Resolution occurred on site. Rosenwinkel and his team knew the importance of healthy plants and beautiful gardens on opening day—not always a quality of construction management teams.

I'd call his approach helpful, or targeted bullying—something Americans have a reputation for doing well—being in charge without being arrogant—maybe a tad naive, maybe a tad brash—dependable for getting work finished on time and within budget. That was Rosenwinkel; I'd be pleased to work with him again, any job, anywhere.

With the soft opening beginning to loom, I was still way too rarely seeing Kelvin on site. When I asked the GDawg, he told me he had heard that Kelvin sent his family home. Kelvin's story had become hazier and hazier. One night next to the MOC swimming pool, it was nearly midnight and the GDawg and I were relaxing with a cooled orange juice. The temp was still hovering around 100F. He leaned over to me and quietly shared that a couple Emiratis showed up in his office, asking questions about his boss, Kelvin. The GDawg said the Emiratis were part of a CTF oversight committee and they wanted to know what Kelvin was up to.

I listened but I didn't put any more into this than I had the first time Kelvin told me his desert stories. We were getting these gardens built—that was all on my mind. Players change. White-collar mercenaries in, white-collar mercenaries out. Didn't make a difference—still had to get the job done on time.

Then someone new turned up on site—for one day only, thank God. But that visit had later ramifications. Theuns' replacement as sponsor began as the worst sort—or so it seemed—a young bean counter, a recent graduate from Australia on her first assignment in the Middle East. Fortunately for me, by the time she had passed the interview stage, psych profiling and in-processing—by the time she arrived on the job, my team-building work was in place; the inner team of "can do" people on the project was already working like a smooth, well-oiled unit.

She visited the site once as part of her induction training—she was, after all, my new paymaster. I briefed her on everything, showed her around the work site, then the nursery. She must have been satisfied because she never returned to site or contacted me. Good to go, I figured.

This landscape—the Empty Quarter—had certain effects on newbies. Large project work in this desert landscape sand-blasted individual false pride. The Liwa Qsar job site was a smug-free zone. The diversity of nationalities, intensity of daily effort and the immovable opening date wiped superficial smugness off most everyone in less than a week; and the others... they never visited twice. This was what the freshly graduated Australian project manager met. I watched. My only interest was to get great gardens done on time without any new hurdles.

Despite my not attending any of her weekly Abu Dhabi carpet room meetings, the new sponsor left me alone and did her paymaster record-keeping like a champ. A shame she did not leave the office—must have been because of her university lesson on delegation. Or maybe, even though she was Australian, she found this desert just too damn intolerable. Since I never had to confront her—maybe she did have good job smarts.

In any case, I was supported by senior people across all disciplines who knew the problems of the landscape work—the last to get done—the need to cajole all associated and preceding works. In these fast-moving, tight-deadline, complex jobs, some work just had to be coordinated and done in the field, to get done well and on time. No time for Abu Dhabi carpet office meetings.

Carpet office? Project work site offices never have carpet. But head offices downtown? Well furnished, clean and wall-to-wall carpets. The unspoken? People in carpet office meetings most often did not know how to get work done on project work sites.

I must talk about the weather.

Day in, day out, all I saw every day, besides my work, was sky, sand and wind. How? How did or could I see wind? The wind shape-shifted its personality and I could feel it, a lot like Blackwood described the desert in "Descent into Egypt"; but here it was real and always around me, in my face, over my shoulder, always nearby, but never friendly, never welcoming. Always carrying a threat, real or implied—a lot like Kelvin had once described to me.

On the Liwa Qsar project site and at the MOC, everything that JeanClaude, during our transect road trip, had told me about this ugly sand desert, played out every day in real life. We all confronted a killing heat. The General Contractor had constructed shaded rest areas with benches, fans and well stocked supplies of cooled water at central locations around the project for use by the labourers, for everyone. And the low humidity? It dried out everyone's throat and nasal passages. Drinking water regularly was a must.

Then there was that wind—even on quiet days it whipped up enough fines and sharp sand to coat our eyes, ears, every piece of exposed skin. Often a full shower at the end of the day did not seem clean enough. The "cooler" nights were never long enough. And the morning sun always brought the heat of the day too soon.

We all learned quickly, sit on concrete and have your eggs scrambled. We were all breathing the heat of greater than 45C for hours at a time. Everyone had their metabolism destabilized.

The heat, however, did work well for one item—hybrid Bermuda grass. Its success depended upon solving complex irrigation issues—supply and tertiary distribution systems. Once they were installed and tested, we were underway.

But none of it would have worked without the input of one great man, Bankley Cuthbert, Esquire. He treated me like his own son, very helpful. He shared his decades-long experience at the Emirates Golf Club courses with hybrid and "native" grasses, soils and irrigation regimes. That aided me in making sure for the Liwa Qsar lawns around the private swimming pools in the VVIP villas, we planted the "certain-to-succeed" and best-looking hybrid Bermuda grass.

Sod? No way! Too hot and dry. No nursery grew it. So, we did not use sod, we used plugs. The stuff grew and spread like wildfire—desert heat and regular irrigation did the magic. Before they knew it, Green Tree was using their new reel lawn mowers. I had to thank them for getting the equipment and manpower to stay on top of the small patches of lawn around the villas.

As we achieved successes in the hottest summer with establishing the date palms and lawn areas, the Green Tree nursery staff was busy pruning and prepping all shrubs and deciduous trees in the hardening-off areas. We approached the fall tree, shrub and ground cover planting with hope, and confidence we would have successful landscaping for the soft opening, only two months away.

***

Native Plant Crisis

Something strange happened at the end of September. I got an email from JeanClaude. He doesn't normally keep in touch; but he played a big part in getting me on this project and helping me get all the right people in place. He asked me how the project was progressing and if I had time to chat with him on the phone.

I answered that I was satisfied with progress at the moment. We arranged a phone call that night. He told me that Fairuz had mentioned Kelvin's absence from the job site and strange activities in the desert. He asked me if I had any details. I told him I had none—didn't see Kelvin at all anymore. I told JeanClaude that I was doing all my work with the American ex-NFL guy, Gary Dolford. JeanClaude didn't respond. He let it drop. He wished me the best on the project.

After we closed the conversation I wondered what was going on with Kelvin; the entire situation was beyond me. Not part of my work—especially at this stage of the project. And even JeanClaude behaved strangely. I let it go because I couldn't spare any time. Little did I know; but as always happens on these large projects in the oil-rich Middle East, unexpected changes and shakeups were about to happen with the gardens.

Inside the protective outer walls of Liwa Qsar, as we moved into the final months, the courtyard gardens were taking shape. For me, seeing that happen with healthy plants and water fountains was great fun.

Then a shock! The young Australian who had replaced Theuns issued an instruction, received from her Emirati management, that all plants at the Liwa Qsar project be native. With only six weeks until soft opening, I contacted Fairuz.

He agreed to meet me at The Library in Dubai. I had to drive 300km from Liwa Qsar construction site to get there. All along the way I felt the pressure of my work, worrying about this new native plant spanner in the works.

I arrived early. Fairuz wasn't there yet. But my feelings, my tensions as I walked in? Calmed, relaxed by the fragrances and music in the air. I inhaled deeply again and again, then found a seat, ordered a mint tea and waited quietly listening to the delightful music. All my tensions gradually melted away. I especially liked the soft, slow, soothing background lute music. It was dreamy. And I was in a dream when before I knew it Fairuz was standing in front of me.

I stood up and we greeted each other professionally, shaking hands.

"Thank you for making time. But this peaceful lute music has put me into another world. Should we talk here?" I asked.

"Definitely, I'm going to order *kaouwa*, maybe I should order one for you too?"

"Perfect."

Fairuz relaxed into the chair next to me and began, "You like the music of this region?"

"I like the delicate peacefulness of what I'm hearing now in The Library."

"What you are hearing is modern, *Khaleej*. Much of the modern comes from Gulf roots but modified for modern tastes. Permit me to explain. We had conversations when we met earlier about the environment, the landscape in which Emiratis have been born and live. In all cases, in the Hajar mountains, the oases or on the coast, our music is about the bravery required for what we face in the landscape. The sweetest sounds... the traditional music is never as peaceful as that modern lute we hear now in the background." He paused briefly and looked me in the eyes.

"As I was saying, our sweetest sounds, music and poetry, come from our celebration of successes after very much hard work–drinking water, agriculture, animal husbandry and pearling. That brings us to your landscape question. Native plants? There is only one that unanimously stands out with historic and cultural value. Date palms."

Now my project concerns returned. I explained that there were no native plant nurseries in the UAE. I also explained that all the project plants had excellent drought, heat and wind resistance. He suggested that we keep our plant palette as it was—if I may say so, excellent common sense.

He told me a story—about what some people call the "devil palms". I'd never heard of that before.

He said, "People call them devil palms because they don't have edible fruit or any of the other benefits of date palms."

I asked, "Devil palms?"

"You likely know them as *Washingtonia filifera and robusta*—it's a good thing there are none on the project—saves you lots of trouble."

We discussed further the ethnobotany of the Liwa Oasis. He suggested that among our 1,000 date palms on the project, we should plant some high quality and high visibility clusters of regionally popular, highly productive local date palms.

We both knew that the date palms normally sold to contractors were either not good producers or just varieties currently out of favour. Fairuz then met local landowners who agreed to donate some offshoots from locally known, named, historical and popular varieties.

Then I arranged with Green Tree to receive the young date palms, and, at visibly important areas within the project, plant them with interpretive labels. Fairuz made sure that the managing Emiratis and CTF leaders adjusted their expectations for native plants. The value of his assistance was inestimable.

Fairuz was the Emirati champion of this project.

In the oil-rich countries, I have found it rare in project work to have anyone local other than a contractor's sponsor take even peripheral interest in the project. Fairuz was an exception. Without him, this project might have been an opening day disaster.

***

Final Months

In the month of September the soft opening was racing at us like a freight train. Every contractor's labour work force was at 110%. Everyone was running. The days were long and the nights were longer. Everyone knew the soft opening had to occur on schedule.

But there was even more than frenzied construction. The operations people were gearing up. Hotel services, restaurants, shops—all were training staff and receiving goods. There were nonstop flows of people and goods in and out of the buildings. At the same time all the architectural and landscape finishes were being finalized. Exciting times for some. Panic for others.

What is soft opening? Soft opening is an unofficial opening when every part of construction is finished and all operational personnel are in their stations. Everything might be a little off the mark. Off the mark? This is where jargon like snags and punch list are the top items in everyone's to-do list.

All the trades submit requests for inspection and consultants walk through the work. Everything that is not quite right or just off the mark is noted for corrective measures. That is the aura of the soft opening.

Oftentimes, as was the case at this project, the owner offers management staff the opportunity at the soft opening to stay at the hotel for a substantially reduced rate. In essence these guests are the guinea pigs. They are the first ones to experience the operational efficiencies or inefficiencies—to find what works and what doesn't work.

Then at Liwa Qsar, every contractor and operations team

had two months to correct deficiencies until the hard opening. The hard opening is a full media blitz with VIPs and VVIPs. On my side, every plant must be healthy, natural form and welcoming. The items of paving, walls, lighting, pergolas, signage—all the hardscape stuff should look new, clean, fresh. And Green Tree had the hardscape under control.

So everybody was busting it in the two months between soft opening and hard opening. The hard opening? I had no duties on the day. I, in suit and tie, floated ambiguously around the perimeter of activities, observing. Helicopters coming and going, full of Emirati leaders and A-level glitterati. Every top-end four-wheel-drive vehicle arriving at the entry—Bentleys, Maseratis, Lamborghinis, Rolls Royces, Porsches, Mercedes—all filled with guests and spotlessly clean. Each carful added four or five more attendees.

Outside the main entry were a series of majlis like traditional Emirati tents. They were authentic, just like could have been found anywhere in the past centuries around the edges of the sands. In each tent, different groups of guests gathered and met friends and relatives before entering. Inside the lobby were separate areas for men, women and families. Additionally, there was a large indoor area for the official festivities, speeches, etc.

The men gathered in a series of reading rooms which focused on traditional movements of Emiratis from the edge of the seas to the desert oases. Men were singing and clapping traditional music with stories of landscape and seascape hardships; and their successes overcoming. The women gathered in the shop areas where traditional handcrafts were featured.

The entire area was chockful of large incense burners giving off huge clouds of frankincense and myrrh. Arabic coffee and half-ripe dates were in abundance and offered to each guest. The men were dressed in their finest whites; and the Emirati women had their finest decorated black abayas. It was civilized, refined and filled with joy. A success!

***

The Party

Following the successful hard opening, CTF organized a shindig for all its Liwa Qsar staff in the sixth-floor restaurant of a downtown Abu Dhabi hotel. During that CTF evening social function, I was happy and proud—chuffed.

I had to find a very important key person for this Liwa Qsar project success. I looked around for the Green Tree MD. I heard CTF had invited him to the party. He deserved it. Green Tree's hardscape and softscape efforts had contributed big-time to the successful hard opening.

The MD made my recommended improvements quickly after our initial meeting. The Green Tree team worked smoothly after these changes. His field logistics specialist had taken over the management of all maintenance work—smooth transition.

Thomas George and his people were superb. All plants coming to site had been pruned, hardened off, properly prepared, beautiful in both form and health. Made settling in easy. As easy as professionally possible in the arid core of the Empty Quarter. Made opening day reveal a charm!

I found the MD and generously thanked him for his part on this one-of-a-kind, first-in-the-world project. This party was a perfect ending. I also made a point to find and thank Theuns' replacement sponsor—interesting, she was—earned her spurs on this one.

As I prepared to close out my presence on the project, the Australian young lady who had replaced Theuns had called me to ask some insightful questions. I had already overseen

Green Tree's transition from construction to twelve-month maintenance. She asked who would monitor the quality of that maintenance; and who would oversee the hiring of and transition to the permanent landscape maintenance team?

Those were sharp questions about quality expectations on this five-star resort destination. And the answers? Well, I might be returning periodically. She'll be okay. She'll be a good professional real estate project manager.

The party was the first relief I had in eight months. A welcome relief. I was bushed. Job done—to this point. I still had a huge snag list and the final financial close-out to do.

Anyhow, I planned, after finishing up at the MOC, to spend time in Dubai reviewing what had happened on this project which had consumed, as I had hoped it would, all my energy, thought, logic and... my everything. I had found the landscape project cocoon. Soon I would have the time back at my Dubai studio to take a deep breath and download. Where did I stand personally and professionally?

Meanwhile the party was still going on. I thought I had seen everyone, so I was preparing to leave when I bumped into the GDawg. We toasted each other with Champagne. But someone was missing. Hadn't seen Kelvin.

I asked him where Kelvin was. The GDawg told me that Kelvin had gone into the twilight zone and that's all he knew, except that a bunch of Defense Advanced Research Projects Agency (DARPA) military came to either pull Kelvin out of the twilight zone, or follow him in!

I was astonished, at first. "What are you talking about," I asked. The GDawg wouldn't say a thing.

After a little to-ing and fro-ing, the GDawg told me the bottom line was that a couple weeks ago Kelvin had resigned from CTF—bang—finished.

"What happened?" I asked. He began a shocking story.

The GDawg told me it all started months ago, before he had arrived on site, with that incident in the desert, the first time Kelvin passed out on a walk and had to be rescued. It escalated after that.

Apparently, Kelvin had two further episodes just after the

GDawg arrived. Kelvin then kept going out more frequently and especially in the middle of the night. He came to confide in the GDawg, asking the GDawg to cover his absences more and more. Finally, Kelvin even stopped going home to Abu Dhabi on the weekends to see his family. Then he relocated them back to New Zealand. All this about three months ago.

Then, as the GDawg recounted, everything had become quite awkward until about ten weeks ago, just before Kelvin resigned, when a caravan of about eight humvees arrived at site. Then three helicopters arrived, including the personal helicopter of the Crown Prince himself.

I remembered seeing them all arriving on site. I had asked Rosenwinkel what was up and he told me it was just a typical VVIP drive by.

The GDawg's story was different, he gave me details. "The humvees were all desert camo colours and were marked only DARPA on the doors. Same with two of the helicopters. Kelvin buzzed my cell on the day and told me to come at once to his office.

"I got there just before a posse of desert camo troops arrived. In the DARPA group, most were Americans, spoke that way. All had sleeve patches that said DARPA and something like International Joint Operations Task Force. There were others, two or three speaking Arabic. The head guy spoke softly to Kelvin and Kelvin asked me for privacy, so I left the room.

"I went out to the humvees and talked American football with the drivers. They showed me the inside of the vehicles—a quick look. Did they have the equipment—sensors of all sorts—electromagnetic wave equipment, broadband satellite uplink to an overhead stationary satellite, sending/receiving real-time data via numerous digital filters, more stuff that I'd never before seen!! And they had drones, a whole team just to program, fly and monitor the drones!!"

The GDawg continued, "Afterwards, the next day, Kelvin tendered his resignation, effective immediately. That night he came to my cabin in the MOC to say goodbye. The next morning Kelvin and all the humvees and helicopters departed. That was it. Well, a couple of them stayed. We put them up in the MOC, surprised you didn't notice—but we were busy as hell in the run-up to the hard opening." Then the GDawg went quiet.

I had to persist, to ask him over and over to tell me what really happened. As if his job depended on it, he was hesitant. At last he relented and suggested we go outdoors, away from others. We walked outside onto the garden terrace, overlooking a huge mangrove (*Avicennia marina*) conservation area. And do I remember that night!

More than anything, I remember the mangroves—they gave off a strange, almost otherworldly... stink—that's what I have to call it—somewhere just the wrong, the disgusting side of medicinal—damn near choked me into coughing seizures. Same for the GDawg.

We looked at each other and made an immediate about face—went back inside, to the hotel entry lounge. We found a quiet corner in the lounge, away from the flow of crowds through the lobby. We ordered two whiskies to give our throats and nasal passages a good clean out. Then we ordered two more just to be sure and talked around Kelvin for a while. Finally the GDawg relented, swearing me to confidentiality. Here is what the GDawg told me, put into my own words; because his words were just too colourful to repeat verbatim.

Kelvin returned again and again by himself on foot into the Empty Quarter sands just out of sight of our project, never the same place twice. Out in the desert by himself, twice a day. He always kept his GPS beacon live. He started the middle of the night visits. Then on one full moon night—he had an episode where he again experienced body penetration, as he had by now become accustomed. But this time the energy forces, having simultaneously penetrated his urethra and anus, continued into his body cavity, both arriving and uniting simultaneously at his seventh chakra—wrapping it—bathing it—energizing it.

The energy field usurped all Kelvin's gross senses of sight, smell, touch—only his sense of hearing remained. And it was heightened. He heard the energy melding with his seventh chakra and then each of the two forces began to flow upward in, as Kelvin described, a double helix, wrapping his spinal cord, energizing it as they moved upward chakra by chakra. It was at this point where Kelvin always failed to be able to describe what happened next and how it all finished—how he returned to what we all call... normal.

He used words like metaphysical, transcendental... always concluded—not senses, not imagination, not words—indescribable. But, as the GDawg put it, "Kelvin was not normal. He had a strange burning in between intelligence and emotion—a burn, a fire, a heat—unlike anything he had ever experienced. It had no physical symptoms. Figure that one out, CJ."

And the GDawg continued, "After this full-moon experience, Kelvin walked the dunes every day and night for hours—he was chasing for that experience. His Liwa Qsar work meant nothing. His family meant nothing. Then the DARPA people came."

That's how the GDawg told it. I was speechless. I knew there was something strange in those sands. JeanClaude could not stop talking about strangeness in the sands when he drove me out here eight months ago—but JeanClaude—I took a lot of his stories with a grain of salt—but... this time....

I hadn't heard from JeanClaude since his September email. At that time, he was with colleagues in London at Kew. He asked me how the project was progressing. He knew how crazy a hospitality project could be leading up to the soft opening. I told him we expected the soft opening on schedule; but I was beat. The Empty Quarter had taken the best out of all of us. He replied with ambiguity, saying he would be seeing me in the sands again. And that was all. I figured that was JeanClaude being JeanClaude.

Me, I was feeling lucky, just about to get out of there after a crazy number of months trying to undo FUBAR—and being successful. But the stories about Kelvin—I didn't know—just plain weird. That's a shame because I was impressed with his landscape background and his morphogenetic explanations. Maybe there was something to it; but honestly I didn't care. White-collar mercenaries are often like ships passing in the night.

I was glad to be wrapping up this job. I still had snags, as-builts and change order closeouts to do. This had been a fine celebratory party but what had happened out in the sands at Liwa Qsar, though the details were still unclear, was certainly beyond words.

***

This Can't Be

Defend us in battle,
be our protection against the wickedness and snares of the devil.
May God rebuke him, we humbly pray;
and do thou, O Prince of the heavenly host,
by the power of God, cast into hell
Satan and all the evil spirits
who prowl through the world seeking the ruin of souls.
Amen.
-Saint Michael Archangel

The snags were mechanical paperwork. The landscape contractor was cooperating. The guys from LandID did all of the snag and as-built legwork. I just made control over the critical items. But closing out the change order documentation—that was another story.

It became a *majlis* story. The tracking of all cost over-runs and under-runs was carefully monitored by the landscape contractor, the general contractor, the landscape architecture consultant and the CTF quantity surveyor. At the end, the landscape contractor submitted his list. His list was checked by the landscape architecture consultant. Then it all came to me—the entire package. For each item, I had to mark yes or no. Yes, I approve the extra cost or no, I don't approve the extra cost. I forwarded the whole package to the CTF quantity surveyor.

Then the process went dark for the expats, the white-collar mercenaries. The process went live to a *majlis* tent in the desert to be scrutinized and discussed by key Emiratis only. They were the owners of every project operative: CTF, the contractor and the consultant. They and they alone decided the final contract value. This was normal. I never saw paperwork from those *majlis* sessions. But that's okay. If I heard nothing, I knew I'd done my job well.

I still had some final paperwork outstanding on the movement into 12-month maintenance. It was twilight when I finished. As I parked my SUV at the MOC and started walking to my cabin, I almost bumped into a guy coming out of the date palm grove shadows. I said to myself, was that a big box of Frosties in that guy's hands? I must have said it out loud because the guy said, "Frosties? Damn straight, gotta have 'em."

I thought that's a familiar voice then the penny dropped. I said, "Steve? Is that you? Tangier roof top—StoneSteve—what, 20-25 years ago?"

"CJ? Can't be—what a strange world!"

I said, "Can't believe my eyes! What are you doing here?"

"That's a long story, CJ. C'mon over to my cabin and have some Frosties with me—real milk this time."

We walked over to his cabin. He poured out two big bowls of Frosties, handing one to me before I started, "Steve, my job here is finished. I'm on the way out—how about you?"

Steve said, "I'm just beginning."

"What are you doing?"

"The usual comms stuff, like Tangier—only the technology has advanced 20 years better and with DARPA the tech I have now is 50 years better than our rooftop stuff in Tangier."

I said, "Tangier—those are some memories—my ankle problem and crutches, the Amsterdammers, Bree..."

Steve interrupted, "Bree!? I followed up on her stories—the ones she told me when we got her out of that human trafficking crap back there—her stories about West Africa, the Sahara—

well, that all panned out in its strange way. We tracked it back to Dahomey—there was some weird shit but let me cut to the chase..."

I interrupted him, "Wait a minute—there's more to the Bree story. A long time ago I lost my wife Sachy and kids in an automobile accident—killed me internally for years—then I ran into Bree again—we spent time together and hit it off in a strange kind of 'birds of a landscape feather' way. We got married in the mountains of Switzerland and then, in those same mountains, she died." I didn't want to say more.

"Who can guess how the world turns? You okay?"

"Yeah, I'm okay—this project has been my life these last eight months."

Steve said, "This project? You've got to hear this! Bree's stories plus that Anquietas from the Petit Socco Curios shop and our apartment building *shaoush*, Sidi Hamete, started to weave together and that thread of a story explains why I am here."

"Steve, I'm still in the dark—what is this all about... Kelvin... West Africa... Sidi Hamete... what?"

"Let me give you a simplified outline—want any more Frosties? Mind if I finish them?"

"Help yourself, get on with the outline—help me understand what's going on."

Steve needed no more prompting. He said, "Here are the corollaries that make what we are doing today matter:

1. Human nature needs rules and boundaries.
2. This is a planet rich in life.
3. Anquietas are (seem to be helpful) guardians of good.
4. Some of us thought that Bree was onto something in the Sahara that was detrimental to humans or the earth. In the end, we concluded that she, like you, had been under some kind of West African spell—and that was all."

"Hang on Steve, Bree?! Under a spell?!!"

"Definitely, let me finish—you wanted to know why I was here.

5. And here in the Empty Quarter, we thought what Kelvin found in the sand was something detrimental to humans or the earth. You see, we were still keeping Bree's original experience in play... just in case. But, after careful consideration, we concluded that what Kelvin actually found was a piece of debris from one of our decommissioned satellites."

"What??"

***

StoneSteve

"What don't you understand?" Steve asked.

"I knew Bree well—we were married—lived together for years—shared our most intimate experiences in the landscape—in Morocco and Switzerland—she never mentioned West African spells... but me, you know what happened to me in Tangier—it took me years to figure it out and then have it removed by a New Mexican shaman—but I never heard anything about weird spells from Bree—nothing is adding up."

"I don't know what you expect from me, CJ, I'm sharing our fundamental findings after careful and detailed analysis. And here we found, buried in the sand, a part of a decommissioned satellite."

"What kind of satellite?"

"Now, that is confidential. That will not be made known—the US puts a lot of defence satellites in orbit—suffice it to say it was not a telecom/internet connectivity satellite."

I was quiet for a moment. Too much information input for me.

"Here's what got us fussed here. The Emiratis wanted to know what was going on with Kelvin. And we learned Kelvin was planning to put his Empty Quarter experiences online—live stream them. We were concerned that any misrepresentation would upset US relations with the UAE. So we stepped in. Then things got crazy."

"What do you mean?"

Steve didn't answer. He must have been thinking what he

could say and what he couldn't say.

Then Steve asked, "Did you know we found Kelvin dead in the desert? We think a Belgian guy did it, a JeanClaude—he has a Ted Kaczynski profile and CJ, we know you and he spent time together..."

"Dead? What happened?"

"Some Emiratis found him a couple days ago. They took him to a hospital and they declared him dead on arrival, victim of a stroke brought on by extreme dehydration."

"That's it? But... but... it doesn't add up. Kelvin was really well organized; and JeanClaude? He didn't seem like a Kaczynski bomber—he was freaky but not like that."

"CJ, I'm only sharing what I've been told."

In disbelief, I said, "I thought JeanClaude was one of the good guys—information gathering—under cover—The Company. Isn't that who you work for, too?"

"Not that simple, CJ. All I can say is that you will not have any of this come at you."

"I'm still not clear, Steve. Bring this story up to date—Kelvin—JeanClaude..."

Steve said, "We've been friends a long time ago in Tangier, right?"

"Yeah, we had some strange times and a lot of fun."

"So please understand that like you, I've made my career. And my career has a 'chain of command' thing."

"What do you mean?"

"Aside from our reminiscences, I can only tell you what is official and what I am permitted to tell."

"Why all the prelims, Steve?"

"Well, the next is strange. Maybe take it with a grain of salt; but don't expect any further background or details."

"Now, you've got me wound up—where is this headed?"

"You wanted an update, right? Here is the current chapter. There was fear that Kelvin had uncovered something that he shouldn't have. We came to verify what he found. Then before we could question him in detail, he was found dead out in the sands. The autopsy noted in addition to dehydration and stroke, there were traces of some strange plant-based poison;

and JeanClaude's movements in the week surrounding Kelvin's death put him in a research facility in Kew prior to arriving here in the UAE on a private plane before returning to his home country, Belgium. This theory is one of many we are exploring. Are you with me now, CJ?"

I asked, "Why would JeanClaude kill Kelvin? What do you guys figure?"

"That's above my pay grade, CJ, but I've heard JeanClaude was a clandestine operator whose profile was 'take care of loose ends', a wetworks specialist—I can't figure it out, maybe you can."

I was all twisted about. My Liwa Qsar project was complete. The Frosties were gone. It was desert dark outside and I still had to clean out my cabin.

Shaking my head in disbelief over what I had just heard, I called it quits. I said goodnight to Steve and headed to my cabin. I inhaled deeply the desert night air. This was a deep breath that felt more like a deep sigh. I inhaled the Empty Quarter's mystery. It was all around me. I shook my shoulders and told myself to relax. Between the GDawg and Steve it was all too much. What a weird way to end this project. I thought the project ended with a great hard opening; but this epilogue from StoneSteve? Didn't sit right.

The next morning, I saw Steve packing out.

I asked, "What's up?"

'We're outta here, got orders first thing this morning. No more studies. No more work. Me? Can't wait to get back to the States. How about you?"

"I still got a bit of paperwork; but I'll be out of here before the weekend. The project was fun, hard but fun."

"I hear that; maybe we'll bump into each other again?"

"Yeah, here's my email address—drop a line—maybe we can get together for some alumnae function at our university?"

"Sounds possible, take care."

We shook hands and I headed over to my construction office. On the way over, I reviewed all the stuff that Steve, the GDawg, JeanClaude and Kelvin had brought to this landscape architecture project. They brought noise—big time noise—not since my time in Kuwait had I had such a brouhaha surrounding my garden work.

Glad this all happened at the end of the project—unnecessary complications... except... I thought... all this "life" in the Empty Quarter, according to Kelvin?! This was the stuff that was Bree's world... her Sahara faery realm. Was I living the last chapter of a bad dream? Or was it all nothing—like the conclusion Steve and his people apparently reached. And what about that strange story of JeanClaude killing Kelvin?

I forced my energy back into the Liwa Qsar project. Just a bit of paperwork and I'd be on my way back to my studio in Dubai. I couldn't wait to put my feet up, and get a good night's sleep without having an alarm wake me for another day in the heart of the beast.

6-The End

This is the end—my friend.

Eileen

Back in my Dubai studio—what a relief. My first day back in the city—the place where humans dominate—even though it is coastal edge of the Rub al Khali. I didn't even want to write those words, Rub al Khali, anymore. Why? Too much history. Too much empty. Too much fighting for survival.

My project Liwa Qsar was an exception. It was beautiful, it was successful.

But the desert, the sands, the inland Rub al Khali—not for humans, not for life. And it took away my colleague, Kelvin, in a most mysterious manner. I wanted to run away from it. It was not an ecosystem for me.

Off the record, our Liwa Qsar project may be, in the not-too-distant future—ripped, rasped and disappearing—lasting no longer than a tent in the roaring Rub al Khali. I was like all of the workers and managers out there—beaten unrecognizable by the sands, shredded.

The next morning I woke up sweating in my studio bed. The sands were everywhere. And Dubai did not give my hoped-for relief. Mirage. This is the land of mirage. And I couldn't tell the difference...

I was confused by the way my Liwa Qsar project wrapped up in the last 24 hours. Something was not right. I washed my face with cold water. Looked out the window of my studio. It was 9AM and the sun was already too bright. I, though in an air-conditioned studio, felt the heat like I was outside. I was still confused.

Trying to get straight, I checked my to-do notes. I had to call CTF for them to pick up my SUV, their company car. They said their people would come by before noon. My work had been 7 days a week intense for so long... without that pressure, I felt something big was missing.

I hit the showers, shaved and made coffee and toast for breakfast. I wondered if Eileen was still in Dubai. I hoped so. Maybe she would have insight on Steve's story about Kelvin's murder by JeanClaude. The very thought still did not make sense. And that was not all about what I heard from Steve. He talked about Kelvin's desert experience like it was something bad... but Kelvin and the GDawg described the desert experience as having something positive about it.

I was still puzzling over it when the CTF people arrived to pick up my SUV—that was just about the last to-do item of my Liwa Qsar project.

I had a few small admin details to finish online. Then, all contractual items complete, I checked my local bank account. My last monthly paycheque and completion bonus had been deposited. That gave me some relief, considering all the turmoil that had surrounded Theuns and his replacement. Financially, CTF had taken good care of me. They were happy with the result.

But I was still troubled. I had to figure out the source. Was it real or just an Empty Quarter mirage? First things first. First thing on top of everything was Steve's unbelievable story. He had flummoxed me with his explanation of incidents in the Empty Quarter. I had to ask what Eileen knew about the DARPA team blaming JeanClaude for Kelvin's murder in the Empty Quarter.

I dialled the old number I had for her here in Dubai—it had been 8 months since we last spoke. She picked up. We had a short, friendly, personal conversation wherein she suggested we meet for a snack at 3PM that same afternoon in the MOE at Paul's and talk business there.

Eileen, an American working in Dubai for the Analysis Corp., and I had been friends since Casablanca nearly three decades ago when we had to defuse a late-night cheap hotel incident involving Bree and three West African men. Some years later, Eileen entered my life again when I was working in SoCal, Los Angeles. Eileen had put me in touch with a very large project in Saudi Arabia which also started my info-gathering efforts.

Since then, except for the last eight months, I have been regularly in contact with her. She has always been helpful and a willing friend. She knew that I had a close professional, personal and info-gathering relationship with JeanClaude. Only natural that I seek her understanding of Steve's JeanClaude story.

She and I arrived at Paul's about the same time, shook hands, and took a table. They were mildly busy. We weren't there to eat, rather to talk. I ordered an espresso and she ordered an Earl Grey tea. And we got down to business.

"Nice to see you again—escaped from the Empty Quarter, have you?"

"Job finished. It was just what I hoped it would be—fully engaging. It was a wild ride—fast moving carousel. I think it is still turning..."

"Tell me, that's why I am here."

"Really weird, Steve, a guy from way back in Tangier where he was my neighbour—used to call him StoneSteve—he was a good, a helpful guy who got me out of trouble with the Tangier authorities. Anyhow, he turned up out at Liwa with a team from DARPA. Let me cut to the end—he told me that JeanClaude had killed, out in the sands, assassinated Kelvin Isley, a key CTF expat manager. I knew them both and the story just didn't add up. It didn't affect my work—my question to you is about JeanClaude. They told me he had left the country. Could any of this be true?"

"Here's what I know. JeanClaude has never been involved with wetwork, the elimination of anyone endangering our national security. And I have seen nothing with his name in my watchlist incoming. So, what you have heard sounds like BS. In fact, I know he was here in the UAE and to our knowledge he is still in country. That answers your JeanClaude question."

"That helps but do you have anything else about Liwa and my project?"

"What's going on? We have nothing about Liwa Qsar..."

“I’m just a bit curious. Seems like the sands out there were churning up something...”

“Anything specific?”

“I don’t know a whole lot—just a bunch of stories about something unexplainable in the sands—like what Bree sensed way back when she was in the Sahara. My past work around these Arabian Peninsula deserts has uncovered loads of unanswered questions that get lost in time; but what has happened out there was in real time... maybe I should forget about it—but it feels like a niggle. I’d really like to free myself of all this...”

“What’s stopping you?”

“Good question—my project is finished and I have to get on with my own life, as you well know since my arrival in Fujairah. But JeanClaude was a friend... and the sands... they have captured me...”

“Like I said, there is nothing about Liwa and your project... but...”

“But what?”

“But there is one more thing to be on the lookout for while you are still in Dubai—a shady fellow, the Professor. We believe he is here now. He has been on our watchlist a long time.”

“The Professor? That Jesuit I knew in Cairo?”

“Yes, exactly. The Professor is a gemologist—trafficking East Africa gemstones—it is the network we are watching—he is active in that area—lots of trafficking—lots of smuggling. We are observing his connections but his quantities of gemstones alone are not excessive. Just keep your ears and eyes open.”

“I can do that.”

“If I hear anything I’ll let you know; but your professional life, what are you going to do? And by the way, Alan is still at Atlantis...”

“Thanks for that tip—I’m going nowhere near that guy. I’m thinking I will talk to the big developers in Abu Dhabi and Dubai—CTF, Masdar, Emaar, Nakheel—to see if there are on-going critical projects—maybe talk with a couple huge American A/E/CM firms here in the UAE.” I sounded upbeat but deep down I wondered about even taking the path that had not been fruitful before my Liwa Qsar project. Dubai was still buzzing, running hot with new project construction.

"Design work? Or..." she asked.

"Design work?! I think not. Design, planning, managing in carpet-world—too much chitchat, too much sitting around—too little to keep me engaged. The intensity of that Liwa Qsar project is what I need, otherwise... Bree and... well that part of my life is a dark hole that I don't want to visit."

"Well, I can't help you there; but like I offered before, if you need something to get by locally, I have some options."

"If I recall, my Christopher Janus ID will allow me back in the US, right?"

"Yes, without problem, but remember you'll be without any bank accounts, financial support, etc—you'll be starting from scratch on everything personal and professional. But yeah, you can enter the US without scrutiny—basic document-wise your US background is clean and clear."

We had both long finished our drinks. We agreed to keep in touch and departed, as always, good friends.

***

Colleagues

I passed the next week relaxing in Dubai–on my own "Big Bus Dubai Tour". I visited, not the bustling cafés of The JBR Walk and its various clones but some of the lesser-known neighbourhoods. The ones that had history before 21st century modern Dubai. I hung out on Diyafa street near the port in between Jumeira and Satwa–an area some call Little Teheran.

I visited the small cafés and workshops of Hor Al Anz, in Deira. And if I wanted more Western, high-pitched action I headed over to the MOE. It had lost its prime destination status to the heady mix of Dubai Mall, Dubai Fountain and Burj Khalifa just adjacent to Business Bay.

And speaking of business, I made my first contacts at the Dubai and Abu Dhabi developers. In the first place I wasn't looking for downtown carpet-world jobs but that is what the HR people were trained to offer and trained to expect. Result? Zero. Same as before! I think they wanted the younger people–so it goes.

I found myself passing more time at the MOE because they were still enforcing proper dress standards. I liked that more conservative social environment. The sports WAGs (wives and girlfriends) and media-hungry Western ladies who dressed in bikinis or even less in public were not frequenting the MOE. The MOE felt civilized.

I ate at all the different Indian restaurants in the mall. There were five, and each had a different menu. If I wanted more native Indian character I went to Al Fahidi street in Bur

Dubai, just off the Dubai Creek near the Old Textile Market. Exploring the side streets thereabouts, I uncovered Indian restaurants with layout and character running the full gamut from high-end to basic-labourer quality–from North India to South India, from pure vegetarian to halal–and price–all with enjoyable preparations. And the variety? Plenty–good fun.

I talked to Green Tree and my other landscape contractor contacts–I even called Marty, the plant supplier middleman from SE Asia, in my search for a very large project in need of someone with my skills. Zero.

Late one night, at 10PM, after my 5-minute walk back to my studio from the MOE, when I was punching in the key code to my building, I heard the voice of an older gentleman softly call my name.

"Christopher, Christopher."

I stopped trying to enter my building and turned around. Couldn't believe my eyes–it was the gemologist person Eileen had told me was trafficking in gems. I knew him–from Cairo–years ago, as Professor, a Malta-born, cultural anthropologist academic dedicating his life to field research. When our eyes met, he smiled and stepped toward me–limping just as I remembered when we first met at the Giza Pyramids.

"Professor, what are you doing here in Dubai?"

"Christopher, please come with me."

I looked closely. He pointed to a taxi waiting just behind him.

"Why? What is going on?"

"We need to talk about the Empty Quarter. Come with me, the night is still young. This is important."

I got in the taxi with the Professor and he had the driver take us to The Pointe on the Palm Jumeirah. Along the way the Professor would not answer any of my questions. He said, "Wait, till we leave the taxi."

The taxi stopped in front of a Lebanese restaurant, Al Safadi. The Professor paid the driver and we headed into the restaurant on foot. I followed the Professor, slowly as always with his limp, as he led the way through the busy air-conditioned restaurant to the terrace on the water. Outdoors was warm but with a slight cooling breeze.

There weren't many people. A waiter offered to show us a table but the Professor knew where he was going. He went to a lightly populated corner of the terrace, to an isolated table surrounded by hedged shrubs. The table already had one person sitting at it. That was where he was headed.

As the Professor reached the table, the person sitting there stood up, turned around and said, "*Bien venue mon ami*!"

It was JeanClaude. JeanClaude!! I was surprised and thought something was in the works. We shook hands and sat down in privacy protected by plants.

I looked at my two companions—both men with decades of academic and real-world stature. A cultural anthropologist and an ethnobotanist. I could see where these seekers of mysteries might have things in common. I knew them both but never knew they were friends or colleagues. And JeanClaude? The centre of recent Empty Quarter mysteries. What could be the reason for this meeting?

When the waiter arrived, the Professor took over for ordering. Like a lifelong eastern Mediterranean, he ordered a fantastic range of cold *mezze—baba ghanouj*, vine leaves, *labneh, moutabbal, hummus, tabouleh, fatoush.* The Professor drank *ayran* while JeanClaude and I drank pomegranate juice. Nobody said anything. When our order came, with pita, warm flatbreads, we all ate in quiet.

After we finished, JeanClaude said to me, "I suppose you have questions?"

We sat and talked, all three of us. Espresso after espresso until the waiter came at 1:45AM to tell us we were the last in the restaurant and that they had to close in 15min.

***

Download

In Dubai, Palm Jumeirah, at The Pointe, late evening, in the midnight hours, outdoors on the coastal edge is pleasant and conducive to conversation—high 20sC, light breeze and a view of the landmark Atlantis Dubai.

It was as comfortable outdoors as it can be in Dubai. Three North Africa and Middle East specialists, relaxed and sharing a meal—perhaps you wonder what we talked about?

"Questions? I have a ton, like how is it both of you are here and how do you know each other and what the hell happened to Kelvin? And JeanClaude, were you there?"

"Easy *mon ami*, the night is still young. First, about Kelvin. What do you know and who told you?"

"My old friend from Tangier, a comms specialist with DARPA, told me..." I paused, looked around and began whispering, "...you killed Kelvin in the Empty Quarter not far from Liwa Qsar with some kind of plant-based poison because Kelvin was going to livestream what he found there in the sands. Is that what happened?"

"Not at all, *mon ami*. To the best of my knowledge Kelvin is dead. And he might have been killed for the reason you heard; but I think people, clandestines, associated with DARPA, killed Kelvin. The Professor, Fairuz and I were deep into every aspect of Kelvin's efforts and his discoveries; but he had his own interests, purposes and schedule. We were not with him 100% of the time."

"Still sounds mysterious to me. Look, I had my job to do. I was fully engaged. And the sands and Kelvin's thing—I just didn't have time. Tell me, how is it that the Professor is here with you, with us?"

The Professor intervened. "Let me tell my own story. In fact, Christopher, after your own explorations in the Pharaonic landscape, and your project history around the Arabian Peninsula, I am surprised you haven't shown more interest in Kelvin's discoveries—he did describe some of them to you, did he not?"

"Well, he did; but I was here to get the project done. It was important that I do it right and it was in serious trouble on many fronts. Like I said, I didn't have time to go wandering in the sands like Kelvin. Professor, tell me, what brought you here?"

"Now, we are getting to the point," said the Professor. "If I may..."

JeanClaude interrupted, "I'll let the Professor continue in a moment; but I must set the context, the local foundation. As you know at the beginning of your Liwa Qsar project, you met with me and Fairuz. Later Fairuz brought Kelvin's behaviour to my attention. I don't know for sure how DARPA got involved but they have their own silo of resources. Anyhow, after getting together with Fairuz, then hearing about DARPA's interest, I started accessing my own sources. I accessed some of DARPA's early draft reports. Some weird stuff—though interesting.

"Having read them, I decided to talk with the Professor—after all this is his native neighbourhood. If I can summarize DARPA's early reports—they gave credence, CJ, to your Moroccan experiences with your Tangier apartment *shaoush*, the building watchman Sidi Hamete, who as a child worked in that small, arcane bookshop of the Petit Socco in the Tangier medina. They confirmed that there were beings on Earth, like Sidi Hamete, called Anquietas. They are here to be active on the battlegrounds of good and evil to effect positive solutions. That describes your experiences with Sidi Hamete, does it not?"

I nodded.

"They dug deeper. They were able to track his lineage back to Vienna where he was longtime in the Hapsburg court, a confidant of both Sissi and Maria Teresa. They went even deeper, tracking his lineage from Vienna to Anatolia and ultimately in the court of Alexander the Great on the island of Failaka on what is now known as The Gulf or the Persian Gulf. And that's right, his history included activity in the Persian Gulf, near here."

JeanClaude paused. I felt confident when he spoke. He was different from Steve. And Steve had commented that he only could give "the company line". To me that meant it might not have been the truth about what really happened. And here I was with JeanClaude. His explanation was easily believable. I was getting into it. My Liwa Qsar duties were finished and I had the chance to reassemble the small details I had heard from Kelvin himself and his right-hand man, the GDawg.

JeanClaude continued, "It gets weirder still. Their draft report said that DARPA had an alien, not Anquietas, captured in New Mexico about 70 years ago, who confirmed details about the Anquietas and their special powers. They are hermaphrodite-like. Reproduce with all the knowledge complete from last generation. New versions rebirth as knowledgeable youths out of aging old form. Anquietas display aging when so many social and political changes in the human environment begin to undermine the Anquietas powers. Then it's a cocoon to butterfly thing, yielding a new body.

"Don't you see, CJ, how all this ties into my ethnobotany explorations and your portal experiences?" This was really too much for me; but JeanClaude was on a roll and continued.

"They're an advanced clone that not only ages but also they are emotionally rich while being detached, kind of like old-time, austere Vedic Indian yogis. I think the Vedic cosmology may be a usable baseline for discussion."

Vedic cosmology, I thought. Didn't, what was her name? Vrndadevi. Back when I was in Ban Muang Thailand, didn't she tell me about heavenly and hellish planets and how the earth is in the middle of all that—in the middle of the battle between good and evil?

Before I could say anything, the Professor said, "What is accurate or not in those DARPA reports is not for me now; but

I can add that there are many Biblical references to life forms not easily understood by us. Life forms beyond human, having either good or evil behavioural traits."

It was my turn to try to understand how these key people all fit together in this Rub al Khali episode. "Thank you, Professor. I wonder, how does Fairuz enter in? He and I worked closely on Liwa Qsar, together solving many problems. Just two weeks ago, on the television, I saw Fairuz on the dais with the Crown Prince and other VVIP Emiratis for the official hard opening of Liwa Qsar. That was exactly where he should be. I know, JeanClaude, you and he are friends but..."

"For him—he had a conflict after his Western education," JeanClaude said, "he had roots, sympathy with the Bedu and their traditions and stories—enter the *djinni.* He told me that perhaps Kelvin had encounters with the *djinni*—so of course he was interested."

I was trying to keep it together because what I was hearing was like an on-line episode of Alex Jones or David Icke mixed with details from Simon Pegg's *Paul.* I had to get something real out of this. So I asked, "But what was found out there? What did Kelvin find? What did you guys find? Anything more than what Kelvin told me? And why are DARPA so worried about a streaming podcast?"

JeanClaude said, "Well, *mon ami,* there are fundamentally two questions you have asked. What's out there and why does DARPA fear publicity. First. What's out there—Fairuz, the Professor and I had a chance to sit with Kelvin out in the sands—the same general area, though he could not be exact where he had such strange experiences. None of us experienced anything like he had.

"But, as best I recall, and Professor correct me if I'm wrong, Kelvin shared in his words 'what I thought or what they shared—goes back tens of thousands of years—first time they were here. This planet so rich in life, water, sun, soil—they decided it was essential to protect it.

"'These beings from another planet do not deal with hard metals as we know them. They manage the stuff of emotions—they have a science of emotions and that is the basis of the devices they placed here on earth. The closest thing we have on this planet is the energy source in the earth's core.

"'They have a means for weaving emotions and that high energy into a mode of transportation that enables easy movement over the vastness of space. Faster than the speed of thought. The entire construct is beyond the limited senses we humans have. They visit periodically in a maintenance effort.' Whatever Kelvin encountered was not observable by our eyes and ears. He felt it. He never saw anything. Professor?"

The Professor sat saying nothing. We were all quiet for minutes before JeanClaude spoke again.

"Kelvin said his understanding was it was a device meant to limit activity in the area, however one may interpret that. So they fly by every few hundred years or so to monitor things. Their guy had technical trouble back in the 1940s and they found him—good and helpful—that's our source. What was his body and how did they communicate, stuff of science fiction imagination—maybe nothing but Artificial Intelligence developed by DARPA, for all I know. But that was in one of their drafts."

JeanClaude added, "As I interpret, the beings that placed that device and the Anquietas are different but they both are attempting to reduce the amount of stressful energy on this planet. And your second question, why DARPA does not want publicity—DARPA is funded by politicians and politicians seek control to feed their greed and envy. They probably will revisit their find after they get a plan to enrich themselves over it. They are servants of the seven deadly sins (pride, greed, wrath, envy, lust, gluttony and sloth) and woven through those are dangerous threads of evil. The battle goes on no matter what."

***

What Do I Really Think?

I had my own opinions. But they were foggy, wrapped in some kind of mental *shamal.* Still I was not clear what of substance had they found with Kelvin. My 8 months enveloped by the inland Rub al Khali influenced my opinion on what was found—only the desert winds—only the eternal shifting sands.

Something from my past was niggling me. Couldn't put my finger on it. Then one night as I was falling asleep—no, I was already asleep when it emerged... in Arabic, in a dream... sand fever—sand fever.

Hadn't heard that since my days in Egypt's Great Sand Sea. Maybe Kelvin had sand fever. What was sand fever? Near the Great Sand Sea, I met some people, native to Egypt's S'h'ra, who described sand fever as the passive danger the sands emitted on quiet days. Sand fever? Something to fear—like all other emotions—without material substance. But fear it causes.

I was looking for a measurable bottom line. Each of my colleagues had a different story.

Fairuz, they told me, was still sympathetic to *djinni.* He had said, "That explains why the US government wanted no publicity—they did not want anything to disrupt their political 'status quo' approach to the UAE and the Arabian Peninsula at large."

I had spent a lot of time with Fairuz. His words were, in my opinion, free of *taqquiyah,* free of *tawriya.* He had always been straightforward and helpful. He knew there was something inexplicable in these sands. And in the end, faced once again with the inexplicable, he had chosen to accept his ancestors' explanation—*djinni.* He had a strong Western education—an education that did not include the inexplicable—there was always an answer—you just had to find it. Fairuz was faced with that conundrum.

I thought about Fairuz' conundrum—isn't this the nature of human life on this planet—always without clarity—always with the seven deadly sins? This place can seem like its own hell.

Our after-dinner conversations went further. The Professor? His was a different story altogether. He was a Jesuit who on his own went beyond the basics. He had said, "Whatever happened out there had nothing to do with the story of Jesus and basic Roman Catholic theology." He understood that the Roman Catholic hierarchy would be happy if, whatever it was, it was covered up because their interest was in social matters. The last thing they wanted was a discovery that would question their theology.

The Professor recounted an off-beat exchange with Fairuz. It was on the subject of whatever it was in the Sahara and Empty Quarter—it made life hell. Just look at the people's life in those regions. It obviously made the efforts for modern scientific and social progress extremely difficult if not impossible.

The Professor told me: "Fairuz wondered if the Ashkenazi people may have implanted something to hinder the people of the region." That was history well beyond my understanding. When I questioned the Professor he went on and on about Red Knights, Khazarians, I don't know what all. I couldn't follow any of it. My thoughts drifted. I really longed for something simpler, something easy to understand. Long game for planetary dominance? That sounded like fantasy, science fiction.

I'd had enough of that. I had to interrupt. "What is this long game for planetary dominance by Jewish peoples?"

The Professor was succinct. "The idea is contentious, aggressively debated from both sides. The bottom line is they are encouraging, among the liberal West, tolerance of illicit sexual activities and a new world order because they know that forced diversity is the source of degradation, destabilization and evil. They are certain that the new world order will quickly collapse, with people seeking order and clarity. Their long game plan is to take charge of the world when that dissension is at its peak."

First time I'd ever heard that. But the Professor provided an historical perspective to support those conclusions. In the end, the Professor said that Fairuz' Ashkenazi theory might be on to something. But that theory, while having credence as a theory, was a speculative theory only.

And myself? I had a bunch of my colleagues and friends involved in this strangest of landscape stories. It was and is still a mystery. It could have been the result of aliens from another planet. It could have been evil personified. It could have been "spirits". But Kelvin was logical and clear—he certainly had all his faculties. This was not a figment of his imagination.

These conversations seemed at odds with what I recalled from Kelvin's morphogenetic explanations and the GDawg's recollections. Kelvin felt a kind of enlightenment—a positivity that he could not find words to describe. Had nothing to do with Jewish anything. Had nothing to do with extraterrestrial aliens. Had nothing to do with human politics.

I shared that in a series of questions to JeanClaude and the Professor, concluding once again with "What happened to Kelvin? What did he encounter? Was it some kind of portal—some kind of landscape portal? Help me out. None of those explanations fit logically."

JeanClaude saved his opinion till last. Looking directly at me, he said, "*Mon ami*, you are a landscape man and your existential interest in gardens and plants keeps you close to my ethnobotanical heart. If I may, for one time, speak for both the Professor and myself..." The Professor nodded. "... your practical application in landscape architecture sets you apart from the Professor and I as academic researchers." Then looking at the Professor, "Don't you agree?" The Professor nodded again.

"Your experience with plants as a bridge or portal to an existential effulgence (your own words) has a direct bearing on the experiences of Kelvin. But I have no idea how to link them. Frankly, *mon ami*, I am in the dark."

The waiter had used all his patience. It was time to close. The Professor, as all good Eastern Med hosts would do, took over paying for our dinners. I excused myself and washed up in the WC.

I was washing up when JeanClaude came in. He came to the sink next to mine and began washing his hands. Then he abruptly stopped and turned toward me saying, "Let me share this brief private moment with you. Some things should only be between you and I. As I have described previously and now as I know you must have experienced yourself, there is something unique about this desert—something from beneath its surface that has an undefinable effect on humans—their gross and subtle senses. *Mon ami*, let me tell you and you alone what I have learned from inspecting a very large range of US intelligence information silos. The key concept is tesseract. Tesseract is like a portal, maybe like your portals. It is about the suspension of time and its relation to material nature. These are about measurements beyond the speed of light—maybe the speed of thought. Tesseracts can be accessible only by mind melding with the source of earth core gravitational energy. That is why experiments are ongoing in the Empty Quarter and the Sahara. That is what DARPA is hiding. Are you following?"

"Following? Following what?"

"*Mon ami*, these are portal experiments that have time travel implications."

"I'm into plants, gardens and landscape, JeanClaude, not into changing the world."

I looked into JeanClaude's eyes. They went quickly from excitement to disappointment.

Then he said, "Forget we talked about this."

"That won't be hard, I've had enough of this deep science and humanity big picture thinking. No offense to you, but I know when I've reached my limit." With that we both walked out of the WC, saying no more.

For me this was a merry-go-round, a carrousel without stop, without answers. Internally I was troubled. We were trying to understand experiences beyond human understanding. Impossible therefore to put human vocabulary to them. I was glad to call it a night.

I walked with them to a nearby dock where they had a cruiser. They climbed aboard and before leaving said they were going a short distance but could not tell me where, for their and my own safety—you never know what those DARPA types may get up to.

After they left their mooring, I hailed a nearby taxi and went back home—not really sure about what had transpired out in the sands during my Liwa Qsar project or during our conversations that evening.

As I went to bed that night, I lay there thinking about landscape. About my professional lifetime of international culture and landscape experiences. I knew culture and landscape were linked. I still didn't know how.

I reviewed my first-hand landscape experiences—the Sahara; the Empty Quarter; West Africa; Jungfrau Region deaths; Arabian Peninsula desert legends (Emerald tablet, Lazarus and the date palm oases)—how the powers in the landscape bewildered me. Does design... or can design emerge from all that? Or is design just a flimsy mental construct—rightly a fad, a passing fancy—true pop-art?

***

A New Path

The following days, I turned over and over the most recent of my landscape experiences—the sum total of my last 8 months in the Empty Quarter.

Seekers? Searchers? JeanClaude? The Professor? Fairuz? Me?

Me? Yeah, me too. We were all chasers, regular chasers—letting uncertainty guide us into chasing the unknown existential. They have been chasing all their lives—like me on the subjects of landscape and culture... of design. I had been chasing design all my life until Vrndadevi in Ban Muang and later Bree. They convinced me that my chase was futile in a variety of material and spiritual ways.

Nothing I heard from JeanClaude or the Professor gave me hope—this beast of a landscape, the Empty Quarter, had flummoxed everyone. I needed to look further afield. I needed to draw on my knowledge, my life experiences to find just where my path forward might be. It certainly wasn't in the Empty Quarter. The job had been good, but the Empty Quarter landscape and its powerful uncertainties, I'd had enough of it.

Something else became clear—no more chasing, seeking, searching for the existential glories. I can see why people seriously turn to religion, because this material world doesn't have answers—just endlessly evolving paths to disappointing, even frustrating unknowns... and another bunch of questions.

Searching is not the goal or the path for me. I am seeing all of us racing down a blind tunnel. Maybe our energies are misdirected. Maybe our souls are searching for something beyond the earth, beyond this material world—maybe each of us, in our own way, has been and still is searching for God—isn't that the conclusion of all great thinkers, all great philosophers?

So where does that leave me? Search for another job, another huge project out in the sands? The sands? Danger and no answers? I put enough in the bank from the Liwa Qsar project to be financially comfortable for a while; but I couldn't sit around doing nothing. I concluded that I had a simple choice—two paths:

1. Seek a new project, a new cocoon... in the sands? That's unlikely; or,
2. Make a change to my life.

Change to my life? Isolate myself? A monk's life? Liwa Qsar was an old-fashioned cocoon to shield me from the loss of Bree. The hurt, the pain. Why should I hide from it? I had learned from her. Learned not to always be running for something I was imagining. In her haybarn garden on the Grosse Scheidegg in Grindelwald she showed me not just the hard work of gardening but also the daily "joys" of being so close to the plants and the landscape. I felt it. We shared it. But now she is gone.

Perhaps I can honour her memory by living a life like I shared with her in her garden—nurturing the plants and using everything they offer to make a good life—sensually, emotionally, intellectually, spiritually and economically. Not hide from her loss but glorify what I learned from her. I had to think about it. I had to try to distil the essence and see my path forward. A monk's life? Leave my profession behind? Not sure. Leave the sands behind? Not a bad idea but this is where my likely work opportunities lie.

I walked over to the MOE. It was still hot and humid outside—6PM. Inside, ahh, air-conditioning—like everything everywhere I've worked in the Arabian Peninsula. Oil. Gas. Power plants. Desalination. Big energy. Plentiful water and plentiful air conditioning. But I had personal issues to resolve.

The MOE was bustling with people. Bustling. And it was noisy. Noisy not by piped-in music but by the rush of socializing people. All people, all ages, all nationalities, all classes. All with jobs. All earning money. All rushing.

I never rushed when working with Bree in her haybarn garden. It was almost as though there was something called "plant speed". And the closer we came to the plants, the more the aura of "plant speed" surrounded us, enveloped us. That was a very nice feeling. It was a feeling without any passionate rush. It was a soothing peace from long hours of hard work that strengthened our "plant speed" connections.

In the MOE, I found a busy Indian restaurant and merged into the crowd of customers. When I finished dinner, I walked home. Back in my studio, with my stomach full, I put my feet up. I was starting to drift off when memories of the words of Vrndadevi, from Ban Muang, came to my head. She had said, "As the nature of sugar is sweetness, the nature of our soul is service."

In our talks she said to try it–unmotivated service yields what she called a "transcendental satisfaction". And why? I remember the clarity she shared, "... because that transcendental satisfaction can only be experienced when the soul is in its rightful position–when it is rendering service." On the day our discussion went deeper; but service was the essence.

I thought about when I ran away from my parents. The parents who gave me, via their service, the essential skills to be successful in life. I thought... perhaps it is time for me to return that service to them. I mulled that over... and over... and fell asleep.

The next morning, I woke with my mind still engaged in that possible new path. My parents? I didn't even know if they were still alive. And if they were alive, I didn't know where they could be. My mom's from SW Florida and my dad's from Detroit. But they were divorced a long time ago. My first task would be to find them... and if they think I'm dead? I have some awkward paths to follow.

Eileen had said I could get back in the US on my Christopher

Janus passport—so that won't be a hurdle. I showered, shaved, squeezed some orange juice and brewed a stiff coffee.

I made a plan. I had a contact, my Executor, Kurt. Maybe he was still operating his boutique landscape architecture practice in Santa Monica—SoCal.

***

Kurt

Get in touch with Kurt? Yeah, I had to do some preliminaries. I dug into it. I cranked up my iPhone to see if my old friend and boss Kurt was still in business in Santa Monica. He was. His office had a tidy, chic, online presence. I was pleased to see it. He had been my Executor and for all I knew he did his duties, thinking I had died in Cairo.

Years ago... we had links... we had ties. Maybe they still existed. Maybe he would remember. Maybe he wouldn't be shocked to hear my voice. What would I say? What would he say?

This was really weird. What might I say? "Hello Kurt, this is CJ, I'm not dead. Are you okay?" What should I say? I mulled that over most of the day—got nowhere.

I thought, "Aw hell, enough farting around—9AM his time is 9PM here. I'll just get on with it."

I walked over to the MOE, grabbed a meal, walked around a bit, wasted time window shopping till 9. While I was walking around I thought about my parents. I abandoned them a long time ago; but they are parents and I am an only child. Kurt, he is my only connection and my only connection to them—if they are still alive. I had logic on my side and butterflies in my stomach as I walked back to my studio.

Finally, I took the big step and dialled. It rang and a voice picked up.

Show time. "Hello, is this Kurt Milligan?"

"This is Kurt, can I help you?"

"Is your office busy? Are you looking for help?"

"Who's this?"

"You sitting down?"

"What's the gig?"

"No joke—you sitting down?"

"Okay, okay, who are you and what do you want—a job or something? Is this a 'You've Been Framed' spoof?"

"Right, enough's enough, you asked for it—this is CJ."

"CJ? Christopher Janus?"

"The same."

"Get back Jack!"

"It's a long story if you've got some time..."

"You didn't die in Cairo?"

"Correct!"

"I knew it! I thought so! I was never convinced! You've got a whole lot to account for—start talking."

"To summarize..."

"Hang on! I've got to sit down—are you for real?"

"I've never bullshitted you, Kurt; and I won't start now!"

"I can't believe it, but I am happy to know my instinct is still strong—you didn't die."

"Here is the short form. I've been working as a landscape architect all around the Arabian Peninsula. So I am still a landscape architect. I remarried, an American girl living in Switzerland, and we had a good thing going. But in a horrible accident she died; and I am on my own now."

"CJ, I read all your journals and learned about your first wife and family and how that devastated you—for years. I also read about Bree—that's who you married, right—in Switzerland, right?"

"Yeah, I've had two horrible low-spots in my life and the second one, Bree, just happened. I'm in Dubai, hoping to rebuild my life. You helped me after Sachy and now you are the starting point for me to get on a new path—the loss of Bree. Deep hurt—I need a new path."

"What's the gig? I'm shocked but pleasantly surprised you are still alive. We've got lots to talk about—what's this new path deal? No landscape architecture?"

"We can talk shop but here is what is driving me now. We

are both getting on in years and I am wondering about my parents. Neither of them understood the depth of my hurt when Sachy and our kids died—but here I am with nothing—I was thinking I would try to see them again if they are still alive. Have you been in touch with them—being Executor and all?"

"It went like this, CJ... your Amsterdam bank contacted your parents; and I, as your Executor, had nothing to do with them except sign off on the bank's records. But a couple years later, your parents sought, via the Amsterdam bank, how to contact me. We talked. I told them your death was an unresolved mystery for me. They asked me to contact them if I ever got new information because I told them my efforts to understand if you were truly dead came up empty. They left their contact information with me—that might be about 5 years ago now.

"We talked quite a bit on the phone that day. They were in their 80s, reunited and at, let me check... living in a large home on the edge of a golf course in west-central New Mexico—your dad was proud of it. He had hired a private architect—designed a cross between Spanish Mission style and hacienda with an arts and crafts motif. If the inside is anywhere as nice as the outside—spectacular. I Google-Earthed it. Your dad told me the main house had 4 beds, 4 baths and the attached casita was 1 bed, 1 bath. Sitting on a small knoll overlooking the adjacent golf course, it had an interior courtyard and a number of small stone terraces on three sides. It was a good site, well developed. He dug his own well for water and built in an area with low wildfire risk.

"I figured the reason they made their retirement home so large was they had hoped that you might somehow be alive and maybe come to live with them. I'll send you the images if you'd like."

That felt like good news! "Hang on to those images, I'll look at them when I return."

"Return? You're coming to the US? Do you want me to tell them you are coming to the US?"

I thought, this is complicated. My parents are older and I didn't want to shock them. And since Kurt has already had contact with them; and voiced his doubt about my "death"...

"Kurt, would you please contact them—let them know there's news from the UAE that I am working here. Let them know you will try to contact me. Then from that point we can move forward. How does that sound to you?"

"Sounds like a plan."

"You do have time and are willing to help me?"

"What are Executors for? Sure thing!"

"Let's get on with it, this week. Email me or call me after you've talked with them. Then we can figure out the next step. I really want to visit them—as soon as practical—but I don't want to blow them away."

"I'll get right onto it. But hey what's this new path stuff?"

"I'm going to try to help them as my top priority."

"And your LA career?"

"It's in the past... listen, Kurt, it is complicated... I've had two wives die in my arms... it took me years the first time with Sachy and the kids and now... after losing Bree? I've got to get a big new focus... my parents, I hope."

"I'll do what I can—get back with you as soon as I talk with them."

"Thanks, Kurt, I hoped we could do this together. This conversation has felt like an encouragement, a healing. That's all I can ask for. And before I visit my parents, I'll come see you—we can talk shop then—your office still in the same building in Santa Monica?"

"Yeah same as always... and I have so many questions for you..."

"Kurt, let's keep this conversation private—just between you and me, okay... hey, are you still single—surfing and pulling the beach girls?"

Kurt laughed. I laughed. He said, "Some things never change—though the waves change—the ocean is always there. Call me anytime."

"Take care, Kurt, and thank you ever so much."

So the conversation ended.

I hung up, took a long, hot shower. Everything in the Empty Quarter surrounding Kelvin, JeanClaude, Fairuz, the Professor and Steve—all too much—too confusing. The hot shower gradually washed the confusion away. A huge burden released. I thought about my change in direction—the threshold of professional retirement. In so many words... I hadn't thought about it like that before.

The hot water running over my head helped bring more clarity to my life's quests. I still believed in plant portals and special powers in the landscape. But so much of my efforts had been "chasing the snark". The portals are still there. Bree showed me how personal that portal experience was and to cherish it in our own garden. She convinced me of the megalomania of thinking I could gift any part of that experience to anyone else. Opened my eyes to humility–instead of chasing fame.

And the powers in the landscape? Another "tilting at windmills" effort. The powers are there, I don't doubt that, but thinking that any power, other than God, is in control... and that I could understand forces larger than this planet with my limited and faulty senses—truly "tilting at windmills"!

I needed a more local focus. And there is the issue of service—serve my own needs or serve others. Vrndadevi explained that nicely in Ban Muang. Human nature.

I needed to give my love and service—I've lost all my efforts to have a family but if my parents are still alive... One step at a time. I have to hear what Kurt finds. I was fatigued. I hit the sack

***

The Change

Kurt spoke with my parents. Afterwards, he gave me a play-by-play.

"Your Mum, Kate, answered. I told her I had news for her."

"Yes?" I was eager to hear.

Kurt continued, "About CJ."

She said, "What?"

"He is alive."

"What?!!"

"Then I heard her shouting to your dad, 'CJ's alive.' Then I heard her sobbing and your dad, Sam, took over on the phone."

Kurt continued relating the phone call, "He asked for details and I told him I had heard from you via email. He asked where you were. I told him the UAE; and that you were planning to come back to the US shortly. I told him that you had asked me to get contact details. I learned from him they still had their family residence but had recently moved into an old folks' home in Taos, called Enchanted Village. I told him that as soon as you closed out your current responsibilities in Dubai, you would be coming back here. He asked when and I said in the next month or so. I told him I would call them back as soon as I got your confirmed travel plans."

Kurt gave me my parents' location and contact details. I thanked him and told him I would immediately put in motion plans to arrive in LA. I closed our conversation telling him

I would be in touch with him when I would have my return flight details confirmed. Then we could discuss how I would go to meet my parents in New Mexico. I looked forward, upon returning, to seeing Kurt, my long-time professional and personal friend.

I busied myself over the next week with numerous details in preparation for leaving the UAE. Then I called Eileen to share with her my plans for retirement and return to the US. She was happy for me and encouraged me. Things were coming together. But I still had a big hurdle. I thought it was time and important for me to contact my parents. I couldn't wait.

To say the least, I was nervous about calling them. I hadn't seen or spoken with them since the deaths of my wife Sachy and our three kids—more than 25 years ago. And no doubt they had been thinking I was dead for more than five years. This was going to be a whole lot more difficult than my first call to Kurt. I was worried. Kicked it around in my head for half a day and then decided—hell, just get on with it. My dad's there, he can handle it.

I dialled their mobile number. I only got a recording. "Please leave a message." I left this message.

> I have been working in the UAE and will wrap up in the next month. Then I plan to come visit you. Kurt will meet me at Los Angeles International Airport and I will contact you again as soon as practical after I have arrived back in the US. Looking forward to seeing you.
>
> Love CJ

I spent the next two weeks finally closing the last of my personal responsibilities and preparing for departure, for my return to the US—had been away, I don't know, two maybe three decades... As soon as I got my confirmed reservation, I notified Kurt when I would arrive at LAX (Los Angeles International). Because of project responsibilities, he could not meet me at LAX. But he did explain how I could get a shuttle from the arrival terminal to LAX-it, where I could find a taxi and for $40-50 get to his Santa Monica office in less than a half hour. Everything was in place.

***

Prodigal

Sixteen hours' flying time—direct flight—via the North Pole—DBX-LAX. After take-off it struck me. Nearly three decades had passed since I set foot in the USA. I wondered what might be. Didn't have to think twice—I was on my way.

The flight, though overly long, was amazing. Amazing? The Northern Hemisphere geography from 40,000feet. It began on take-off from DBX. All beneath for the first hours was an Arabian Peninsula nothingness—an all-sandy-beige, threatening haze, albeit from a safe distance.

And then Northern Europe all green. The arctic all white. Canada and the west coast of the US all green. Trees, plants, soil and water—such a natural, such a material wealth.

The best entertainment part of the flight was the movie I watched just before landing—Eddie Murphy in *Beverly Hills Cop.* Arrived LAX early afternoon their time. Airport terminal was busy. Every international airport terminal is busy these days. Sometimes hard to tell the difference because they all have the hectic feel, the hectic anxiety, the hectic emotion—a hurried tension.

Got out of the terminal quickly and easily following Kurt's instructions found the LAX-it shuttle and was in a cab in 10 minutes. Gave the cabbie the Colorado Blvd address in Santa Monica. He said the best way would be via Lincoln Avenue, no need for the freeway which was slow this time of day. The cabbie looked scruffy, reminded me of Herb Striet from Tangier—50s, a bit pudgy and a couple days unshaven—not clean and sharp like the Dubai taxi drivers. But his car was alright—washed, windows closed, air-conditioning working.

He asked me if I minded listening to his music. Hell, I was open to anything. I was looking forward to a taste of modern America.

I said, "Go for it."

He turned up the volume—AC/DC—classic loud, head-rocking music from the 80s. *Moneytalks.* The inside of the car vibrated like a huge rock'n'roll venue. He drove peacefully, 30-35mph along Lincoln Boulevard, like he was listening to Brahms. But AC/DC and *Moneytalks,* I got into it. Guys making money making fun of making money. But the music was good. I thought, "Definitely back in the USA."

Funny, as we drove across town on Lincoln Boulevard—LAX, Marina Del Rey, on to Santa Monica, it kind-of looked the same as I remembered it. Heavily developed lower-level urban roadside. Nothing boarded up. Very few for lease or for sale signs. Small business busy—big -time.

We had lots of traffic lights, traffic density was moderate—steady, no delays. No street side parking. Few roadside pedestrians. Fewer bikes. Car and truck country—even in the city.

After a 20-minute ride, I got out at Kurt's office—the same place I had worked as an intern and later for 5 years before I took that big Yenbo new town project in Saudi Arabia. As soon as I walked through the front door—BOOM—it was all different—big time.

He had a new elevator pitch on the wall next to the inner door. *Power of Landscape.* As I was looking at that graphic Kurt came to welcome me inside. We shook hands and hugged.

After lots of short, choppy, chit-chat Kurt asked, "How do you like the new entry? I've updated this waiting room and our client meeting room."

I looked around an indoor garden sitting area—his "waiting room"? I was in a ventilated, skylight-covered Hawaiian mini courtyard, warm, fresh and lightly moist, filled with fragrant floriferous broadleaf plants and tropical climbers.

"Spectacular, Kurt!"

"Wait till you see the rest—the client meeting room..." He

led the way.

"Wow!" I gasped.

I was speechless. The meeting room had a central table for nine; but... the elephant in the room—270degree curved full room height ultra-HD screen, a landscape scene from nature. He used a controller to cycle through a couple larger than room size images—Pacific Ocean surf, coastal redwood forest, giant redwood forest and other large powerful live landscape images.

Kurt said, "I had a friend who had been years with Apple digital graphics put the technical setup together. He had sources for the images—it's all programmable. Each has its own emotion. Check this out." He put up a glowing California wildflower scene from the low hills around Lompoc.

I felt the SoCal design aura descending all over me. A bit like old times. "Kurt, you ought to get some sand desert images from the Empty Quarter. It might help your clients to realize how fortunate they are to live here."

"Welcome back, CJ. You always bring ideas with you. Now, I've got an idea, should we get on over to Trader Vics and carry on where we left off?"

"Don't think so, I'm beat. What's your schedule?"

"Before we go any further, I've got to tell you that your parents called me after they got your message. They told me, just what I figured, that they hope you can stay in New Mexico at their house and if all goes well, they will leave Enchanted Village and live out their days at their residence in Grants."

"What?"

"That's right. That's what your dad said. When did you last see them? Before you came to work for me—30-35 years ago?"

"I hope it works out with them—it's been so long—glad my dad's hopeful. That's good news. I'll get there as fast as possible; but today I'm wrung out from the 16-hour flight—don't you have to go to work?"

"I'm free the rest of the day."

"Great, let's go someplace quiet."

"Let's go over to my place, sit, relax and talk—I've got a cot if you want to spend the night. We can kick back."

"That's just perfect."

I adjusted my case to backpack and climbed on the back of his Harley.

Off we went on Pacific Coast Highway, leaving Santa Monica behind on the way to Malibu. Wind in my hair, pleasant temp, sunshine, blue sky, Pacific Ocean to the horizon. Back in SoCal.

***

Malibu Surf

We opened a couple beers and went outside on his porch—nothing but fresh air between us, the sandy beach, the Pacific Ocean, the horizon and the sky. I felt relieved. I asked, "One bedroom, one bath in approx. 1500sqft—what's it worth these days?"

"I've got a larger site around me; and believe it or not close to 3mil according to Zillow but that depends on the buyer. I get loads of requests from people who want to trash my place and rebuild with 4,000 or more sqft and they'll pay a shit-ton more—but I love my place. It is my door to relief. You know the pressures of work in SoCal. Here is where I take the exit."

I listened and I thought I was hearing Kurt talk about portals. I didn't say anything, I was tired.

He asked, "Do you want to take a walk along the beach—take your shoes off, get some sand between your toes?" Sand, I thought, what's the difference between Malibu beach sand and Empty Quarter sand? I didn't say anything. Kurt brought out two more beers and before I knew it all I could think of was a good night's sleep. Kurt set up the cot in his living room and I crashed.

Before I knew it I smelled freshly brewed coffee. It was morning and Kurt was running around in his baggies like he was going to go surfing. I got up, folded up the cot, showered and shaved. Felt a whole lot better. Kurt was making pancakes. We ate and went back out on his porch and sat letting the pancakes settle in.

Then Kurt opened up.

"It's great to see you and all that bullshit but...what the hell have you been doing?"

I felt much stronger after a good night's sleep and Kurt's American breakfast. I was alert and ready to get into it.

"Same as you, pursuing my landscape architecture career." I smiled wryly when I looked over at him.

"Not good enough. I went all the way to Cairo to try and get your 'death' figured out. I got nothing. Until about 4 hours before my flight back when a strange looking American cowgirl handed me a package with photocopies of your Cairo diaries and design journals covered with a cryptic note saying you were alive but I shouldn't talk about it if I wanted to keep growing my business—something like that. Let's start with that!"

"That's easy. That was Eileen—as my Executor you will have probably read some of my writing..."

He interrupted, "I read them all!"

"Then you have read about the matter in Casablanca—that was the first time I met Eileen. She and I solved a problem with a small group of West African troublemakers. Well, she found me, years later here in SoCal when I was working for you. She arranged for me to get the job in Saudi. She always dresses like a cowgirl—so she was probably the one who handed you those photocopies."

"So what were you doing?"

"Now we're getting into it. I was into landscape, cultures and design..."

Kurt interrupted again, "I know all that—what really happened?"

"It sounds funny to me now but then I was searching for the Pharaonic landscape and I got into a bad way in the Sahara—something in those sands started to take away my professional aspirations and my emotional history—it was internal—coarse sandpaper erasing intellectual and emotional roots—I don't know how to describe it any better—but somehow I was able to walk away and with the help of a couple professional colleagues I recovered. And that is when I really got together with Bree in Switzerland—we got married. Great stuff. I felt like a brand-new life had begun."

Kurt butted in, "Can you talk about it?"

"Long story Kurt. Short story—Bree and I were hiking in Switzerland and had an accident. She died in my arms. Kurt, two wives have died in my arms and I don't want to talk about it. Don't push."

"You have my sympathy—but I have to ask you about Switzerland, the Alps, the yodellers and what you called the summum bonum of landscape design? Do you still hold onto that and what that might mean for design here in SoCal—did you ever think about it that way?"

"I've been away a long time—a very long time out from under that design umbrella that is SoCal."

"I know you've been away, but..."

"Design has always been a part of me; but you know, the client who pays for our services gets what they want—we aren't really freelance artists."

"Yeah, I get that but talk to me about where you've gotten to with design, and is any of it applicable here in SoCal?"

"Feels like a warm day is coming. Is it too early for a beer? Hey, it's a weekday, why aren't you at work?"

"The guys at the office can handle it besides, having you back—it's like a holiday. I'll get us a couple beers."

He went inside. I looked out at the Pacific, listened to the waves crashing and enjoyed the cloudless blue sky—high pressure system over us—for sure it would be a very warm day.

Kurt came back with the beers and said, "Okay, get on with it. We were talking about design, your international experiences and if they might apply to SoCal."

"So many things over the years—if you've read my diaries and design journals, you know my Moroccan, Thailand and Swiss Jungfrau Region experiences. If I summarize, I still believe that garden rooms are essential and the sequence of experiences moving through those garden rooms is also essential. But above all that design theory is the importance of maintenance—without healthy plants and dare I say, loving maintenance—all that design theory is useless fluff."

Kurt said, "That sounds little changed from the old days."

"That's right. Doesn't really work for commercial/retail landscape architecture, does it?" Rhetorical question. Kurt knew it.

I continued, "Maybe you wanted me to address SoCal more directly."

Kurt nodded.

"Well I got a look at LA on my taxi from LAX to your office and here's what I saw: poorly maintained ice plant verges that used to be well maintained, ficus street trees where nobody walks, poorly kept grass, malfunctioning irrigation systems, poorly maintained medians, few pedestrians, wide busy streets, a lot of single-storey retail, hair and nail salons, gas stations, a few two-storey townhouses, motels, fancy 3-4-storey apts with California native plants—salad fashion—awkward, not refined, not cottage garden style, one-storey medical centres, so many roadside plants looking like dry kindling ready to burn, telephone/power lines in the right of way, Santa Monica Freeway verges looking scruffy in danger of burning—like the water has been witheld—what do I think about it?"

"Yeah, get to the meat!"

"It looks like crap design and crap maintenance. It may be that government regulations have pushed native plants and lower water usage. Everything looks strained and like brush waiting to fuel a wildfire—IN THE CITY! I find that hard to believe. And on top of that I saw public realm tagging everywhere—homeless encampments under every bridge along the way—government is allowing that?!"

Kurt had a look of shock.

I continued "The only exciting, inspirational stuff I saw was in your office—that Hawaiian garden and those life-size landscape images in your meeting room. That's some very fine, powerful work, Kurt."

I had more to say, "...the feel of those images is so strong—demonstrates how strong the landscape impacts human culture... Kurt, what are those connectors?"

Kurt looked surprised at my question. He had no answer.

But after a quiet moment, he did say, "It makes clients peaceful and receptive to my sales pitches."

I said, "I've been seeking the existential reality of those 'connective landscape/cultural tissues'—coming up with nothing definable—and that has made me open to the paranormal or the supernormal—beyond our senses, beyond our imagination —some call it magic realism—I called it at the best of times transcendent effulgences—something stronger than what others call auras."

Kurt said, "Off the deep end again, you are."

"Let me finish. I've stopped looking for the big stuff. But I have a question for you—how do you get on with a government that doesn't maintain the plantings, that seems to have a wildfire death-wish and lets bums live on sidewalks in the public realm—that's a real downgrade to human civilization, don't you agree?"

"I can't disagree—homeless in underpasses; political correctness, wokeness, environmental activism—all are part of daily life in SoCal. I don't like it. I vote against it but I tolerate it. I have the surf and my firm is doing well."

I had an opinion, and shot it out, "Here's what I think after my short time here—anybody staying in these urban shitholes should be aware of the consequences of doing so and should be prepared. There is a trend—an obvious downhill trend. I couldn't live here. It looks like you've taken the easy road and are capitulating to the current, lazy agenda because it is easier. You abide by the disastrous regulations, pay into the machine via state taxes, and keep your head down in order to make a living."

"Back off, CJ, you're a guest in my house."

"Am I wrong? Do you think the public realm is better quality now than 20 years ago? Honestly?"

Our conversation had gotten heated. We both looked out on the Pacific.

Then Kurt said, "You might be right-on. I come out here to get away from it. They haven't effed up the ocean yet but you're right, the regulations have gone batshit—water restrictions, native plant requirements—there is no buffer between wildfire area and development anymore." Kurt sighed.

I was thinking, Kurt's Malibu beach bungalow aside, that

I had to get out of here. I remembered the Bangkok urban environment—another place where the low quality of the public realm pushed me out. Same thing was happening in LA. I drained my beer and said, "Let's get started with the plans for my parents. I've got to find out if I can even get along with them. I hope so. Let's get down to business."

Then we got serious about how to move forward with my parents. I worked out this plan with Kurt:

> He was to call my parents, Kate and Sam, and tell them I was on my way flying into Albuquerque. Then via Greyhound bus to SantaFe and onward to Taos. Tell them I was enroute and will be in Taos in 2 or 3 days.
>
> Tell them I plan to look for them at their place in the Enchanted Village. If I have any delays along the way, I will call them, otherwise they should expect me at their doorstep in the next couple days.
>
> Tell them I have a reservation at the Taos Inn and can't wait to reunite with both of them.

The next day, Kurt drove me to LAX and I took off that afternoon. Glad to leave LA behind. Sad to see Kurt mired in it all, though his business looked to be doing well.

On my way back to the New Mexico landscape of my youth, I was on a new path to help my parents, in their late 80s, however they needed. Maybe we can all live in the family residence. I can take care of them—all in "plant speed". And maybe I can take care of their outdoor garden, like Bree did at the haybarn. I just might call it Candide's Garden.

***

Land of Enchantment

Leaving LA, I was on a flight where I couldn't get away from the green in the landscape below—there had to be topsoil and water—deserts of SW US—not like the Arabian Peninsula—no way! Coming into Albuquerque, the metro area was large but nothing compared to LA.

As the flight descended, I felt nervous to see my parents after so many years, but those worries were sidetracked as I observed the landscape below our descent. I was overwhelmed by the varieties in the New Mexico landscape.

I recalled simpler times when, as a youth, growing up in New Mexico, I used to ride and ride my bicycle in the countryside—the air in my face erasing the tumult of my parents' disputes in our home. I never thought how the landscape could erase my emotional troubles. I wondered, how would the New Mexico air affect me now?

On the ground, I only had a five-minute walk to the Sheraton where I would spend the night before heading to Taos the next morning. As I was walking, I breathed in deeply and concluded I needed more New Mexico air than a bus ride to Taos would afford. I was thinking to rent a convertible and drive top-down not via Interstate 25 but via the mountains and plains on the west side of the state—the landscape of my youth.

Checking into the hotel, I saw an advertisement for an event at Popejoy Hall on the University of New Mexico campus—Mahler's Third Symphony—that very evening. I tried to buy online; but they were sold out. However, I was told that there may be a few last-minute seats at the box office. I arranged a car rental, a convertible, drove to campus and was able to score a ticket via someone else's cancellation.

I spent the night in Albuquerque at Popejoy Hall with Mahler's Third. I knew about Mahler. You get your money's worth with a Mahler symphony... but what does that have to do with landscape, you may ask? Mahler—large music, large theme. I loved it. They had prepared a wonderful programme, sharing Mahler's thinking on the Third, over his career. They also included his key inspirational references, Nietzsche and Germanic romantic folklore.

The orchestra was huge. The theme was larger still: the relationship between humanity and the natural world—nature beyond words.

Inspired by his time in the Swiss Alps, Mahler drew upon the seasons, the flowers, the animals, humans, angels and love. He progressively used woodwinds, brass, voices, strings, percussion—I was enthralled. Songs of angels reminded me of Bree in her haybarn gardens. The music stirred all my thoughts on music, design and landscape. The mood and meter of his music had variety like a walk through woods and meadows. I got fired up even more to drive the next day through the New Mexico landscape.

I had been nervous about seeing my parents so I was happy for the Mahler distraction. So many things were happening. For obvious historical reasons, I did not want to linger in Albuquerque. I did not want to stir up those Sachy and kids accident memories. Unexpectedly I did feel, for the first time, a detachment I had never imagined. Nevertheless, I figured on zipping out of Albuquerque into the countryside landscape, remembering my much earlier trips to the Taos area for the shaman.

I wanted to feel once again that landscape I felt as a kid. I lowered the convertible top, raced along Interstate 25 and got out of Albuquerque as fast as I could. Exited northwest on US 550 and for the first time the landscape air rushing through my hair and deep into my lungs—it was joyful. I felt the freedom of my youth. I was flying through the New Mexico landscape. Around every curve and over every hill—among the foothills of the Colorado Plateau, Jemez and San Juan Mountains—on US 550 then on State Route 96 and US 84 and US 285 back toward the Rio Grande and the Sangre de Cristo Mountains.

It was gorgeous along the way—the large landscape. But along the roadside from time to time... the sporadic human developments... reminded me of what I had seen in my Empty Quarter transect with JeanClaude. How? Small, single-storey, low-budget construction, weakly maintained. They looked to me like small independent efforts at making a living in the large landscape. Sad, not inspiring. The large landscape inspires, the human impacts are sad. Felt like the 1800s wild west hard scrabble.

I pulled over for a break just above the Rio Chama. Shut off the engine, took a little walk. I was alone in the quiet of the large New Mexico landscape. Found a boulder to sit on and just looked around.

***

Misterioso

...read the following in a mysterious mood...

I was in the Rio Chama basin at a rest spot, elevation 1880 metres. Looking around, I saw in the soils, hills and cliffs pinkish reds from crystals in the granites; and in the sparse yet rich vegetation were lavender blues, greys and greens. This was in what some people like to call New Mexico deserts. In this area the records show 13 inches/year precipitation against what in Saudi Arabia? Less than 6 inches/year. What a difference seven inches makes! Vegetation, soil—from regular rainfall. Or would you prefer barren drifting sands?

Carefully walking down a steepish slope to the banks of the Rio Chama (1840m), I lingered in the shade under a couple poplar trees (*Populus sp.*), observing and thinking. Shade, the flowing year-round river, dependable water—none of this in the Empty Quarter. Landscape has a powerful impact, broad and deep—an existential reality of human culture. I'd learned that lesson numerous times in my career. But I could never put my finger on the connective tissue between landscape and human culture.

While I was absorbed that day in the northwest New Mexico landscape, my thoughts drifted back to JB Jackson, a famous landscape writer influenced as I was by the landscapes of New Mexico and Switzerland. His writings had always interested me because he described landscape as so much larger than our landscape architecture professional practice. He, after decades of observation and research, never could quantify the mysterious though incontrovertible connection between humans and landscape.

I had theorized those existential connections should be the root of landscape architecture design—chased that for decades without result—hunting the snark, in Lewis Carroll's words. Having spent too much time with the hookah-smoking caterpillar, I may as well have been a Lewis Carroll character peering through the looking glass. But as I looked around me at the incredible beauty and variety in this New Mexico landscape, I was enthralled. I felt myself in a wonderland of life's Wonderland.

I began walking uphill. I climbed up the foothill to 1940m. I stopped two or three times to catch my breath—idyllic. The day was idyllic—both the landscape and the weather, sunny, partly cloudy and in the 60s (18C) on the day. Walking, sweating, resting, breathing deeply. I felt an inner healing.

I thought about the two wonderful ladies, each in their own time in my life, who had died in my arms... and for the first time ever I no longer felt the devastating hurt. They both had loved and protected me—saved me from excesses. I had been so fortunate to share life with them.

Found another boulder and sat down. I asked myself, just what am I doing? What is this change in my life? Am I really retiring? I am giving back—serving—becoming a base of love for my parents in their 80s as they approach the ends of their lives. That was clear. That was pretty straightforward. That was my intent.

But retiring? Turning my back on my landscape architecture profession? Uncertainties about the latter. Two things happened in the last 24 hours—Mahler's Third and my internal "rebirth" in the New Mexico landscape. Landscape, culture, design. I thought I had stepped beyond these but... they still were alive in my thoughts. I looked out over the Rio Chama basin in which I sat. I just sat. Quietly sat. Let my internal passion subside.

Landscape—not a thing—an existential reality. What is existential? What is its definition? Who am I? Where did I come from? Where am I going? Life. Death. Infinity. Eternity.

Things that exist no matter how we define them. Questions that we ask that do not have certain answers. That is where human uneasiness begins. Landscape is an existential mystery for humans... but it is also a salve for human uneasiness. Then my thoughts went quiet again.

"Plant speed" and "long game" bubbled into my thoughts. Plant speed had been around since Bree. I liked how she said it—how it was part of her daily activities in her haybarn garden on the Grosse Scheidegg in the Jungfrau Region of Switzerland. Now I see it as something general. Something a person can activate in daily activities. What is plant speed—plant speed in the garden—plant speed in the landscape? Plant speed, in Bree's words, in Bree's world, was her connection with Faeryland. Faeryland was the way she described her experiences, equivalent to existential effulgences. Then is plant speed no different than existential (transcendent) effulgences?

Transcendent effulgences? Human experiences beyond human gross and subtle sensual capacities—some describe as arising from the pineal gland. Plant speed means having portals open for existential effulgences. And that means a person is willing to accept transcendent input from plants, gardens, landscape. The input is an external initiation and normally the human first response is something like: oh, that's beautiful.

That is how it starts. It was those eccentric botanists in Tangier who educated me and guided me toward opening my portals—and how to keep them open.

But what is that other thing that bubbled up? The "long game"? It is an amalgam of plant speed and a loving approach to plant, garden and landscape maintenance. The long game is JB Jackson's understanding of landscape—wide, deep and long—no one can get free of it. It is Bree's approach to the garden and its maintenance. It is like the love people have for pet animals. If you grow that kind of love and care for plants, gardens and landscape... well then, you will realize portals.

Portals are an individual's willingness to let plants, gardens and landscape access their pineal receptors. That gives anyone access to "plant speed" and plant speed is nothing less than micro-macro momentary relief from the tensions and anxieties that daily life brings to each and every human.

Do the maintenance in a service attitude and keep your portals open because the landscape and plants in the garden speak on their own terms, open their own portal connections on their own time. That is the long game.

Plant speed and the long game are what I hope to share with my parents, at their house, in their gardens. I stood up and started walking back to my car. I took a new path.

I was feeling relieved and looking forward to seeing my parents until... something on the ground caught my eye. It was a cluster of blazing stars (*Mentzelia conspicua*). I bent down to take a closer look at the flower that caught my attention. Then I sat down to take an even closer look. Heavenly joy—transcendent effulgence—I lost track of time, purpose and goal as I observed the beauty of that one flower. It wasn't until a large cloud covered the sun causing me a chill that I regained conscious purpose. That flower was outstanding... but, in this Land of Enchantment, I had a goal. I had a purpose. I had to get to SR68 and drive the last 120km to get back together with my parents.

...in my dreams, a botanical lyricist: but it's more...

...gardens, plants, landscape...

They weave the music.

Illustrations

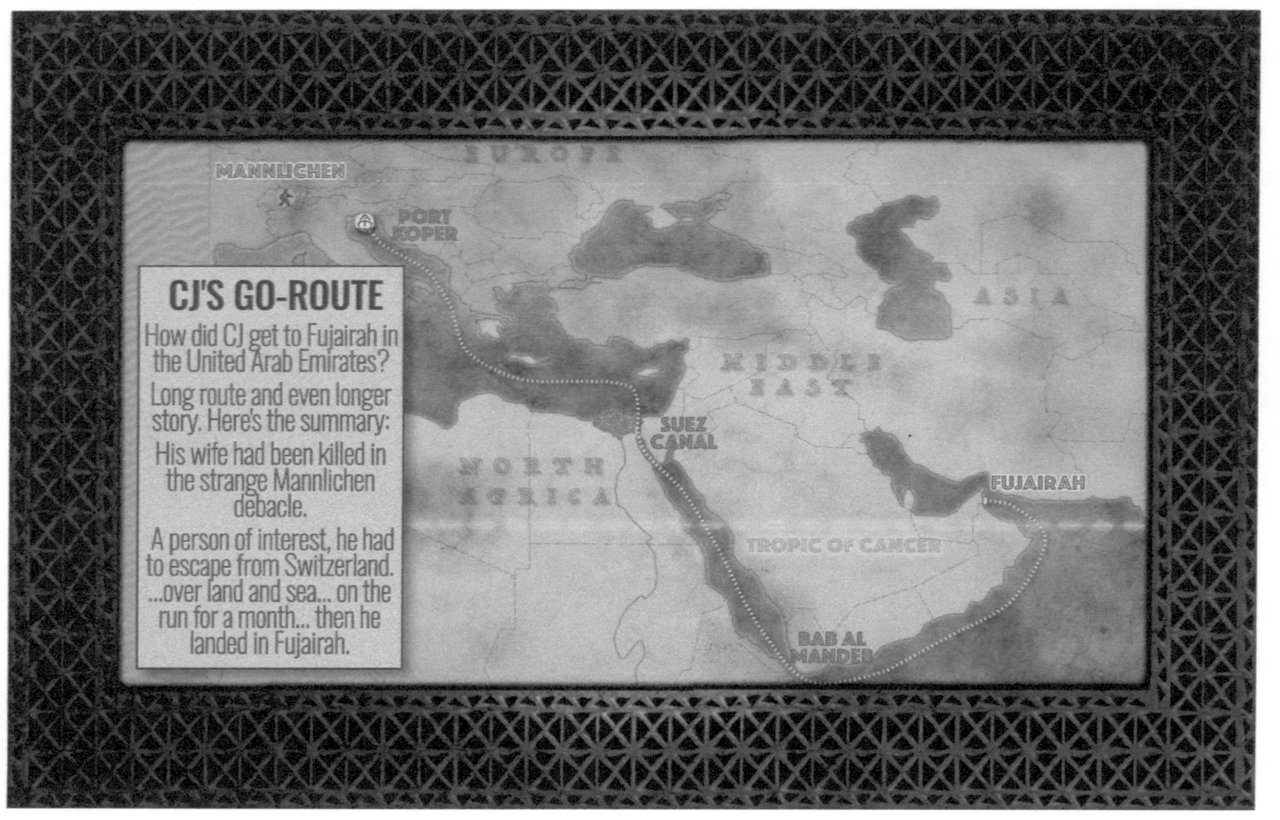
CJ'S GO-ROUTE
How did CJ get to Fujairah in the United Arab Emirates?
Long route and even longer story. Here's the summary:
His wife had been killed in the strange Mannlichen debacle.
A person of interest, he had to escape from Switzerland. ...over land and sea... on the run for a month... then he landed in Fujairah.
EUROPE
MANNLICHEN
PORT KOPER
ASIA
MIDDLE EAST
SUEZ CANAL
NORTH AFRICA
FUJAIRAH
TROPIC OF CANCER
BAB AL MANDEB

LANDFALL
FUJAIRAH, UAE
After 30 days on the run and at sea, CJ stepped
ashore to the barrenness of the Hajar Mountains
on the far eastern edge of the Empty Quarter.

DBX/DUBAI METRO
CJ had been twice before through DBX—on jobs.
This time he was without a job, without a home and his wife had just died in the horrendous Mannlichen debacle.

MOE, DUBAI
CJ saw this from his hotel room in the Mall of the Emirates (MOE). Spectacular hospitality destinations along the Gulf coast. Modern highway and state-of-the-art public transit infrastructure.

HOSPITALITY DESTINATION
Dubai, located on the coastal edge of the Empty Quarter, has opted to provide guests with irrigated, healthy, green... fantastic environments to stroll through.

LIBRARIES
Many hotels provide libraries for guest relaxation.
CJ often used them for relaxed business meetings.
The Liwa Qsar Guest Library displayed Liwa
Oasis realities and traditional efforts at
accommodating the deathly extremes of the
Empty Quarter.

EMPTY QUARTER SUN
No escaping, no shelter.

THE DUNES
No two dunes are alike.
The wind has its way.
...the sands...

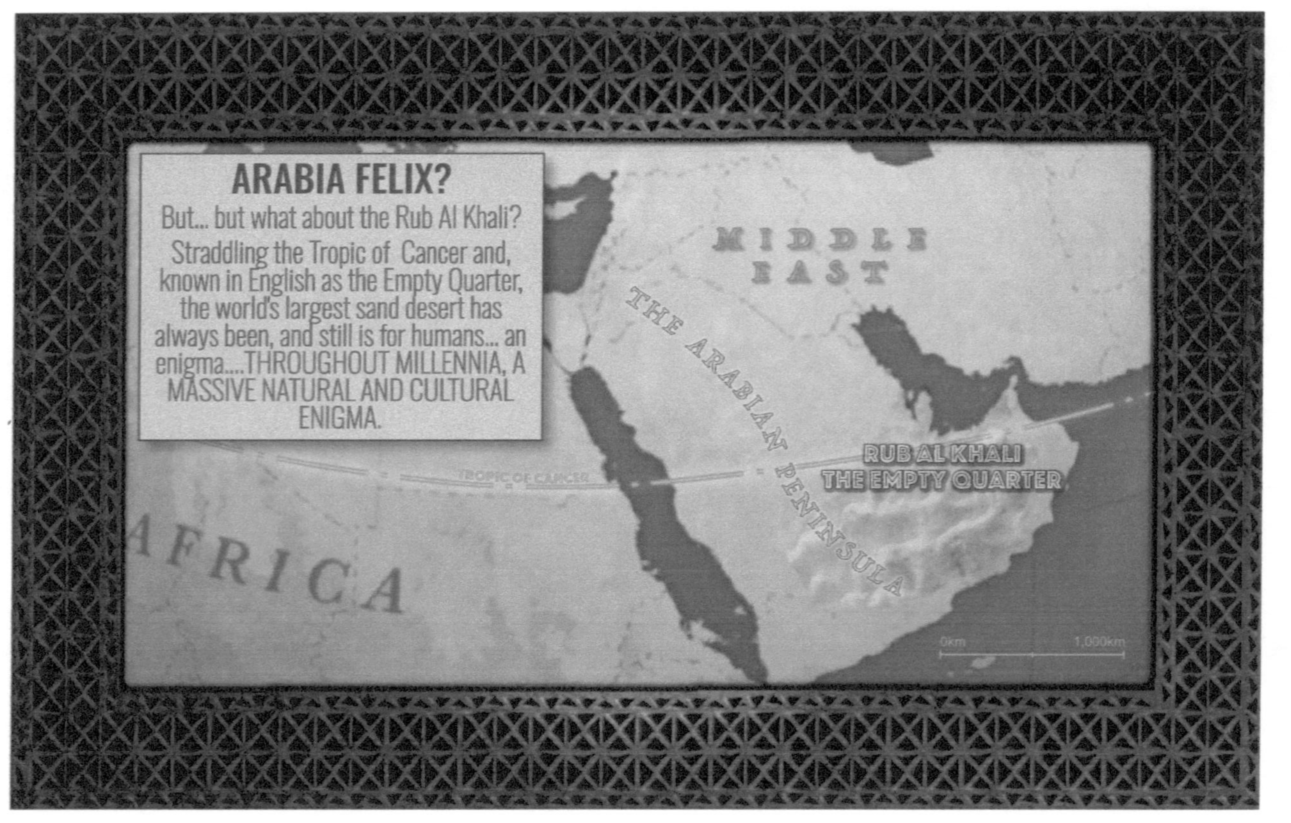
ARABIA FELIX?
But... but what about the Rub Al Khali?
Straddling the Tropic of Cancer and, known in English as the Empty Quarter, the world's largest sand desert has always been, and still is for humans... an enigma....THROUGHOUT MILLENNIA, A MASSIVE NATURAL AND CULTURAL ENIGMA.
MIDDLE EAST
THE ARABIAN PENINSULA
RUB AL KHALI
THE EMPTY QUARTER
TROPIC OF CANCER
AFRICA
0km
1,000km

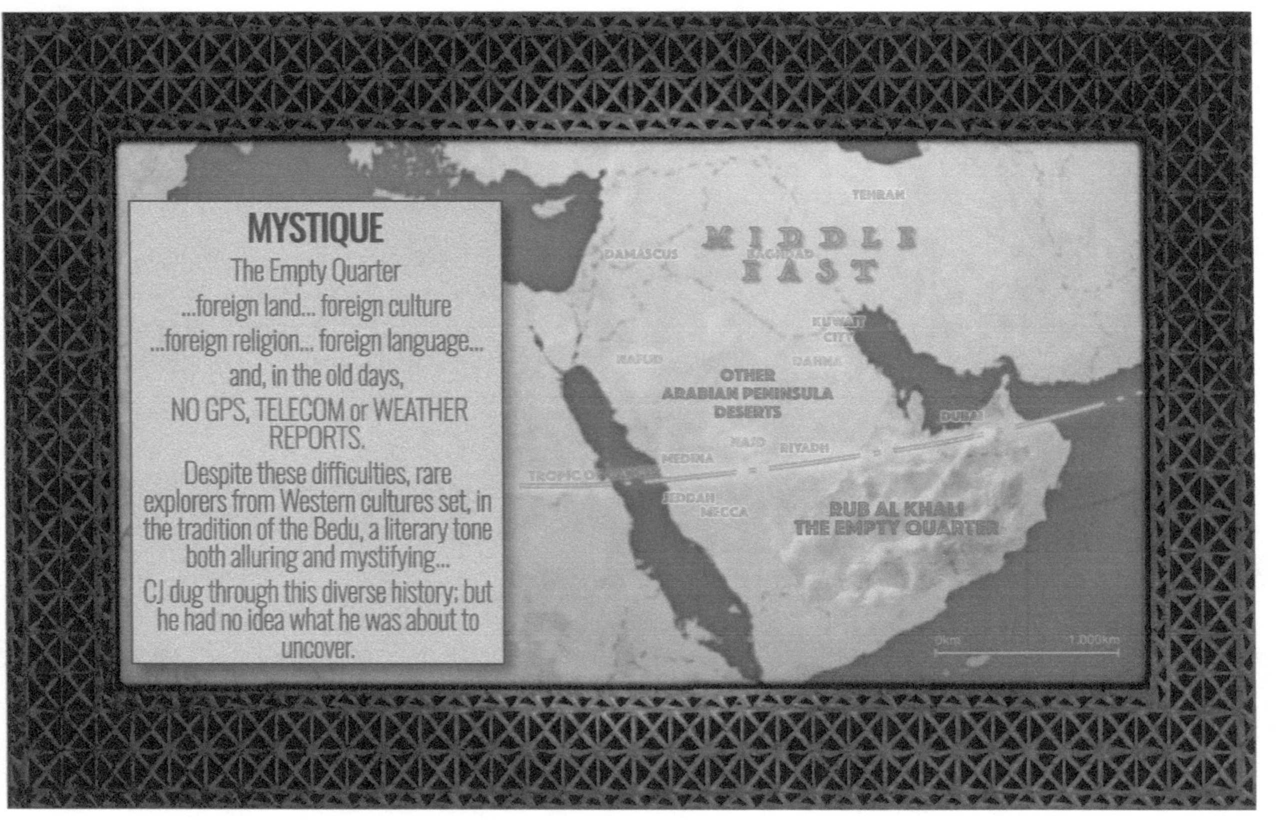
MYSTIQUE
The Empty Quarter
...foreign land... foreign culture
...foreign religion... foreign language...
and, in the old days,
NO GPS, TELECOM or WEATHER REPORTS.
Despite these difficulties, rare explorers from Western cultures set, in the tradition of the Bedu, a literary tone both alluring and mystifying...
CJ dug through this diverse history; but he had no idea what he was about to uncover.
TEHRAN
MIDDLE EAST
BAGHDAD
DAMASCUS
KUWAIT CITY
NAFUD
DAHNA
OTHER ARABIAN PENINSULA DESERTS
DUBAI
NAJD
RIYADH
MEDINA
JEDDAH
MECCA
RUB AL KHALI THE EMPTY QUARTER
0km
1,000km

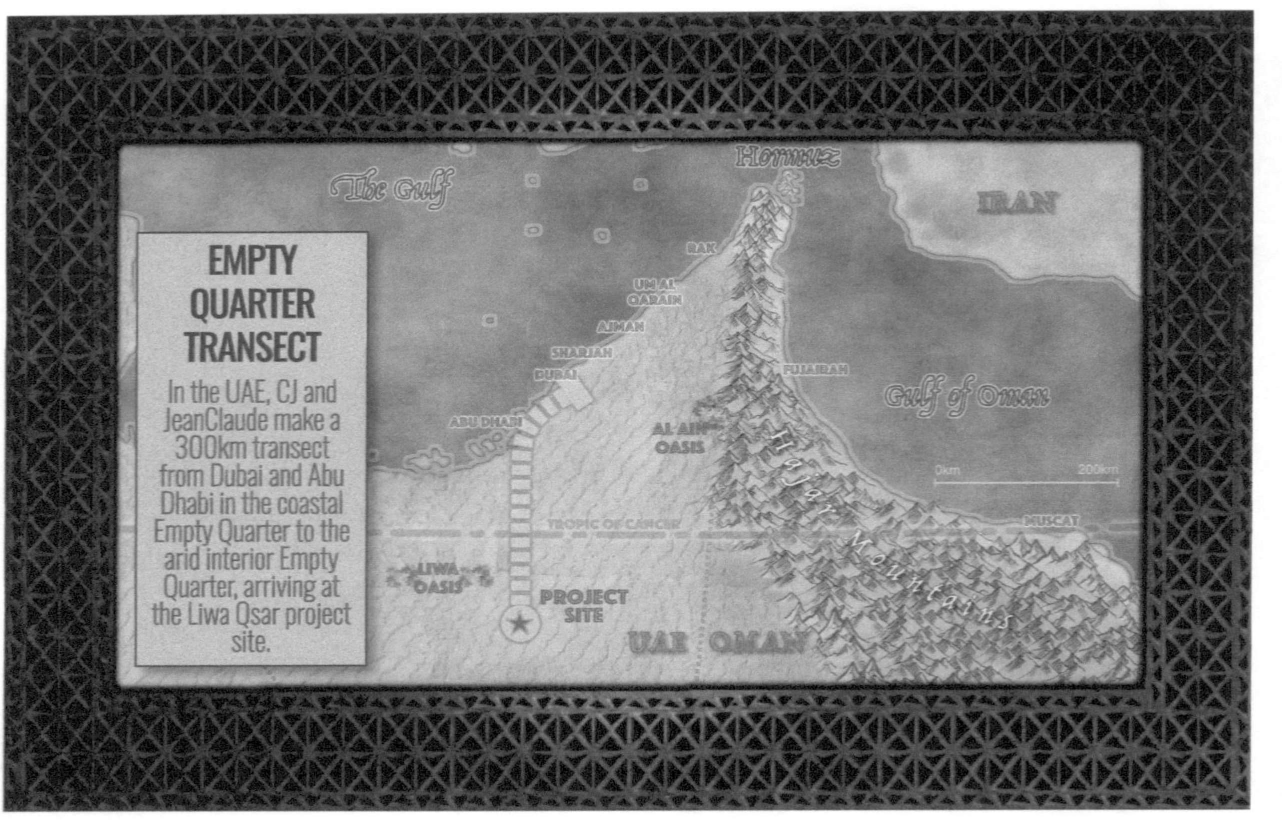
EMPTY QUARTER TRANSECT
In the UAE, CJ and JeanClaude make a 300km transect from Dubai and Abu Dhabi in the coastal Empty Quarter to the arid interior Empty Quarter, arriving at the Liwa Qsar project site.
The Gulf
Hormuz
IRAN
RAK
UM AL QARAIN
AJMAN
SHARJAH
DUBAI
ABU DHABI
FUJAIRAH
Gulf of Oman
AL AIN OASIS
Hajar Mountains
0km
200km
TROPIC OF CANCER
MUSCAT
LIWA OASIS
PROJECT SITE
UAE
OMAN

RUB AL KHALI FROM SPACE

Salt flats—sabka—in between the ever-shifting huge red sand dunes. No signposts. Without Garmin, without Kestrel... no chance.

RUB AL KHALI
ON FOOT
Empty? Not agreed by all. But no
current human habitation. Even in
pre-Islamic records—no human
habitation. But there are stories,
there are legends.

EMPTY? NO PLANTS?
Well, not exactly. But you have to search for them. Most of the time they can be found here and there in the sabkha flats--the same place JeanClaude went when he found the Xygophyllum.

The Empty Quarter
...is death just the flip side of beauty?
THE
23 CLUB
THE 23 CLUB?
On a very late night trip driving from Dubai to Abu Dhabi, Fairuz explained to CJ how to become a member of The 23 Club--driving from Dubai to Abu Dhabi in 23 minutes or less.
...strange cross-cultural differences in foreign lands, foreign cultures?

GETTING THERE
Regular watering, grading and rolling
of the gatch and sand haul road was
required daily to be able to access the
Liwa Qsar project site.

THE WORK
A massive logistic and construction effort established the Liwa Qsar project.
SITE OFFICES

LIWA QSAR COMPLETE
A protective micro-environment to
observe and study the Empty Quarter.

DESERT?

Some people think the New Mexico landscape is a desert. CJ, with his Arabian Peninsula desert experience, found this New Mexico landscape rich with soil, flora and fauna—anything but a desert.

A blazing star found CJ.
WHAT CJ FOUND
...or about what found CJ. It's only mysterious if your own portals are closed.
Mentzelia conspicua
CJ found blazing stars.

"The Landscape Architect" Series

In this Book 6, *Dubai Sands*, we find CJ in the United Arab Emirates—Fujairah, Dubai, Abu Dhabi. Struggling to overcome personal and professional disaster, he takes one last project—a 5-star hospitality destination deep in the infamous, death-dealing Empty Quarter. Can he survive in this landscape?

The Landscape Architect series is about CJ, Christopher Janus. He wrote it all. The six stories are his collected memoirs. He was into asking questions, discovering and writing. And above all he was a landscape architect deeply intrigued by foreign cultures, landscape and design. The six stories track the arc of his beginning interest in landscape architecture followed by his growth in the profession.

Who is CJ? CJ is an American, born in the Midwest, raised in New Mexico—a hard worker who found his muse in the landscape. At university in the late 1990s he grew to embrace landscape, literature and all the fine arts with humanitarian, environmental and spiritual sensibilities. He became a landscape architect and despite his heart-felt attraction to the New Mexico landscape—inspired by the works of Ansel Adams, Georgia O'Keeffe, and the writings of JB Jackson—he travelled the world because, like it or not, life had its own plan for him. CJ's personal life and professional landscape architecture career are woven through with drama in landscape, foreign culture and design—all presenting him with unrelenting dilemmas.

The series reveals the twists and turns in his professional landscape architecture development. But the series explores further. CJ, drawing upon his fine arts history, becomes obsessed with experiences in nature and the landscape beyond the five senses. Beyond the five senses? The paranormal? He recognizes his limits yet always strives to achieve more.

CJ chases nature, its landscape and plants to their existential roots. He describes his interactions with cultures, landscapes, gardens and plants of the world—where the unexpected and downright strange become daily facts of life.

CJ, like his landscape architecture profession and its practitioners, obsesses over design. In one of the major themes in the series, he tries to get to the root of the gossamer, ever-evolving landscape design theory.

Unique in this series, CJ, not a tourist, uses his expatriate life across the Middle East, North Africa and Europe, attempting to weave the threads of his foreign landscape and cultural experiences into a pragmatic design theory.

Throughout his adventures and to his surprise, he discovers, on the good days, not the normal landscape architecture world, rather an enlightening and exciting ethnobotanical world influenced by the likes of Lord Byron, HG Wells, Algernon Blackwood and Rod Serling. And then there are the "not-so-good" days... strange cultures and even stranger landscapes.

Previously in Book 5, *Orient Espresso,* we found CJ in Egypt, Vienna, the Jungfrau Region of the Swiss Alps, Istanbul, Bahrain, Kuwait and the United Arab Emirates. CJ's professional career flip-flopped—a combination of his own fateful choices and the capricious nature of international landscape architecture work in the Eastern Mediterranean and the Gulf Region.

"The Landscape Architect" series began with Book 1, *Tangier Gardens,* where CJ, introduced as a student of landscape architecture, goes to Morocco for a term abroad design study.

First edition 2025

Illustrations and cover art by copyright owner.

Edited and formatted by Lin White, Coinlea Services,
http://www.coinlea.co.uk

ISBN: 979-8-9993102-1-7

Published by copyright owner
https://flahertylandscape.com

Acknowledgements

All illustrations prepared by author. Base photos by author unless as acknowledged below.

Base maps from 2022 Google Earth: https://earth.google. The following illustrations base images have been provided in 2024 as listed below:

Illustration: 3-DBX/Dubai Metro image from project by Agura Consultants: http://aguraconsultants.com/projects/.

Illustration: 8-The Dunes image from ZamZam: https://zamzam.com/blog/saudi-arabia-deserts/

Illustration: 12-Rub al Khali from Space from Map Tiler: https://www.maptiler.com/satellite/

Illustration: 19-Desert? image from Google Earth: https://earth.google

Illustration: 20-What CJ found images from https://www.inaturalist.org/guide_taxa/824750

Colophon

Books are crafted. Colophons are the end credits of literature.

Books have a typographical tradition that to this author go nearly as deep into human culture as does the landscape.

So when it came to selecting the manuscript text, Baskerville, originally by John Baskerville in the 1750s, was my clear favourite because it reaches back into history where alchemical roots still had gravitas.

Baskerville has an enduring elegance not unlike an attractive landscape—crisp, high contrast, generous proportions and refined beauty.

When it came to chapter headings and scene headings, Matthew Carter's relatively modern Skia provided a Mediterranean anchor. Skia is Greek for shadow and the letter forms take inspiration from stone-carved 1st century BC Greek writing.

Baskerville and Skia truly link the Western world with the Middle East; and that linkage is the context of CJ's search—to understand the existential links between human cultures and the landscape.

Ends of chapters are indicated by the author's line drawings of a coffee pot typical of the United Arab Emirates.

Cover Art

On this book's cover, upon examination, you will find but the sands. That is the Empty Quarter, the Rub al Khali.

This was daily life for Christopher Janus while he was living nearly a year in the United Arab Emirates.

Dedication

Dedicated first of all to my wife, her photographs, support and understanding. Then to everyone who has interest in landscape, culture or the profession of landscape architecture.

About the Author

An international award winner and frequently invited conference speaker, Edward Flaherty practiced landscape architecture over the past 5 decades on very large projects where he has lived as an expatriate in Africa, Europe and Asia.

In the United Arab Emirates, he has made his home in both Abu Dhabi and Dubai.

Professional details at LinkedIn, https://ch.linkedin.com/in/edflaherty1

Discussion Guide for Dubai Sands

As I wrote this story, a couple big picture items kept me busy. I never fully resolved them, so I ask you, the readers, to discuss them and share your thoughts with me by commenting on my blog via this link: flahertylandscape.com.

1. Does human culture relate to the landscape? If so, then how?

2. What is the power in plants, gardens and landscape that induces peace in humans?

3. How do human cultures change? How do ecotypes in nature change? What happens at the edges of adjacent ecotypes and the edges of adjacent human cultures?

I look forward to hearing from you. Thank you.

Call to Action

Dubai Sands is the last book in the fictional autobiographical series, "The Landscape Architect". In the series, CJ tracks the intriguing events he experienced in his expatriate personal life and professional career in landscape architecture amid the strange cultures and even stranger landscapes of Europe, the Middle East and North Africa.

If you enjoyed reading about CJ's adventures in Dubai and the sands of the Empty Quarter, then please write a short review and share it on my blog flahertylandscape.com.

You might also enjoy reading Book 1 in "The Landscape Architect" series, *Tangier Gardens,* where CJ, introduced as a student of landscape architecture, goes to Morocco for a term abroad design study, expecting sandy beaches, colourful exotic markets and timeless pedestrian cities. But when he encounters aggressive landscape and culture, he is bewildered, loses focus. Could he recover? Could he finish his assignment?

www.ingramcontent.com/pod-product-compliance
Lightning Source LLC
Chambersburg PA
CBHW031336020726
47499CB00005B/1287

* 9 7 9 8 9 9 9 3 1 0 2 1 7 *